Second Chances

MJ Duncan

This is a work of fiction. Names, characters, places, and incidents are products of the author's imagination or are used fictitiously and are not to be construed as real. Any resemblance to actual events, locales, organizations, or persons, living or dead, is entirely coincidental.

Copyright © 2013 by MJ Duncan

All rights reserved. No part of this book may be reproduced, stored in a retrieval system, or transmitted in any form or by any means–electronic, mechanical, photocopy, recording, or any other–except for brief quotations in printed reviews, without the prior permission of the author.

Cover art © 2013 by Jade

ISBN: 0615855830

ISBN-13: 978-0615855837

Prologue

"Oh shit!" Charlie yelled, lifting her arms to try and block the shoe that was flying at her face. Really, she could understand why the redhead was pissed at her, but throwing things was just a little overdramatic. "Watch it!"

"Fuck you, Charlie Bennett!" the woman screamed, picking the brunette's other red heel up off the floor and chucking it at her with a frightening level of accuracy.

"Hey!" Charlie yelped as the second heel smacked her in the forehead. "Jesus! Those are Louboutins, for fuck's sake!"

"What's my name?" the irate redhead demanded, hands placed firmly on her hips as she stared hard at Charlie.

Charlie swallowed thickly. "Um…Marissa?" she offered hopefully.

The redhead growled and threw her hands up in the air in irate disbelief as she spun in place and began searching for her clothes, which were strewn around Charlie's bedroom. "This is what I get for picking up some random chick at a bar," the woman–whose name, Charlie was willing to bet, was *not* Marissa–muttered under her breath as she stepped into her skirt.

Charlie groaned and pulled the sheet up to cover her naked chest as she watched the redhead slip her bra back on. She had been sure the woman's name started with an "M" and she wracked her brain to try and remember what it was. "Melissa?" she tried again, and she actually flinched when the woman stopped buttoning her shirt to glare at her. Nope, not that one either, apparently. "Sorry."

"My name is Michelle," the redhead growled. "Not Mackayla." That was the name Charlie had called out as she climaxed. "Or Marissa. Or Melissa. Michelle."

"Right. Michelle," Charlie repeated, nodding even as she silently kicked her own ass for screaming her ex-girlfriend's name while having sex with another woman. Again. This was actually the third time it had happened in the last year, and she would be the first to admit that it was pathetic considering the fact that she had been the one to call things off with Mackayla back in college. "Sorry."

The redhead rolled her eyes and shook her head as she waved off Charlie's half-assed apology. "You know what? Forget it. I..." Her voice trailed off and she shook her head again. "Just forget it."

Relief swept through Charlie when the redhead–Michelle, she reminded herself–stalked out of her bedroom without further incident. When the front door of her condo slammed shut with enough force to rattle the windows, Charlie flopped back onto the bed and groaned. "I could have sworn her name was Marissa!"

She laid in bed for a while, watching the play of shadows and light on her ceiling as she listened to the quiet but ever present hum of city traffic below. The sound used to be comforting, she usually drew strength from the idea that there were so many other people around her all the time, but now it just reminded her how alone she really was. She knew that she should be happy. She was just a few months past her twenty ninth birthday, had her dream job as a writer for *Sports Illustrated*, a National Magazine Award already sitting on her shelf, and she was perhaps only a year or two away from making Senior Editor at a disgustingly young age. She was young, beautiful, and successful in a city that loved people who were young, beautiful, and successful. She had everything she could have ever dreamt of having when she moved to New York after graduating from Wesleyan, and yet she was miserable.

The nights she didn't spend out in the field or at the office were spent either alone in her apartment with Chinese take-out and a movie on HBO, or in the arms of a woman whose name she really couldn't be bothered to learn. Her best friend was also her colleague, and she knew pretty much nobody outside her work. Her love life, as evidenced by Michelle's dramatic storm-out, was a train wreck. A collection of meaningless one-night stands and fractionally longer flings that never lasted more than a month or two. It was her fault, she knew, that she compared every woman she dated to Mackayla, but she just couldn't keep herself from doing it, and the results were always the same: she became frustrated with them for not being who she wanted them to be, and left.

"Fucking hell," Charlie murmured as she rolled out of bed and pulled on a pair of soccer shorts and a t-shirt.

The hardwood floors were cool against her bare feet as she padded down the hall to the kitchen, and she sighed as she grabbed a beer from the fridge. She twisted the cap off the micro-brew, her eyes landing on her worn leather satchel on the dining room table, and it was only then that she remembered the letter she had been handed earlier that day.

She dropped into her usual chair at the table and reached for her bag, easily finding the thin white envelope nestled between a copy of last week's edition of Sports Illustrated and the legal pad she doodled on when she was bored out of her mind during meetings. She took a long swallow of the crisp amber lager as she eyed the envelope speculatively, trying to remember if she had ever heard of Blake University before. She was pretty sure she hadn't, but the return address told her it was located in New Hampshire, of all places.

Curious as to why, exactly, a school she had never heard of was sending her mail, she slit the envelope open and unfolded the letter that was folded neatly inside. Her eyebrows rose in surprise as she scanned the letter, astonished to find that it was a query offering her a guest lecturer position at the university for the coming school year.

It was an enticing offer, complete with housing provided by the university, and she wondered what in the world she had done to make them even consider her for the position. Sure, she had guest lectured before in the past at NYU, Cornell, and Columbia, but those had always been one-and-done type things. She would go in, give a lecture, smile, wave, answer a few questions, and then leave. But Blake's journalism department wasn't asking her to come give a talk–they were offering her what basically amounted to a one-year professorship.

Teaching full-time was something she had never considered before, but the idea was certainly intriguing. Intriguing enough that she actually retrieved her laptop from the coffee table in the living room to look up more information about the university. She scanned the school's webpage as she nursed her beer, and the more she learned about it, the more she actually began to consider the offer. She knew that on any other night she would probably roll her eyes and toss the papers in the trash, not even bothering to respond with a brief and insincere "no thank you". But tonight, with her forehead still stinging from the second heel that had slipped past her guard, she saw the offer in a different light.

Chapter 1

"You're seriously doing this."

Charlie laughed and nodded, even though she knew her best friend couldn't see her. "Yes, Adam. I'm really doing this. I actually crossed the New Hampshire border over an hour ago." She could practically see his scowl and she smiled as she ran a hand through her hair, enjoying the way the shorter strands of her new hairstyle felt running through her fingers. It had seemed only right for her to start this new adventure with a new haircut, and she thought the choppy, chin-length bob her stylist had given her was perfect. "It's gorgeous up here."

"It's gorgeous down here, too," he retorted. *"Seriously, Charlie!"*

"Don't be such a crybaby. I know for a fact that Billy called you up to his office not even an hour after my sabbatical officially began and gave you everything I'd been working on. Now it's your turn to show them what you got."

Once she had decided to take the teaching position, she had gone to the senior editors at the magazine and made her pitch. It had gone even better than she had dared dream it would, and she didn't even need to threaten to resign–her ultimate ace in the hole because *ESPN the Magazine* had been banging on her door for months now trying to get her to come over to their team. It was obvious that Billy Davis and the rest of the Senior Editors weren't particularly pleased with her desire to take a year to go off and teach, but they didn't fight her on it.

"*I still don't know how you talked them into giving you a sabbatical like that,*" Adam grumbled. "*I mean, anyone else would have to quit!*"

"I just appealed to their better nature," Charlie drawled, rolling her eyes and glancing at her GPS that was showing she had a half-mile until her exit.

"*Bullshit. They don't have a better nature. They have a bottom line.*"

"Yes," Charlie chuckled, "but thankfully they seem to believe that my career and their bottom line are connected, so they caved. Don't hate the player, bro. Hate the game."

That actually got Adam to laugh. "*Gorgeous little five foot nothing brunettes such as yourself should not be pulling the 'don't hate the player' card. Except...well, you are a bit of a player, aren't you? Have any more shoes fly at you lately?*"

"Nope," Charlie said as she slowed to allow the car in the right hand lane to pass so that she could ease into the slow lane, mindful of the little U-Haul trailer that she was towing. "I've given up girls for a while. Going to focus on myself. Maybe try and write a novel or something."

"*Can it have lots of lesbian sex in it like that Lynn Turner book you gave me to read?*" he asked playfully. "*I would read the shit outta that.*"

"I bet you would, you pervert," Charlie chuckled. Her GPS announced that her exit was coming up next, and she smiled as she scanned her surroundings, eager to learn everything she could about the small town that would be her home for the next nine months or so. The mountains on either side of the highway weren't the Rockies by any stretch of the imagination, but they were stunning. "Look, I'm here. I'm gonna have to get off the phone so I can figure out where I'm going."

"*Sounds good, Charlie-girl,*" he replied, his tone softening. "*I hope you find what you're looking for up there.*"

Charlie smiled and nodded. "Thanks. You're going to come up and visit, right?"

"*Oh, gee...I dunno. Will I come to see my best friend who will be surrounded by sorority girls in tight little t-shirts? You can bet your glorious ass I'll be coming to visit.*"

"Just make sure they're legal and not one of my students," she told him with a laugh.

"*Whatever,*" he chuckled. "*Now, go. Stop bugging me and shit. I got stuff to do.*"

"Love you too, Mr. Snow," she retorted, grinning as she disconnected the call before he could respond.

The downtown area of Hampton, home of Blake University, was just a few miles from the highway and Charlie felt herself relax as she drove down Main Street, her attention more focused on the quaint brick buildings that lined the boulevard than the street itself. It was like something out of a movie. Hand-painted signs and multi-colored awnings dotted the boulevard, making each individual business stand out from the rest. The trees along the sidewalk were tall and leafy, providing both a feeling of nostalgia to the area as well as shade, and there were more than a few clusters of people just standing beneath the sheltering boughs chatting. Everything about the downtown area, from the quaintness of the buildings to the completely unhurried pace of the people on the sidewalks, was a complete antithesis to hurried, purposeful stride so commonly seen in Manhattan and, rather than being put-off by those differences, Charlie was charmed. The stark contrast between her old life and the one she was about to begin was, if anything, proof that agreeing to teach for a year had been the right decision.

"Turn right, in one quarter mile," her GPS instructed, and Charlie started to pull over into the right lane without checking her mirrors.

She was barely over the lane line when she felt her steering wheel shudder under her hands and the sound of crunching metal filled the air. She had hit another car with the trailer she was towing.

"Shit," she hissed as she pulled back into the left lane, causing more drivers to sound their horns in protest of her reckless driving. "No, no, no," she murmured, her heart racing as she carefully worked her way over to the curb. She could already hear the *cha-ching* of her premiums going up, and she knew that the minute she told Adam about this, he would laugh and tell her that it was the Fates' way of telling her to get her ass back to New York. When she was safely at the side of the road, she yanked her keys from the ignition and banged her forehead against the steering wheel. "Fuck!"

Responsibility weighed heavily on her shoulders as she dug around in the glove box for her insurance information, and she offered up a silent prayer that whoever she had hit wasn't a total dick about it. She found what she needed wedged between the cover and title page of her owner's manual, and climbed out of her car to inspect the damage and trade information.

A light breeze out of the south ruffled her hair, sending it flying into her eyes, and she huffed an exasperated breath as she swiped it out of her face with her left hand. "I'm sor–" she started to apologize as she heard a car door slam shut, but the rest of her apology died in her throat when she saw who she had crashed into. "Oh my god."

"No way," the woman murmured, her bright blue eyes registering pure shock as she looked at her. "Charlotte?"

Charlie swallowed thickly, trying to find her voice that had suddenly abandoned her. She had daydreamed about someday running into Mackayla Thomas again many times over the past few years, always wondering where in the world she had disappeared to, but never in her wildest dreams had she ever expected it to actually happen. She cleared her throat softly in response to the questioning look Mackayla was giving her, and nodded. "I go by Charlie now, but yeah." Her eyes swept slowly over the blonde's lithe figure, appreciating the toned muscles that were left on tantalizing display by her hiking shorts and fitted white tank top. Mackayla had always kept her hair short, but it was even shorter now, styled in an extremely flattering messy pixie cut that framed her angular face perfectly, and when her eyes landed on Mackayla's lips, she found herself licking her own unconsciously. "How are you doing, Mackayla?"

"Mac," the blonde corrected, running a hand through her hair as she tried to get her racing heart under control. Out of everyone she could have possibly expected to literally run into that morning, Charlotte Bennett was not even on the list. The last time she had seen her was eight years ago, and the brunette, tired of waiting for her to be ready to finally come out of the closet, had walked away from her at the end of their junior year of undergrad. How they had managed to avoid each other that last year was still something of a mystery to her, and yet here she was, in the middle of downtown Hampton, looking better than Mac remembered. "What are you doing here?"

"Moving," Charlie replied, waving a hand at the trailer she had sideswiped the blonde's Jeep with.

Though she wanted to ask where Charlie was moving to, a sick, twisting feeling in her stomach had Mac desperate to get away from her. If she had to stand there and look at the brunette any longer, she would either lose her temper and start yelling or just break down crying because *goddamn it*, she thought she was finally over her. "Do you have insurance?"

Charlie nodded, chewing her lip thoughtfully at the strange tenor to the blonde's voice, and held out the paper with her insurance information on it. "I don't have anything to write with though, sorry. Maybe you could just take a picture of it with your phone?"

"I've got some business cards and a pen or twenty in my Jeep," Mac said, trying her best to look like she wasn't about two seconds away from losing it. She turned back to her cherry red Wrangler that was banged up on the front half of the driver's side, and quickly pulled a few of her business cards from the pocket in the door along with a blue pen.

Charlie watched as the blonde leaned over the hood of her mangled car and quickly copied down her information, and she licked her lips nervously when Mackayla turned back to face her. "Good?"

"Yeah," Mac murmured, nodding as she handed Charlotte back her printout. She waited until the brunette had pocketed the paper before she offered her one of her cards that she had written her insurance agent's information on. "Look, here's the name of my guy here in town, in case you need it. I'll get the claim started when I get home."

Charlie nodded her thanks as she took the card Mackayla was holding out for her. "Okay. Yeah." She ignored the blonde's tidy scrawl and flipped the card over to read the embossed lettering on the other side. There was a light blue, blocky B in the center of the card and inscribed over it in black was *Mackayla Thomas, Assistant Professor, English Department,* followed by her office information, voicemail number, and email. She ran the pad of her thumb over the lettering, her heart swooping up into her throat as she realized that there was a very real chance she would be seeing more of the blonde over the next nine months. "Wow. So you really did end up becoming a professor," she murmured. "Congratulations."

10

"Yeah. Thanks." Mac shoved her hands into her pockets. "Look, good luck going wherever it is you're moving to. It was…" Her voice trailed off and she sighed, her eyes slowly tracing Charlotte's patrician features. Charlotte had always been a pretty girl, but she had grown into a beautiful woman. Her chestnut-colored hair was just as thick and luscious as she remembered, though cut in a sexier, more mature style, and the short shorts and fitted emerald green t-shirt she wore showed that she was just as fit as she had been back in college, if not better. She wore minimal makeup, just a little lip-gloss and some mascara to highlight her bright green eyes, and it was clear that the years that had passed since they had left Wesleyan had been good to the brunette. She didn't know why Charlotte was in New Hampshire, and she hated the way her heart felt like it was breaking all over again, but she was glad to see that Charlotte looked healthy, happy, and whole. "It was good to see you, Charlotte," she murmured.

Charlie felt her heart skip a beat as Mackayla flashed her a quick smile before she turned and walked back to her car. She was still standing beside her car when Mackayla drove off, and she waited until the blonde was out of sight before she climbed back into her car, ignoring the speculative looks she was getting from the people on the sidewalk. She looked at Mackayla's card again and smiled as she slipped it into the empty cup holder in the center console. She didn't have any false illusions that Mackayla would just immediately forgive her for walking away from her like she did, but the small smile the blonde had given her before she disappeared was enough to give her hope that the coming school year would give her the opportunity she needed to maybe find a way to correct the biggest mistake of her life.

Chapter 2

A feeling of calm that had eluded her since she had run into Charlotte swept over Mac when she stepped into the foyer of the two-story colonial that she shared with her best friend and fellow faculty member, Spencer Walsh. She hung her keys on an unused coat hook in the built-in locker system that kept most of their shoes and other outdoor gear organized, and sighed as she made her way down the hall to the kitchen, where she could hear him listening to a podcast of *Mike and Mike in the Morning*.

It was impossible to keep from smiling when walked into the kitchen to find Spencer hunched over the table with one arm wrapped protectively around a large bowl of cereal. He was wearing nothing but his favorite pair of sky blue lacrosse shorts that were a leftover from his playing days at Blake and a frown, and his sandy blond hair was a picture-perfect definition of bedhead with the way it stuck up in every possible direction.

"You are not going to believe who I just ran into," she said without preamble as she dropped into the chair opposite him at the table.

"Is this one of those times where you really want me to guess, or are you just using a rhetorical question as a segue to telling me anyways?" he mumbled around a mouthful of Fruit Loops. "And can you talk quieter, please? My head hurts. I'm still waiting for the Tylenol to kick in."

Mac chuckled, remembering how smashed he had been when he stumbled home the night before with a cute little redhead on his arm. "I'll bet. How is…whatever her name was? She was freaking loud, by the way."

"Gone. And oh my god, I know. Right? It was distracting," he grumbled. "Like it isn't hard enough to try and keep my rhythm when I'm totally shitfaced like that; her screaming totally threw me off."

"Poor baby," Mac teased as she reached for the box of cereal and grabbed a handful to snack on. "But, back to what I was saying."

"Right," he said, nodding obediently. "Because it's all about you. Who did you run into?"

"Did I mention that I quite literally ran into her? Like, literally, literally? I'll probably have to get half of my driver's side repainted."

"You did not, but I will take it down to Bill at the shop for him to have a look at it if you want." He waved his non-spoon hand in a circle and arched a questioning brow at her. "So, who is this mystery woman that has you looking like you're about two seconds from flipping your shit."

"I do not," Mac grumbled, tossing a few pieces of sugar-coated cereal into her mouth.

"If you say so, dude. But, still, a name for this girl would be really fucking helpful, because my head really hurts and I don't wanna play a guessing game right now."

"Charlotte Bennett," Mac said, crossing her arms over her chest and arching a brow at him. He knew her entire sordid history with the brunette and, despite the fact that she was still reeling from the encounter, she had to laugh when he choked on the mouthful of cereal he had been trying to swallow. "Breathe, Walshy."

"Seriously? The chick who dumped you because you weren't ready to come out in college because your dad is a freaking religious whackjob and you knew that he'd cut you off the minute you did? That Charlotte Bennett?"

Mac nodded. "Yeah, that one. And she goes by Charlie now."

"And..."

"She's even more stunning that I remember," Mac groaned, sighing dramatically and shaking her head. "God, I hate when they get better looking after they've dumped me."

"Okay," Spencer said, sitting more upright in his chair and pointing his spoon at her. "First of all, I believe Ms. Bennett has the honor of being the *only* person to ever turn down your fine ass, so enough with the dumping business, Ms. Love 'Em and Leave 'Em."

Mac grinned in spite of herself because he was right. Ever since Charlotte had walked away from her, she'd had exactly zero serious relationships. Sure, there were girls that she had dated for a while, but she never let herself get emotionally involved with any of them. If Charlotte leaving had taught her anything, it was that she never wanted to hurt like that ever again. She waved a hand in a circle in front of herself and prompted, "And, second of all..."

Spencer nodded. "Second of all..." His voice trailed off and he frowned. "Yeah, there wasn't any more. Don't pay my hungover ass too much attention. But, hey, at least you probably won't see her again, right? Because, I mean, the only thing around here is Blake, and what did you say she did?"

"No idea. She had always wanted to write for *Sports Illustrated*, but I don't know if she ever managed it or not. She had a U-Haul trailer and she said she was moving so, really, I don't have a freaking clue."

"Wait!" Spencer slapped his hand on the table excitedly, making his cereal bowl rattle and sending the milk inside it sloshing dangerously toward the lip. "You said she goes by Charlie now? Charlie Bennett?"

"Yeah," Mac said, frowning. "Why?"

"Dude, my favorite columnist in *Sports Illustrated* is Charlie Bennett!"

Mac arched a brow at him and shrugged. "Okay…"

"Wow. I'm telling you–she knows her shit. Damn, I would totally kill to be a full-time writer for *Sports Illustrated*. That would be badass."

Mac rolled her eyes. "Look, is there a point that you're getting at with all of this, or am I just supposed to sit here and listen to you fangirl over my ex-girlfriend?"

"Sorry," Spencer murmured, shaking his head and refocusing his train of thought back to the matter at hand. "But, anyways, my point was that there's nothing around here but the university, so she was probably just driving through and we'll never see her again."

"Yeah, you're probably right," Mac said, nodding slowly as the adrenaline that had been pounding through her veins since she came face to face with Charlotte began to ease. "She was just driving through."

"Yeah," Spencer repeated, nodding as he shoved another heaping spoonful of cereal into his mouth.

"Yeah," Mac sighed. "So, what do you have planned for today?"

He rolled his eyes and covered his mouth with his hand as he answered, "I gotta run over to campus to meet this new guest lecturer that I'm supposed to be mentoring."

"The journalism department scored a guest lecturer?" Mac arched a brow in surprise. "How did you guys do that?"

"Hell if I know," Spencer muttered. "I know it was arranged before graduation and everything, and that Cheryl Davis was supposed to mentor them originally, but then she backed out because her mom's going through chemo and everything, and it got passed down to me."

"You didn't think to ask who it was?"

Spencer shook his head. "Nah. I mean, what's it matter? It's probably some academic tight-ass from who knows where just looking to pad his resume a bit."

"Way to go into this thing with a winning attitude and everything, Walsh," Mac chuckled.

"Whatever, Thomas." Spencer lobbed his spoon at her and laughed as she caught it easily. "What are your plans for the afternoon?"

"I need to get over to my office and work on my syllabi for the semester," Mac said, throwing his spoon back at him.

Spencer snagged the spoon out of the air and got up to put his dirty dishes into the dishwasher. "I thought you were done?"

"Almost. Just have the one for my advanced creative writing module left to do. Then I need to go over the final edit that I got back yesterday to approve or ignore the changes made to *Convergence* so it can go to print," Mac said, referring to the sequel to the novel she had released the year before.

"Sweet. You wanna drive over together?"

Mac nodded and looked at the time. It was just after one thirty, so by the time they both showered and changed, it would be just about time for him to head over for his meeting. "All right. Yeah, we can drive over together. You want first shower?" Their four-bedroom house, while an architectural delight with its dove gray siding, black shutters, bright red front door, gabled roofline, and meticulously restored interior had been built in 1935, so there was only a single bathroom upstairs with a shower that they shared.

"Do you mind?" Spencer asked, wrinkling his nose as he looked down at himself. "I'm still kind of gross, if you know what I mean."

"Right," Mac drawled, nodding as she waved a hand at the stairs. "Go for it. Just save me some hot water."

"Will do." Spencer ruffled her hair as he walked behind her and laughed as she took a swipe at him. "Too slow, McFly!"

Mac laughed and waved him off. "Whatever, Walshy. Go. You reek of debauchery."

"Jealous?" he teased as he backed down the hall.

"Maybe a little," she admitted with a smile.

"You wanna go out tonight and find a hot little brunette to pick up?"

Mac shook her head as his description of the type of women she usually dated brought up a memory of how Charlotte had looked that afternoon. "I don't think so."

Chapter 3

The furnished house the university had leased for Charlie for the school year sat right on the northernmost edge of campus. It was a cute little Cape Cod bungalow with dark sage green siding and white trim, and the flowerbeds around the walk were overflowing with colorful perennials. The porch, while not overwhelmingly large, was deep enough for a couple of Adirondack chairs, and Charlie smiled as she walked up the paver walkway to the shining black front door.

"Here we go," she muttered as she slid the key she had been given into the pewter deadbolt. She held her breath as it turned over and she pushed the door open. The door swung open easily, and the breath she had been holding spilled from her in an appreciative hum as she saw the interior of the house she would be calling home for the next nine months.

The walls of the small foyer were painted a rich butter yellow, and there was a hand-woven rug just inside the door that protected the light hardwood floor from the dirt and grime that the seasons would inevitably bring inside. There was a rectangular mirror with coat hooks mounted on the wall beside the door, and Charlie nodded to herself as she wandered through the doorway on the right that led a comfortable living room. The color scheme from the foyer carried into this part of the house as well, and on the far side of the room there was a small brick fireplace surrounded by built-in bookshelves with a flatscreen television sitting on the mantel.

She ran a hand over the back of the beige upholstered sofa that faced the fireplace as she walked through the living room to the dining room, which was wholly unremarkable with a small table that had four chairs around it and a boring print hanging on the wall. The kitchen at the back of the house was more than twice the size of hers in New York, and she bit her lip as she surveyed the space. The cupboards were painted a bright white, the counter was a dark gray quartz, and the appliances—while obviously not top-of-the-line—were stainless steel. It was a kitchen for somebody who enjoyed cooking, and Charlie felt a little bad that her entire catalogue of culinary skills consisted of cereal, macaroni and cheese, baked chicken breasts, and whatever pre-packaged side she could cobble together.

A one-car detached garage and a small patio were visible through the window above the sink, and Charlie hummed approvingly under her breath as she walked back through the kitchen, dining, and living rooms to the foyer to explore the hallway that was on the left of it. The first of the bedrooms was small, probably no larger than ten-by-ten, with a desk in front of the large picture window that overlooked the street. Next was a full bath that had a quaint black and white octagonal tile floor. Though it was not particularly large, Charlie was relieved to see that it had a full tub and a shower, because she did enjoy her occasional soak with a glass of wine. The bedroom at the end of the hall was a little bit larger than the front room, though not by much. The queen-size bed that was centered on the wall opposite the door took up most of the space, and Charlie chewed her lip nervously as she opened the closet.

"Oh thank god," she murmured when she saw that it was not as small as she had feared. It wasn't outstandingly large, either, but her things should fit easily enough. She sighed and glanced at her watch as she worked through her mental checklist of everything she still had to do that afternoon. As much as she wanted to start getting moved in, she had a meeting with Jack O'Connor, chair of Blake University's Journalism Department, in twenty minutes, so getting settled would have to wait.

Because her house was so close to campus, Charlie decided to walk over so that she could leave her car and the U-Haul trailer that was still attached to it sitting in the driveway. The day was gorgeous, sunny, with the light breeze from the south stirring the air enough to keep the humidity at bay, and Charlie smiled as she made her way up a small bluff which afforded a stunning view of Blake's campus.

"Oh, wow," she murmured, taking a moment to soak up the magnificent view before starting down the hill to where the majority of the campus buildings were located. Large oak trees dotted the campus, casting an almost continuous shade over the wide sidewalks that wound beneath them. The colonial style buildings were red brick with white trim and black shutters, and Charlie was struck with a warm feeling of nostalgia because they were so similar to the ones at Wesleyan.

She checked the campus map she had saved on her phone when the sidewalk she was on split, and saw that if she took the left path that it would take her where she needed to go. After not even ten minutes of walking, she was almost to her destination, and she smiled at the idea of such a quick commute. It certainly beat having to deal with hurried Manhattan commuters in the subway to get to work every day. The Green in the center of campus was impressive, easily the size of two football fields, crisscrossed with sidewalks, and Reed Hall, home of the Blake University Journalism Department, sat on the western edge of the Green near the imposing four-story library that anchored the southern edge of the large lawn.

Reed Hall was three stories of towering brick, and Charlie chewed her lip nervously as she made her way through the double doors that were propped open. Several hallways branched off of the main entryway and she double-checked her notes with Jack O'Connell's office information on them before she headed for the wide, dark wood staircase that ran along the right hand wall.

She found his office easily once she reached the third floor, and she took a deep breath as she knocked on the open door, drawing the attention of the redheaded man in a dark blue polo shirt that was hunched over the desk writing furiously on a legal pad. "Professor O'Connor?"

The man at the desk looked up and smiled. "It's Jack, please," he said as he stood and waved her inside. "Charlie?"

"That's me," she said, smiling as she extended her hand. "It's so nice to meet you."

"The pleasure's mine," Jack replied, shaking her hand firmly before motioning at the chairs opposite his desk for her to sit.

She set her satchel on the floor beside the chair and took her seat, nervous excitement fluttering in her stomach as she looked into kindly green eyes that smiled back at her.

"You found the place all right? I know we're kind of out in the middle of nowhere here."

Charlie nodded. "No problem at all."

"Well, I have to say, I am quite excited to have you here. When I spoke with Juliette Newhouse at NYU, she had told me I was wasting my time contacting you about the position."

"How do you know Professor Newhouse?" Charlie asked, leaning back in her chair and smiling at the mention of her old advisor.

"We did our PhD work at Columbia at the same time. She speaks quite highly of you."

"I'm glad," Charlie said. "She was a wonderful teacher, and an even better mentor."

"Well, it seems like you were quite the student, too," Jack said, pulling Charlie's resume out of another file and looking at it. "You've won a National Magazine Award; by looking at the statistics for your online articles, you have a very large and loyal fanbase; your personal blog has over two million followers, and you're not even thirty."

Charlie smiled. "I peaked young."

"I guess," Jack replied, chuckling. He dropped her resume to his desk and shook his head. "I have to admit, I was surprised when I heard from you regarding the position. I wasn't expecting any response at all, to be honest."

"You caught me at a very good time," Charlie murmured, tucking her hair behind her ears.

Sensing that there was more to the story that the brunette was not willing to share, Jack nodded and obliged her obvious wish to change the subject. "Right, well, teaching. I put those five seminars we discussed onto the course catalogue for the semester, and you actually have a wait list for each," Jack said as he slid a manila folder full of class rosters across the desk to Charlie.

Charlie gave him a surprised look as she reached for the folder. "You're kidding."

He chuckled and shook his head. "I'm not."

"Wow," Charlie murmured as she opened the folder to look at her lists.

"The two seminars on Sports Journalism have some of the longest wait lists for the department this term."

"Okay, so now I'm even more nervous about this whole thing," Charlie muttered under her breath.

"Don't be. I'm sure you'll be great. And if you have any questions, Spencer Walsh will be able to help you out. He's a fourth year assistant professor and a Blake alumnus, and I think you two will get along well."

"I'll take any help I can get," Charlie replied, closing the folder she had been looking through and folding her hands on top of it.

Jack smiled reassuringly and glanced at his watch. "Spence should actually be here any time..." His voice trailed off and he smiled at the new face that appeared in his doorway. "Now."

"Am I late?" Spencer asked as he ambled into Jack's office in a pair of khaki cargo shorts and a black polo shirt. He ran a hand through his hair and smiled at the department chair.

"Not at all," Jack assured him. "We were just going over the sections Charlie will be teaching this semester."

Spencer's smile faded slightly as he looked at the brunette who was turned in her seat and looking at him. Her legs were long, lean, and perfectly tan, and even though she was sitting down, he could tell that she had curves that could drive a man or woman to absolute distraction. Combined with her sexy, purposefully messy haircut that brought to mind the indescribable look women got after they had been bedded, she was easily a twelve on a scale from one to ten. It didn't matter that he had never seen a picture of Mac's ex, the brunette was exactly her type and there was no way there were two women named Charlie walking around Hampton right now. "Charlie?"

"It's short for Charlotte," Charlie said, smiling as she got up to shake his hand. "Charlie Bennett. Jack was just telling me about you."

Spencer nodded and shook the brunette's hand, feeling like a traitor as he did so. Mac was going to flip her shit when she found out that her ex-girlfriend was the guest lecturer he was mentoring for the year. "Right. Well, don't believe anything he says," he told her, trying his best to look like he didn't already know quite a bit about her. "I'm not nearly the troublemaker he likes to make me out to be."

Jack cleared his throat. "I didn't tell her any of those stories."

"Oh." Spencer grinned sheepishly. "Good."

"I think I would like to hear some of those stories, though," Charlie chuckled.

"Maybe some other time," Spencer deflected, offering the brunette a wry smile. He looked at Jack and said, "So, what's the plan?"

The department chair smiled and tipped his head at Charlie. "Well, she already has some excellent ideas for how to approach the courses she'll be teaching from the angle of print sports media, so you'll just need to answer any questions she has regarding the technical side of teaching–lecture pacing, exams, etcetera."

"Not a problem," Spencer murmured.

"That reminds me, I have my syllabi done already," Charlie added, reaching into her satchel and pulling out a blue manila folder. "I used the sample you sent me and just modified it to fit the parameters of each seminar," she said as she handed it over to the department chair.

"Perfect," Jack said, smiling as he glanced at the top syllabus in the folder. "These look great."

Spencer cleared his throat, feeling like a complete slacker for not having his finished yet, and said, "I'll have mine to you by Monday."

"That'll be fine, Spence." Jack nodded as he dropped Charlie's folder onto his desk. "If you could just show Charlie around campus, help her find her office and the classrooms she'll be using, and then be available to answer any questions she might have, I think we're good here. Unless there is anything else you can think of?" he added, looking at Charlie.

"I think that should cover it for now," Charlie said.

Jack nodded and looked at Spencer. "Are you going to be helping with freshman orientation next week?"

"Yeah. And I'll be around on move in day for the upperclassmen as well," Spencer said.

* * *

"Good."

"Am I supposed to do that too?" Charlie asked. "I mean, I can help if it's needed."

"I think that would be a great idea," Jack said, and Spencer tensed because he knew what was coming next. "Why don't you tag along with Spence and he'll show you around, introduce you to some of the other faculty and the like. Walsh?"

"Not a problem," Spencer answered dutifully, even as he made a mental note to wear a cup when he told Mac that his mentoree would be joining them for the beginning of term activities.

"Perfect! I knew you were the man for the job," Jack said enthusiastically.

"Thanks," Spencer mumbled, running a hand through his hair uncomfortably.

Jack looked at Charlie and smiled. "Well, I'll let Spencer show you around the campus now because he knows it better than anyone. If you have any problems or questions or anything, don't hesitate to give me a call."

"Thank you," Charlie said. She stood and shook his hand. "And, thank you so much for this opportunity."

"Thank you," Jack said. He reached into his drawer and pulled out a key ring. "This one–" he pointed to a longer, brass-colored key, "–is for your office. The other is a master to the classrooms in here in Reed Hall. They're usually unlocked, but it's good for you to have a key just in case."

Charlie nodded and dropped the keys into her satchel. "Got it. Anything else?"

Jack shook his head. "First journalism department meeting is next Wednesday. Freshman move in on Thursday, and their orientation is Friday–I'll let you coordinate with Spencer for how you're going to handle that–and the returning students will arrive on Saturday. The real fun begins a week from Monday."

Charlie grinned. "I can't wait."

Chapter 4

"And this is Sanborn, where our offices are," Spencer said as he pulled open the front door to the building that housed the offices of the Arts departments' faculty. "Which one did they give you?"

Charlie glanced at the yellow post-it that was stuck to the front of the folder she had gotten from O'Connor. "Three thirteen."

Spencer nodded and did his best to not visibly cringe. Three thirteen was down the hall from his office and directly across the hall from Mac's. "Excellent."

"Is there something wrong?" Charlie asked, frowning at the hint of sarcasm in his tone. She had been trying her best to be friendly with Spencer as he had shown her around Reed Hall and the rest of the campus, but there was something about his demeanor that told her he wished he was anywhere other than with her.

"No," Spence murmured, shaking his head. For as much as he wanted to dislike the brunette because of what she had done to Mac, he found himself charmed by her quick wit and the stories she shared about working at *Sports Illustrated*. She was funny, incredibly bright, and he wished she would do something to justify disliking her because right now, besides the whole breaking Mac's heart thing, she was somebody he could easily picture himself hanging out with. Which, in the grand scheme of things, made perfect sense because she *had* dated his best friend for two and a half years. "Sorry. I just have a lot on my mind right now."

"It's okay," Charlie assured him. "If you need to go do stuff, I'm sure I'll be able to find my office on my own. Really, I need to get back to my house and start unloading all of my stuff so it's not sitting in the trailer overnight anyways. I just want to have a quick look at the space to see what I should bring over and what I should keep at home."

The idea of sending her up alone was tempting, but Spencer shook his head. "Nah, it's fine. I need to grab something from mine anyways," he lied. He had everything he needed on his laptop at home, but he had driven over with Mac, so he had nowhere else to go. Besides that, he had a feeling his roommate would appreciate a familiar face being around when she found out that not only was her ex the guest lecturer he would be mentoring for the coming year, but that she would also be taking up residence in the office across the hall from her.

"If you're sure," Charlie murmured as she followed him across the small lobby to the elevator.

"The stairs are usually faster when school is in session because kids going up and down clog up the elevator, but as long as they're not around it isn't too bad."

Charlie nodded. "I'll keep that in mind."

"Yeah," Spencer replied lamely, biting his lip as he reached out and punched the elevator call button.

As they waited for the elevator to arrive, Charlie studied Spencer's reflection in the brass doors. He was tall, easily six-foot-two, and well muscled, with keen hazel eyes and that all-American look that never failed to turn heads. She would bet her first National Magazine Award that he had been an athlete in college, and she wondered if that topic of conversation might make him more comfortable around her. "So, what was your sport?" she asked as the elevator arrived and she stepped inside.

Spencer smiled. "In college? Lacrosse."

"What position?"

"Attacker. You know a lot about the game?"

"A bit," Charlie admitted with a small shrug, "though I never played. My brothers did, though. It's a great game, even if it is completely and totally sexist."

Spencer arched a brow at the brunette and grinned, curious to where she was going with her argument. Not that it wasn't one that Mac made every time he dragged her to a game, but it would be interesting, considering Charlie's background in sports journalism, to hear her take on it all. "How is it sexist?"

"Oh please," Charlie scoffed as the elevator deposited them at the third floor. "No helmets for the girls. No pads. No real gloves. And I'm not even going to go into the differences in what type of sticks they're allowed because that's just beyond messed up. No body checking. Game stopping every two seconds for some lame-ass penalty that wouldn't ever be called in the men's game. If you'll excuse my language, fuck that. Girls can beat the hell out of each other with a stick just as well as the boys can. If not better, in some cases. Bitches be vicious."

Spencer laughed as he directed Charlie down the hall to the right and around the corner to where their offices were. "True. Bitches can be vicious. But I think the idea behind it is–"

"To not respect women as athletes who can actually compete at a sport and instead treat them as pretty little dolls who are *allowed* to go outside and play so long as they not disrupt the societal perception of what is appropriate for 'proper ladies' to do," Charlie interjected.

"I'm going to stop trying to defend my sport now," Spencer muttered, unwilling to get into an argument where he actually agreed with each of the points she had brought up.

Charlie laughed and nodded approvingly. "Wise decision."

"Thank you," he replied with a mock bow and a smile as he waved at the door to his right. "Okay, this is my office. If I'm in, the door's open–which is pretty much the policy around here. It's more for your protection than anything else. If you're alone in a closed room with a student and they claim you assaulted them or something, you have no defense. So, keep it open. If it's closed and you need me for some reason, just call me on my cell."

"Right. I wouldn't have thought of the whole door thing, so thanks," Charlie said, her eyes flicking away from his office to an open door near the end of the hall where she could hear music playing. The beat was familiar, though not loud enough for her to be able to place it, and she wondered who else she would be sharing the floor with that year.

Spencer followed her gaze and grit his teeth, knowing that he was about to walk into a lion's den. "And your office is just down here."

"Okay." Charlie nodded and followed him down the hall. When she was about ten feet from the office with the music playing, she realized that hers was the one directly across from it. *At least they have good taste,* she thought, bobbing her head a little to the beat of *Sports & Wine* as she glanced through the open door. Her heart caught in her throat when she met a surprised pair of blue eyes for the second time that day. Fate, it seemed, was determined to give her every opportunity to try and redeem herself. "Hello, Mackayla."

Mac looked from Charlotte to Spencer, who had his hands held up in front of himself in an *'I swear I didn't know'* type of gesture, and swallowed thickly. "Hey."

The air between the women crackled with tension, and Spencer cleared his throat nervously. "Hey. How's the syllabus coming?"

"Done. Just going through that manuscript now," Mac said. She took a deep breath and looked at Charlotte, forcing herself to at least pretend to be a mature adult when what she really wanted to do was throw something and scream that it wasn't fair that Charlotte was here to remind her of what she had lost. "Hello, again. So you're the mysterious guest lecturer, huh?"

"I...yeah," Charlie murmured, nodding. "Sorry I didn't say anything before. I was just really surprised to see you."

"Tell me about it," Mac muttered. She herself to keep her tone nonchalant as she asked, "So, you're going to take three thirteen?"

"I am. Is that okay?"

"It kind of has to be, doesn't it?" Mac replied dryly.

Spencer cleared his throat and tilted his head toward his office. "You okay if I duck down to my office for a few?"

Mac nodded, grateful that he was giving her some room to handle things. "Yeah. That's cool. I can work on this at home, so we can leave whenever you want. Just remember that it's your night to cook."

"Oh yeah," Spence drawled, brow furrowing with fake confusion. He always tried to get out of cooking whenever possible because Mac was so much better at it than he was. "You sure it's my night?"

"I'm sure. I made dinner before you went out last night, remember?"

"If I say no, will you cook again?"

Mac laughed. "No."

"Right, then I'm thinking Chinese," Spencer drawled.

"As long as you're buying," Mac told him. "I'll be down in a few, and then we can go. Okay?"

"Sounds good." Spence nodded as he backed slowly down the hall, looking as if he were afraid a brawl was going to break out at any moment and that he would have to jump back in to break it up.

Once he had finally disappeared into his office, Charlie asked, "You two live together?"

"Yeah. We met during orientation weekend for graduate school when I came up here to start my master's."

"Well, that would explain why he was so distant earlier," Charlie muttered to herself. She sighed and stepped into the blonde's open doorway, wrapping her arms around herself as she leaned against the jamb. "I didn't know you taught here. Before I ran into you earlier, I mean."

"Why would you?"

The coolness in Mackayla's tone felt like a slap to the face, and Charlie actually winced. "I'm sorry."

"For what?" Mac asked, arching a brow as she leaned back in her chair.

"Everything," Charlie whispered as she stared beseechingly at the blonde, trying to convince her with a look that she meant it more than words could possibly convey. "I'm sorry for everything, Mackayla."

The sound of her name falling from Charlotte's lips like that had always been enough to undo her, and Mac sighed as she ran her hands through her hair. "No. No. You don't get to do this. You don't get to try and walk back into my life like this when it was you leaving that messed everything up in the first place. Do you get that?"

Charlie nodded and swallowed thickly as her heart seized at the pain evident in every aspect of Mackayla's being. "I'm sorry," she whispered.

"Yeah," Mac murmured, licking her lips as she flipped the screen of her laptop shut. "I wish that were enough to fix it, but it's not. I..." Her voice trailed off as she looked up at the brunette, her eyes filling with tears that she refused to let fall. "Fuck, Charlotte. I just..." She shook her head, hating the fact that Charlotte could still affect her like this. "I gotta go."

"Yeah, of course." Charlie sighed as she watched Mac hurriedly pack up her things, and she swallowed thickly as she stepped back to allow the blonde to lock up her office. She wanted to apologize again, to pull Mackayla into her arms and convince her that walking away from their relationship was the biggest mistake of her life, but she didn't. She didn't want to push Mackayla any more than she already had just by being there, and she was afraid that what little hope still burned within her for a future with the blonde would be irrevocably extinguished if Mackayla pushed her away.

And she needed that hope.

She needed it like she needed air to breathe, because being in the same room with Mackayla again made her feel whole for the first time since she had so stupidly walked away from the blonde all those years ago. "I'll see you around, I guess."

"Yeah," Mac said, nodding as she looked at Charlotte. What little bit of her heart that she had managed to heal since the day the brunette left her shattered again at the sight of tears welling in Charlotte's expressive green eyes, and she shook her head. "I'll..." She cleared her throat and blinked hard to keep her own tears at bay. It had been difficult enough to see Charlotte that afternoon when the brunette had crashed into her, but the idea that it was a one-and-done type of thing made the pain she had felt at seeing her again tolerable. But now, the knowledge that she would be seeing Charlotte on an almost daily basis was overwhelming, and she needed to get away from her. "I'll see you around."

Charlie swallowed thickly and nodded as she watched Mackayla hurry down the hall, not even pausing as she strode past Spencer's door and yelled, "I'll meet you at the car!" before she rounded the corner and disappeared from sight.

Charlie's hands trembled as she slid her key into the lock of her office door, her head spinning like she was only moments away from passing out. It took longer than it should have for her to fit the key into the lock and twist it open; but, once it did, she quickly slipped inside, grateful for the privacy the space afforded her. She slammed her satchel down onto the desk and swore softly under her breath as she walked over to look out her window. The tears she had been holding back began to fall as she watched Mackayla run from the building, looking like the hounds of hell were chasing after her, and she wrapped her arms around herself as her tears fell faster and faster until she couldn't have stopped them, even if she tried.

Chapter 5

Four days had passed since Mac had last laid eyes on Charlotte. Four long, tedious days. No matter how much she wanted to ignore the fact Charlotte was going to be at least on the periphery of her life for the next nine months, whenever she stopped moving for too long, her thoughts would automatically turn to her ex. Charlotte's broken, whispered apology played on repeat inside her mind, the echo of brunette's sexy, smoky alto doing things to her body it had no right to do. The memory of the regret dimming Charlotte's normally bright green eyes tugged at her heartstrings no matter how much she wished it didn't. She had tried to distract herself with her work, poring through the edits on her manuscript, but the corrections were few and none required her to think too hard about them. The only solace that she was able to find from her thoughts was when she ran, and she had been spending more and more time pounding the pavement every day.

"I'm going for a run," Mac announced as she bounded down the stairs in a pair of slinky black running shorts and a pale gray tank with her shoes untied.

Spencer muted the Red Sox game he had been watching on the large television beside the fireplace in the living room, and turned to flash her a disbelieving look. "You're going out again? You already went this morning."

"We can't all be couch potatoes," Mac retorted, shooting him a grin as she propped her right foot on the edge of the second stair to tie her laces.

"Hey, I was in department meetings all morning, and I'll be working my ass off tomorrow helping all the freshmen get their shit up to their dorms. I've earned a lazy afternoon."

"I'm going to be right there with you tomorrow," Mac pointed out, switching feet and tying a tight double knot on her other shoe.

"Yeah, and I'm betting that's why you've been running like a madwoman lately. You're going to hurt yourself if you keep this up. You do know that you can't actually run away from her, right?"

Mac's smile faded and she shook her head. She didn't need him to play Jiminy Cricket to her battered psyche. She knew that she couldn't run away from Charlotte, but she was not at all interested in explaining to him exactly how much seeing the brunette again had affected her. "I don't know what you're talking about."

"Yeah, you do. And I get it, okay. But that doesn't make me any less worried about you."

The "worried best friend" plea was a cheap shot, Mac thought, running her hands through her hair in exasperation as she shot Spencer a look that begged him to just stop pushing her on the whole Charlotte thing. "There's nothing for you to be worried about. I'm fine."

"If you say so, Thomas," he murmured, obviously not buying a word she was saying but willing to concede the point for now and let it drop. "Just so you know, that storm watch the weather guy was talking about on the news this morning starts in like fifteen minutes. So take your cell with you, just in case."

"I have my phone right here," Mac said, waggling the armband case she always wore running at him as evidence. She bit her lip as she crossed the small foyer to the front door, and gave him what she hoped passed as a reassuring look as she pulled it open and stepped out onto the porch, calling out, "I'll be back later," as she slammed the door shut after herself.

 She stood on the porch as she fiddled with the Spotify app on her phone, queuing up the David Guetta playlist that she had been running to for the last few days because the pulsing house rhythm *almost* drowned out her thoughts. The neoprene band slipped easily around her bicep and she tugged it tight before fitting her earbuds into place, and she let out a small sigh of relief as she jogged down the front walk to the street. She automatically began to match her pace to the beat as she willed herself to stop thinking about Charlotte, focusing on her breathing and counting her steps as she ran.

 Her route took her north for a couple miles before cutting west toward campus, where she made her way through the paths of the university that she knew like the back of her hand. The familiar setting was comforting in its abandoned serenity, and she felt the weight that settled on her chest every time she stopped moving and started thinking begin to lift as she hit the practice fields that sat between the academic section of campus and the stadium that sat at the northwestern edge of the university's property.

 The stadium was empty when she slipped through the open gates and jogged through the short tunnel that cut under the bleachers. The sky blue Tartan oval that circled the university's football field and the bright yellow goalposts at either end of the gridiron stood in stark contrast to the towering pines that framed each end of the stadium and the dark gray clouds overhead. True to Spencer's warning, the rain the weatherman predicted began to fall before she had even finished her first lap. The drops warm, fat, and heavy, blurring her vision and causing her hair to fall into her face as she ran. She ignored the rain as she increased her pace so that even if her mind wanted to wander, she wouldn't have the energy to do it.

Time and distance became irrelevant as she pushed herself harder and faster, laps blending into a single blurry moment of unending exertion. It was peaceful and relaxing, invigorating and exhausting, and when her legs refused to carry her any further, she slowed to a hobbled walk with a pleased smile on her face, her mind blissfully blank. She yanked her earbuds from her ears and leaned against the railing of the bleachers to stretch, humming contentedly under her breath as she rested her forehead against the cool aluminum.

"Mackayla!"

Her head snapped up at the sound of her name, and her heart caught in her throat when she saw who it was that had called to her. Charlotte was jogging toward her in the outside lane of the track. The brunette's hair was soaked, her flawless skin flushed with exertion and glistening from the falling rain that made the cardinal red soccer shorts and black tank top that she was wearing cling to every one of her delicious curves. Mac didn't want to find her attractive, did not want to remember the way it felt to run her hands over Charlotte's body, but she did. And a jolt of anger surged through her because of it.

"You have got to be fucking kidding me," Mac muttered, her stomach sinking painfully as she turned to face Charlotte.

"Hey, you," Charlie called out as she slowed to a stop in front of Mackayla. Her stomach fluttered with anticipation as her eyes raked over the blonde's body, and she smiled nervously, feeling like a schoolgirl with a crush as she pushed her bangs out of her face. "I tried waving to you when I got out here, but you were lost in your own little world."

"Yeah, I kind of do that when I run," Mac murmured.

A small, wistful smile tweaked Charlie's lips, and she nodded. "Yeah, I remember that about you. How many laps did you do?"

"I dunno. I wasn't counting." Mac combed her hands through her hair and closed her eyes, lifting her face to the sky as she resisted the urge to just run away. For as much as she wished simply running away was the answer to her problems, the fact that Charlotte was standing in front of her now was proof enough that that method of coping was not going to work. She took a deep breath as she forced herself to meet the brunette's gaze, and the question she had been turning over and over in her mind ever since she all but ran out of her office on Friday afternoon spilled from her lips before she could rein it in. "Why are you here, Charlotte?"

"To work out," Charlie replied, frowning. "It's allowed, right? I mean, I assumed that since the gates were open that it was okay."

"Yes, it's allowed. And that's not what I was asking. I meant, what are you doing here in New Hampshire? Why in the world are you here when you had your dream job and everything you ever wanted in New York?"

"I had my dream job, yes," Charlie conceded with a small nod, crossing her arms over her chest. "But that was pretty much all I had, Mackayla. Is it really so hard for you to believe that maybe I need more than just a job to be happy?"

Mac shrugged. "It's not hard to believe. It's just..."

"You don't want me here," Charlie murmured.

"It's not that," Mac argued. She rolled her eyes at the disbelieving look Charlotte shot her and sighed. "Okay, yeah, I don't, to be honest. But, more than that, it's just..." Her voice trailed off and she shook her head sadly as she looked at the brunette. She wanted to hate her. And, honestly, a part of her did. But underneath her righteous anger was a simmering affection that time and heartache had failed to extinguish. She sighed and chewed her lip thoughtfully as she looked at Charlotte, seeing a hint of the years that had passed etched in the brunette's more mature gaze, and she sighed as a fleeting wish that they could go back to when things were good flashed through her mind. The thought was gone in a heartbeat, but she still silently cursed Charlotte for making her even consider it if only for the briefest of moments.

When it seemed like the blonde was not going to finish her thought, Charlie tilted her head to the side entreatingly and asked, "It's just, what?"

Mac sighed and shook her head, her shoulders dropping under the weight of her conflicting emotions. "It hurts, seeing you again. And I know that we're not kids anymore and that *we*–" she waved a hand between herself and the brunette, "–were eight fucking years ago. And I get all of that, I do. But it just...god, Charlotte, it just really fucking hurts."

Charlie swallowed thickly and nodded, her eyes stinging with tears as the brutal honesty in the blonde's admission stabbed at her heart. "I'm sorry. I know it's not enough to fix what happened, but you have to believe me when I say that I *am* sorry."

"I do believe you," Mac murmured, brushing her hair from her face as the rain continued to pound mercilessly down on them. She rolled her eyes, sighing softly as she shrugged. "It just doesn't make it any better."

"I know." Charlie nodded. She licked her lips and added softly, "It hurts me too."

Mac stiffened as a bolt anger shot through her. "You don't get to say that," she said, pointing an irate finger at the brunette.

"What?" Charlie asked, arching a brow defiantly. "That seeing you again hurts me too?"

"You walked away from me," Mac hissed. "From us. You don't get to play the wounded heart card."

"You're right. I did," Charlie admitted, throwing her hands up in the air. "I made a huge fucking mistake and I walked away from the best thing I ever had in my life, okay? Happy?"

Mac fisted her hands at her sides, clenched her jaw, and shook her head. "How could that make me happy? You fucking broke me, Charlotte!"

"Yeah, well, I fucking broke me too!" Charlie screamed back at her, the tears she had been holding back spilling over her cheeks and mixing with the raindrops that were running slowly down her face. "And I get that you're pissed, I do. And I get that you really don't want me here. But I didn't take this position to harass you. I didn't even fucking know that you were here!"

Mac closed her eyes and shook her head. "You should have known."

"Why?" Charlie demanded. "Even better, how? How could I have possibly known? You've kept in touch with exactly *nobody* from Wesleyan. Your old email address is for shit. Hell, you're not even on Facebook."

"You could have looked through the faculty list!"

"Yes, of course," Charlie scoffed, shaking her head in disbelief. "Because, as I was sitting at my kitchen table in the middle of the night, nursing a mild head wound from a flying fucking stiletto that a crazy redhead chucked at me because I screamed *your* goddamn name while I was having sex with her, it was your current place of employment and not my own fucking unhappiness that was at the forefront of my mind!"

Mac sucked a breath through her teeth as a jolt of completely unfounded jealousy ripped through her. "So you could think of me while you were fucking some woman but not while looking at Blake?"

"Oh my god! That's what you got from that? Seriously?"

"What else am I supposed to get from it?" Mac yelled.

"That I was miserable," Charlie answered simply, her voice quieting so that it barely carried over the sound of the rain as the will to fight left her. She sighed and rubbed her forehead as she decided to just lay all her cards on the table. "Or maybe that I regret walking away from you, and that I just needed to get away from my life in New York because I was drowning. Pick any of those explanations that make you happy, because they're all true."

Mac bit her lip and shook her head as she took a moment to absorb what the brunette had just said. She scrubbed her hands over her face to try and clear her mind, because it was all just too much to process. "What do you want, Charlotte?" she asked in a small, tired voice.

"I don't know," Charlie lied.

Mac rolled her eyes. "Yes, you do."

"Yeah, well, I have a feeling that you really don't want me to answer that right now, Mackayla," Charlie murmured knowingly.

It was not hard for Mac to figure out what it was that Charlotte wasn't saying, and she nodded. "Yeah, you're right. I don't want to hear it. You'll be leaving here at the end of the school year."

"And if I didn't? If I stayed?"

Mac groaned. "Don't."

Charlie took a small step forward so that she was able to reach out and lightly run her fingers over the blonde's arm. The goosebumps that erupted in the wake of her touch gave her a small measure of hope and she swallowed thickly as she looked up into Mackayla's defiant blue eyes. "Mackayla."

"Don't," Mac growled, shaking her head as she pulled away, her eyes filling with tears. "Just, don't."

"But–" Charlie started to argue, but before she could get anywhere, Mackayla was pushing past her for the exit.

"I gotta go," Mac muttered, desperate to get as far away from Charlotte as possible. Being this close to the brunette was too much for her to handle, and she just needed to get away.

Charlie bit her lip and nodded slowly. "Okay," she murmured, her voice too quiet for Mackayla to hear.

Chapter 6

It was a little after eight o'clock the next morning when Charlie made her way across the Green to where she had arranged to meet Spencer. She was exhausted. Sleep had all but eluded her the night before, her mind too preoccupied replaying her run-in with Mackayla from every possible angle to allow her any rest. The only positive thing that she could take from their heated encounter was that Mackayla still felt something for her, but that did little to make her feel better when the blonde seemed hell-bent on trying to fight it.

But, it was a new day, the sun was shining and the sky was a cloudless, perfect blue, and she was determined to try and get through the day with a smile.

"Oops, sorry," she murmured as she sidestepped a frazzled looking mother whose arms were so full of pillows and bedding that she couldn't see where she was going. The campus was a zoo, crowded with far too many cars and people for there being only one thousand incoming freshmen, and Charlie sighed as she looked around the crush of people, suddenly doubting her ability to even find Spencer once she actually reached Royce Hall.

Of course, had she been thinking properly, she would have realized that he would be with Mackayla, and that she had never had a problem finding the blonde, no matter the size of the crowd. And, sure enough, not even two minutes later, she spotted

Mackayla's familiar shock of blonde hair standing in the shade beneath an oak tree about twenty yards from the front door of Royce Hall dormitory. Both Mackayla and Spencer had clipboards in their hands, and they looked to be directing a fleet of upperclassmen with trolleys toward different families that looked like they needed help. They were dressed identically in light blue polo shirts, khaki-colored shorts, running shoes, and sunglasses, and Charlie couldn't help but be amused at the fact that even their white-framed Oakleys with bright blue reflective lenses matched.

The sight of Mackayla smiling so easily made Charlie's breath hitch, and she could not help but wish that Mackayla was smiling like that at her. She was tempted to just hang back and watch, to selfishly enjoy the sight of Mackayla being so carefree and happy, to remember the times when the blonde had looked at her with that much joy in her expression, but before she could seriously consider doing so, Spencer was smiling at her and waving her over.

"Here we go," she muttered to herself, drawing a deep breath to steel her nerves as she ambled over to them. She bit her lip at the way Mackayla's jaw lifted defiantly when the blonde saw her, and she forced herself to smile as she teased, "Don't you two look like the Bobbsey twins."

"Like we haven't heard that one before," Spence retorted, offering the brunette a friendly smile as he felt Mac stiffen beside him. He wished he knew what was going on between the two women, but all he got from his roommate was "It's complicated," which was not particularly helpful. Add in the fact that he actually liked Charlie, who he had spent some time with after their department meeting the day before going over lecture pacing and exam schedules, and he was stuck in a no-win situation. "So, how you doing, Charlie? Did you get that lecture schedule worked out?"

"I'm doing well, thanks. And, yeah, got it all figured out. Thanks for your help," Charlie replied, shoving her hands into the pockets of her shorts and looking around. "You know, it's a lot busier than I expected it to be."

"Yeah, well, then I recommend you stay the hell away this weekend when everybody else comes back," Spencer told her. "Because this is a cakewalk compared to that."

Charlie grinned. "Duly noted. So do all the upperclassmen live on campus, then?"

"Pretty much. Juniors and seniors can petition to live off campus if they want, but most don't because everybody is here: either in the dorms, residence halls–which are more like two bedroom apartments–or over on Greek row."

"That's kind of cool, actually," Charlie murmured, nodding as she looked at Mackayla, who she wished wasn't wearing sunglasses, so that she could see her eyes. Mackayla's eyes always betrayed her mood, which would be especially helpful considering how they left things the night before. "Hello, Mackayla."

Mac nodded and offered the brunette a small smile. "Charlotte. Did you finish your run all right?"

The coolness in Mackayla's tone made Charlie's stomach sink, and she nodded. "Yeah, though I doubt I did anything near the distance you did."

Spencer didn't even look up from his clipboard as he chimed in, "And she was back out this morning before the sun came up. Did another, what did you say when you crawled home? Ten?"

"I did not crawl home. And yeah, it was something like that," Mac muttered. She had spent a sleepless night tossing and turning as her mind replayed her encounter with the brunette the night before, and even her dreams, when she had managed to nod off, provided little respite as every one featured Charlotte. She had dreamt of the good times they had shared, of soft kisses and even softer touches, and when she woke up, she grabbed her gear and took off, desperate to forget it all.

Charlie knew that Mackayla used to run like a madwoman when she needed to clear her head, and she frowned as she finally understood why the blonde had run for so hard and so long the night before. She didn't know exactly how much distance Mackayla had covered, but she had watched her rip off five miles at an increasing pace before she had even jogged out onto the track and tried to get her attention. And it had been another eleven laps for the blonde before she finally succeeded. But, instead of saying anything about that, Charlie just whistled and drawled, "Damn. Are you training for something?"

"No." Mac shook her head and looked away toward the front of the dormitory, pretending to be interested in the comings and goings of the students moving in, their parents, and the upperclassmen volunteers who were helping them. "You know I like running."

Before Charlie could respond, however, they were interrupted by the arrival an older student who looked close to tears. "I'm sorry," the girl said as she approached the group, her red-rimmed eyes zeroing in on Mac. "Professor Thomas, can I talk to you, please?" she asked, her lower lip trembling.

Charlie frowned and looked at Mackayla, who was already nodding and motioning across the Green toward Sanborn. "Of course you can, Liv. We'll go up to my office and get away from everybody, okay?"

"Thank you," Olivia murmured. "Hello, Professor Walsh," she said, nodding at Spencer.

"Hey, Liv," he replied gently, his brow furrowed with concern.

"I'll be back in a while," Mac said.

"Take your time," Spencer said, nodding understandingly. "We got this. You take care of her."

"Thanks," Mac sighed, running a hand through her hair as she turned and started walking toward her office.

Charlie cleared her throat once Mackayla and the student were gone. "Can I ask what that was about?"

Spencer looked at Charlie and sighed. "Mac and I are advisors for GLOW here on campus."

"What's glow?" Charlie asked.

"It's Blake's Gay-Straight Alliance group, but we call it GLOW–Gay Lesbian or Whatever," Spence explained. He flagged down a passing student with an empty trolley and hollered, "There are a bunch of families lost on the southern edge of the Green. Go see if you can help out there."

"Will do, Professor Walsh," the kid replied with a wave before he hustled off.

"Sorry," Spencer apologized. "Anyways, yeah. Mac is kind of like the big sister to the kids, giving them all the 'being gay in the real world' type of advice, and I'm like the overprotective straight big brother who is proof that not everybody is a total dick. That's all I can really tell you, which isn't an answer, I know, but we gotta protect our kids."

"No, it's fine," Charlie assured him. "I'm glad Mackayla is comfortable enough to jump in and help with a group like that. I kept trying to get her to join the GSA when we were in school, and she always refused."

Spencer groaned and shook his head. "Yeah, because her father is on the faculty at Wesleyan and she didn't want him to know."

"I know," Charlie said, rolling her eyes. "I still..."

Spencer shook his head. "How did your family react when you came out?"

Charlie shrugged. "Fine. I mean, it took them a few months to get over the shock or whatever, but they're okay now. My mother is actually bugging me for grandchildren and regularly sends me links of donor profiles she likes at a Boston sperm bank."

"Yeah, well, when Mac came out, it wasn't all rainbows and unicorns and shit, okay?" he said, arching a brow at her over the frame of his glasses. "Look, I get that there's some unresolved tension between you guys and, honestly, I understand. Seeing the way you look at each other when the other isn't paying attention, it's just..." He sighed and reached down to turn off his walkie-talkie that had been chattering since she had arrived. "I'm gonna go all overprotective best friend for a minute, okay?"

Charlie nodded and smiled nervously. "Go for it."

"What do you want from her?"

"Somehow I knew that was what you were going to ask," Charlie muttered. "Can I go all super-honest, regretful ex-girlfriend for a minute?"

He grinned and nodded. "Hit me with it."

"I was very unhappy in New York at *SI*. I got the envelope with the offer from Blake on a Friday afternoon, but I didn't open it until late that night, after I'd had a crazy redhead chuck my high heels at me before storming out of my apartment."

"You had a chick throw shoes at you? Even I haven't managed that one before," he muttered with an amused chuckle.

Charlie rolled her eyes and shrugged. "Yeah, well, she didn't appreciate me screaming Mackayla's name as I...um, you know."

"I see." Spencer smirked. "Okay."

"Anyways, I didn't take this job because Mackayla was here. Like I told her yesterday, I didn't know where she was. She all but disappeared off the face of the earth after Wesleyan."

"Yeah, well, there's a reason for that," Spence muttered, and, catching the look Charlie shot him, shook his head. "That's her story to tell, not mine."

"Of course," Charlie murmured. "Look, the long and the short of it all is that there's a lot I want from her. I would like her forgiveness, to begin with. Her friendship. But when all is said and done, what I really want is her. I've always wanted her."

"Then why...?"

Charlie sighed and shook her head sadly. "You have to understand that Mackayla wasn't out to *anyone* and I had been all but forced back into the closet for her. You work with this GLOW group, so I'm sure you've seen firsthand how hard it is to live a double-life. It was suffocating. Especially because I had already come out and I knew what it was like to not worry about who knew I was gay, or suspected I might be gay, or whatever. I couldn't tell my friends about the amazing girl that I was in love with because then they might question all the times they'd seen me with her. I had to put up with my family trying to set me up on blind dates because they assumed I was lying when I told them that I had a girlfriend since she refused to come to any of the family events that I invited her to. Walking away wasn't easy. It killed me to do it, but I just couldn't live like that any longer. I wanted her. All of her. I wanted the world to know that I loved her and that she loved me and that it was, to steal your phrase from earlier, all rainbows and unicorns and shit."

"She's still not over it," Spencer shared.

"I know," Charlie murmured, nodding. "She's made that point perfectly clear. To be honest, I'm not either. But I'm trying to fix it."

"Good luck with that one."

Charlie flashed him a wry smile. "I know, right? You wanna help me out?"

"I don't think so," Spencer chuckled, shaking his head.

"Fair enough." Charlie sighed and ran a hand through her hair. "So, yeah. That's it. You gonna kick my ass now, or are we cool?"

"We're cool," Spencer assured her as he turned his walkie-talkie back on. "You and Mac, on the other hand..."

Charlie nodded. "Yeah. Like I said, I'm trying to fix that."

"Walsh, you there, man? Come on!" the walkie squawked.

"Shit," Spencer muttered as he snatched the walkie-talkie off his belt and lifted it to his mouth. "'Sup, Rock?"

"You have the latest assignment roster for Camden, yeah? I've got a student here who says she got an email last week telling her she was moved over here from Holbrook."

"Yeah. I don't have that list on me. Mac was supposed to run it over."

"Well, isn't she with you? Can't you just read me what I'm looking for?"

"Mac, uh, had something she needed to take care of," Spencer hedged. "Gimme a few and I'll find that information for you."

"Thanks."

"Professor Walsh!" one of the upperclassmen pushing an over-packed trolley hollered as it capsized, sending the luggage that had been precariously stacked on top of it flying. "Help, please!"

Spencer groaned and shot an apologetic look at Charlie. "I need to go help him. Could you maybe run over to her office, get that list from Mac, and then just run it over to Camden? It's the dorm right behind Sanborn, actually, so you won't be able to miss it."

"Of course," Charlie said, nodding. "What was the name of the guy who needed it?"

"Paul Rock. He's a math professor here. Little dude, not much taller than you, with a shaved head and thick, black-framed glasses. Odds are actually pretty good that he's wearing a bow tie."

"I got it," Charlie assured him, smiling at the mental image she got of the professor she was supposed to be delivering the list to. "I'll grab the list from Mackayla and run it over there to him."

"You are a lifesaver, Charlie Bennett," Spencer said, grinning at her before he took off running toward the upperclassman who was wrestling with his overturned trolley.

"If only everyone thought so," Charlie muttered under her breath, shaking her head as she started across the Green toward their offices. She wound her way through a sea of eager, yet terrified looking students and their parents, and sighed with relief as she entered the empty courtyard that led to the front doors of Sanborn.

The third floor was predictably empty as Charlie made her way toward hers and Mackayla's offices, and she knew that, judging by the crowd outside, this quietude was sure to be nothing but a distant memory when classes began on Monday. The hushed squeak of the soles of her running shoes against the linoleum floor rolled down the hall in front of her, announcing her presence, and she chewed her lip nervously as she approached Mackayla's open door. It was obvious that something big was bothering the student Mackayla had come up here with, and she really didn't want to intrude when the student clearly needed to confide in somebody she trusted.

Quiet, muffled crying spilling into the hall from Mackayla's open door gave Charlie pause, and she knocked lightly on the doorframe as she stepped into the threshold. "Sorry to interrupt," she murmured, ducking her head and offering Mackayla an apologetic smile, "but they need the updated roster that you have for Camden. Spencer is being all manly and lifting heavy stuff, so he sent me up here to get it from you."

"Crap, that's right," Mac said, immediately reaching for her back pocket and pulling out a folded sheet of paper. "I meant to drop it off on my way in and totally forgot about it."

Charlie watched Mackayla give Liv's shoulder a reassuring touch as she walked past her to the door, and she arched a brow questioningly as she took the papers from Mackayla. "Thanks."

"Thank you," Mac whispered. "Tell Rocky that I'm sorry."

"It's not a big deal. Don't worry about it," Charlie said. She tipped her head at Liv and asked, "She going to be okay?"

Mac nodded. "Eventually, yeah."

"Is there anything I can do?" Charlie offered, her heart breaking a little at the way the girl's shoulders shook with her quiet sobs.

"No," Mac said, shaking her head as she glanced back Liv.

There was a softness to Mackayla's expression that told Charlie that the refusal of her help wasn't personal, and she nodded as she rolled the pages Mackayla had handed her. "You want me to bring you guys some bottled waters or something after I drop this off?" she offered, knowing that if the girl was so upset that she was still crying, she would need something to drink soon.

"That..." Mac's voice trailed off and she nodded. "That would be nice, thanks."

Pleased that Mackayla was going to let her do something, even if it was something as simple as fetching water, Charlie beamed and nodded. "Well, if you think of anything else, shoot me a text."

"I don't have your phone number, Charlotte."

"Spencer does. You can get it from him if you want. Go help her," Charlie murmured. "I'll be back in a few with those waters for you guys."

Chapter 7

Charlie made her way quickly back down the hall toward Mackayla's office with three bottled waters and a handful of various snacks from the vending machines on the first floor clutched to her chest. The bottles kept slipping as she tried to hang onto the small packages of crackers, cookies, and candy bars, and she was beginning to seriously rethink her altruism because if another bottled water fell on her foot like the one did in the elevator, she was going to scream. The sound of quiet voices talking spilled from Mackayla's open door and she sighed with relief at the idea of being able to put everything down.

"My dad disowned me when I came out, too," she heard Mackayla say and, in her shock, her grip on one of the waters slipped and almost everything else she was carrying fell to the floor. Spencer had hinted that Mackayla's coming out hadn't been perfect, and she had known that the blonde had been hesitant to come out when they were together because was afraid of how her father would respond to it, but it had honestly never crossed her mind that his reaction would be so extreme.

"Shit," she muttered, red faced with embarrassment as she bent over to try and pick everything up. A pair of battered Asics slipped into her peripheral vision and she groaned.

Mac smiled in spite of herself as she looked down at Charlotte, thinking that the brunette looked utterly adorable with a bottled water and three bags of pretzels clutched to her chest as she scrambled to try and pick up everything that she had dropped. "Is everything okay down there?"

"Just peachy," Charlie muttered, blowing her bangs out of her eyes as she looked up at the blonde. Her breath caught in her throat at the amused smile tweaking Mackayla's lips, and she cleared her throat nervously. "Um, hey."

"Hey." Mac arched a brow questioningly as she surveyed the mess that still littered the floor, idly wondering if Charlotte had bought out the entire vending machine. "Would you like some help?"

"Not if you're going to be all condescending about it," Charlie retorted as she duckwalked after a water bottle that continued to roll away from her.

"Charlotte," Mac chuckled. "Thank you for this. Really. May I please pick up that last water that seems hell-bent on running away from you?"

Kinda like somebody else I know, Charlie thought, glancing up at the blonde from the corner of her eye. She huffed and exasperated breath and nodded as she pushed herself back to her full height. "Go for it," she said, tipping her head at the rogue bottle as she walked into Mackayla's office. She caught Liv's eye as she set the drinks and stuff onto the blonde's desk and she offered the girl a small smile. "Would you like a drink or something to eat?"

Liv nodded. "That would be great, thanks. Are you a new professor here?"

"Me?" Charlie asked, shaking her head. "Nope. I'm just a lowly guest lecturer for the journalism department this year."

"She's being modest," Mac said as she walked back into her office with the rogue water and leaned against the front edge of her desk. "Charlotte took a leave from her position as an assistant editor at *Sports Illustrated* to come up here and teach for a year."

Liv looked from Mac to Charlie and nodded. "I see."

"It's not like that," Mac said quickly, shaking her head. "We went to undergrad together."

Charlie bit her lip and just nodded when Liv's questioning gaze landed on her. Though she wanted the girl's suppositions to be true, she was still surprised that somebody who didn't know her history with Mackayla might pick up on the whole thing. What was not surprising, was the hurt that stabbed at her from Mackayla's quick dismissal of the idea of them being a couple.

"Sorry, my mistake," Liv murmured. "My gaydar must be off."

"It's not," Charlie assured her with a small smile. "We're just not together." Anymore, she added silently.

Liv nodded. "Well, I'm sorry that I jumped to conclusions. Are you going to be helping with GLOW this year?"

"I wouldn't be opposed, but we haven't really discussed it or anything," Charlie answered, shooting Mackayla a look. The blonde's expression was inscrutable and she sighed. "Well, I'll let you guys get back to whatever it was you were..."

"You don't have to leave." Liv shook her head as she leaned back in her chair and twisted the top off her water. "We were just talking about my options since my parents disowned me last night after I came out."

"Oh," Charlie said. She offered the girl a small smile and added, "I'm so sorry."

"Thanks," Liv muttered. "At least I have a scholarship for my tuition and stuff so I only have to worry about finding a way to cover my living expenses." She looked at Mac. "Do you know of any places on campus that are hiring?"

"The usual suspects for the beginning of the year," Mac replied. She ran a hand through her hair and rattled off, "The student union, the library, all that. Give the semester a few weeks and you could probably pick up some tutoring."

"What's your major?" Charlie asked.

"Pre-med and biochem," Liv answered with a sheepish smile. "Though how I'm going to pay for med school now is anyone's guess."

"The same way everybody else does," Mac said. "You go into debt up to your eyeballs and you spend the next thirty years paying it off."

Charlie laughed. "I'm still paying off my grad school."

"Me too," Mac muttered, ducking her head and trying to get Liv's attention. "It will be okay. I know it doesn't seem like it now, but you will be okay." She took a deep breath and asked, "What's your course load look like this semester?"

"Pretty full," Liv admitted.

Mac nodded thoughtfully. "Look, GLOW has a scholarship that we keep in our back pocket to help in cases like this. Lemme talk to Spence, and we'll figure something out."

"I don't want to take money away from the group," Liv said, shaking her head.

"You won't be," Mac assured her. "I just don't want you taking on so much that your grades slip. Have you gotten your MCATs back yet?"

Liv grinned. "Nailed it. I got a thirty-eight."

"So you're pretty much guaranteed that spot you wanted in next year's med school class here," Mac said, smiling proudly at the girl.

Liv nodded. "Yeah, I should be hearing something soon on early-admission."

"You'll get in with that score," Mac assured her. "So, what you need to focus on now is keeping your grades up and starting to look into scholarship opportunities for next year. Get a job at the library or somewhere where it won't impact your studying too much, and GLOW will chip in to cover the rest of your expenses for the year since it's really too late for you to be applying for aid."

"You're sure?" Liv asked, arching a brow questioningly at Mac.

"I'm sure," Mac said, nodding. "Now, have you told Alex about what happened?"

"Yeah, I went over to her place last night after my folks gave me half an hour to pack my stuff and leave. She told me that I could just stay with her, since I practically lived there anyways, and that will help keep my expenses down."

"Liv's girlfriend is a second-year law school student here," Mac explained for Charlie, who was looking on with a small, confused smile.

"Ah, gotcha," Charlie murmured.

Liv nodded and screwed the top back onto her water bottle. "Yeah. Well, thanks for listening, Mac," she said as she pushed herself to her feet. "I just needed to vent and..."

"I get it," Mac said, smiling as she pulled the girl into a light embrace. "You'll be okay."

"Yeah, I know," Liv murmured.

"If you need anything, you come to me or Spence. Got it?"

"I got it," Liv assured her as she pulled away. She took a deep breath and smiled at Charlie. "It was nice to meet you."

"Same here," Charlie murmured. "Good luck with everything."

Liv ducked her head and nodded. "Thank you," she said, flashing them both one last grateful smile before she turned and walked out of the office.

Once they were alone, Charlie sighed and dropped into the chair Liv had just vacated. "How awful."

"It happens," Mac said, shrugging as she pushed herself up onto her desk. She crossed her legs under herself and looked at Charlie. "I'll make sure she gets through the year, though."

"With that scholarship?" Charlie asked.

Mac bit her lip and nodded sheepishly. "Yeah."

Easily reading the look on the blonde's face, Charlie smiled and shook her head. "There is no scholarship fund, is there?"

"Not really, but this makes me think that we should get one established," Mac said, shrugging dismissively. "Look, she has a full ride for tuition and books, and if she's living with her girlfriend, it won't be bad. I know she won't run up any insane bills–in fact, she'll probably try and live on Ramen noodles or some shit to not spend money on food–and I want her to succeed. She's a good kid and she doesn't deserve to have her entire future fucked because of her parents' prejudices."

Charlie nodded. "I heard what you told her before I dropped the snacks and everything everywhere."

"I figured as much," Mac said. She sighed and ran a hand through her hair. "That's another reason why I want her to make it. I waited until I was done with undergrad and had my tuition and everything covered up here before I came out because I knew my dad would disown me for it and, look, after you left, he was pretty much all I had left. My mom was already gone."

Charlie bit her lip as she remembered consoling Mackayla after her mother's funeral their sophomore year. An only child of only children, the loss had hit the blonde especially hard because she had absolutely adored her mother. She opened her mouth to say something, but was cut off by a shake of Mackayla's head.

"Please don't," Mac whispered. She cleared her throat softly and sighed. "Anyways, Liv is acting tough about all this, but she knew going into it that her parents probably weren't going to take the news well and she did it anyways."

"That was brave of her," Charlie murmured.

"Or stupid, considering the position she's now in," Mac muttered. She shook her head. "Look, I know you never understood why I needed to wait until after I'd graduated from Wesleyan, but sometimes you have to look at the big picture and make sure that you can survive the fallout."

Charlie swallowed thickly. "I get it."

"Do you?" Mac asked, frowning. "Because you sure as hell didn't back then."

"That's not fair," Charlie said, leaning forward in her chair. "I understood. But you were talking about waiting until you had your PhD and I just...shit, Mackayla, I just couldn't accept the idea of hiding who I was for another five years. If..." Her voice trailed off and she shook her head "You know what? Never mind."

"What?"

Charlie licked her lips and shook her head again. "I could have handled never telling your dad, so long as I got to actually be with you someplace other than my place or a locked room at some party somewhere where everybody was too wasted to notice that we were actually together. You could have come home with me to Boston as my girlfriend and your dad would have never known the difference. When we went down to New Haven for dinner and stuff, we could have held hands or kissed or whatever and nobody would have cared. Nobody would have called your father and told him they saw you with me. But you were so far into the closet that I still look back and wonder how in the hell you ever kissed me back that first night at the Tri-Delt house because you didn't want anyone to know you were gay."

Mac's heart clenched at Charlotte's words, and she could easily read the lingering exasperation that was etched into the brunette's expression. "Was it really that bad for you?" she asked softly.

"No. God, no. I was so happy with you," Charlie breathed, shaking her head as she leaned back in her chair. "It just seemed like things were never going to change. I felt like I was dying a little inside everyday because I wanted to shout from the rooftops that I loved you, and I couldn't. Because you were in the closet, I had to be–and I just couldn't take it anymore. Do you realize that we never went on an actual date?"

Mac's brow furrowed as memories of dates they had gone on flashed across her mind. "Yes, we did."

"No, we didn't," Charlie said gently, smiling sadly and shaking her head. "We would go out and take turns picking up the tab, but because you wanted to stay in the closet, I never got to walk down the street holding your hand. I never got to walk you to your door and kiss you goodnight. I never got to tell my friends about the amazing girl that I was so head over heels in love with because doing so would've outed you, and I would have rather died before I did that. I don't regret any of the time we spent together, Mackayla. I just wish I had been smart enough to realize that being with you even with those limitations was better than not being with you at all." She stared at the blonde for a moment, trying to convey with a look exactly how much she wished she had acted differently back then, and then sighed as she glanced at her watch. "I should probably get back down to the Green," she murmured.

"Yeah, um, me too," Mac said, nodding. She bit her lip as she slid off her desk and she rubbed her hands nervously against her shorts as she looked at the brunette. It had been so easy to blame Charlotte for everything that had happened eight years ago because the brunette hadn't told her anything other than she was tired of waiting for her to come out. But now, having actually heard and understood what Charlotte was thinking back then, she couldn't deny that even though Charlotte was the one to walk away, that she hadn't exactly been rushing to meet her halfway, either. In the end, it was just as much her fault as Charlotte's that their relationship failed. "I'm sorry, Charlotte," she whispered.

"Me too, sweetie," Charlie murmured, the old endearment slipping past her lips before she could contain it. She smiled sheepishly and shrugged. She wanted nothing more than to pull the blonde into her arms and hold her close, but she knew that gesture wouldn't be appreciated, no matter the emotional ground they had just gained. "We should probably get back down there, though, before Spencer begins to think that you killed me or something."

Mac swallowed thickly as the unexpected urge to pull Charlotte into her arms overtook her. The strength of the sudden impulse knocked the breath from her lungs, and she shook her head as she tried to force the idea from her mind. Just because she really and truly understood everything did not mean that she was willing to open herself up to the brunette again. That road was not one she had any desire to travel again. "Yeah," she muttered, nodding jerkily. "Let's go."

Chapter 8

With both Charlotte and the last of the parents reluctant to leave their "babies" at college finally gone, Mac was more than ready to go home and hide from the world until she was forced to see the brunette again the following day. But a strong arm draping itself around her shoulders, steering her gently yet forcefully toward the parking lot behind the library where Spencer had parked that morning, told her that her desire to climb into bed, pull her blankets over her head, and disappear was not going to happen. She knew from the way he had been side-eyeing her all afternoon that he had picked up on the strange vibe between herself and Charlotte, and she groaned as she asked, "What are you doing?"

Spencer smiled, noting that while Mac's tone was mildly annoyed, she still sank willingly into his side. "I am taking your sorry ass to Shenanigans for dinner and a beer or five, and you are going to tell me what the hell went down with Charlie this morning that had you doing everything in your power to avoid her this afternoon."

"I don't wanna talk about it," Mac grumbled, shrugging his arm off.

More than used to his roommate's behavior, Spencer rolled his eyes. "Fine. Don't talk. Eat, drink, hang out with me, and, for the love of all that is holy, do not go running again because you are seriously going to get hurt if you keep that shit up."

Mac bit her lip as the shin splints she had felt beginning to develop on her run that morning flared in agreement with his assessment. "Fine," she huffed, crossing her arms over her chest.

"So glad you're amenable to the plan," Spencer drawled. The lights on a silver LR2 parked under a streetlight flashed, and he grinned at his newest toy. "Get in, hot stuff."

"Wow, and with lines like that, it's a wonder you're single," Mac chuckled as she climbed into the passenger's seat.

"I'm single because I'm too young to be tied down," he retorted playfully as he started the engine.

Mac scoffed and shook her head. "Too young? We're almost thirty."

"I know," he pointed out with a lascivious grin.

Mac nodded and looked out her window as he drove off campus and headed to the small corner bar in downtown Hampton that was their favorite haunt. Drinks were cheap, but even during the school year it was almost completely devoid of students because it was far enough from campus that they couldn't walk to it, and the food could be best described as gourmet pub grub. Henry Miller, the chef and owner of the bar, had trained at New York's Le Cordon Bleu before returning home to New Hampshire to open up the restaurant and bar he had always dreamed of owning.

Shenanigans was crowded with Red Sox fans cheering on their boys as they entered, and Mac wasted no time picking out an empty booth in the back corner of the restaurant. The booth would still give them a good view of the televisions above the bar to see the game, but it would also give her at least some of the space she craved. She smiled and nodded at people she knew as she wound her way through the tables to the booth at the back, and she groaned appreciatively as she dropped onto the maroon Naugahyde bench. "Goddamn, it feels good to sit down."

"I know," Spencer agreed as he slid onto the bench opposite her. He gave the stack of menus that were pinned between a mason jar full of rolled silverware at the end of the table and the wall a quick look, but didn't bother reaching for them. He already knew what he wanted.

"Hey, you two," a familiar voice greeted.

Mac smiled as she looked up at Henry, who was wearing an away jersey to match their team. "What are you doing out front?"

He shrugged and glanced over his shoulder at the television as the guys around the bar erupted in cheers as two Red Sox players tagged home. "I was just checking on the score and I thought I'd come say hi. You two ready for the school year?"

"As ready as we'll ever be," Spencer answered.

"Can I get your drink orders in?"

"Rum and Diet Coke," Mac ordered.

"I'll take a pint of the Shandy you have on tap," Spencer said, folding his arms on the table. "Thanks, man."

Henry smiled and nodded. "Not a problem. You guys ready to order, or do you want to wait until Jenny brings your drinks over?"

Spencer chuckled and arched a questioning brow at Mac. Her smirk was answer enough, and he shook his head. "We'll take our usuals."

"Figured as much," Henry chuckled. "Sit tight. I'll get those drink orders in for you guys. I'm also gonna send out some grilled artichokes and a plate of stuffed mushrooms that I'm thinking of putting on the menu. You can tell me if I should do it or not."

Mac rolled her eyes. "I'm sure they'll be awesome," she assured him. "Everything you make is absolutely out of this world, Henry."

"Shut up, Mac," Spencer mock-whispered. "Free food!"

Henry laughed and nodded at Spencer. "It was good to see you guys again. But, while I'd love to sit and chat, I gotta get back to the kitchen. I'll pop out later to see what you think of those appetizers."

"Sounds good, man. Thanks," Spencer said, grinning as he did a complicated high five, fist bump, handshake thing with Henry.

"You are such a guy sometimes," Mac said, rolling her eyes as Henry left them alone.

"You love me for it," Spencer retorted.

"Are you sure about that?" Mac asked, grinning.

Spencer nodded. "Absolutely. So, you ready to tell me what happened with you and Charlie yet?"

Mac shook her head and turned in the booth so she could see the game. The Sox were up 3-2 in the bottom of the fourth over the Tigers. "Nope."

It was obvious to Spencer that she was still working her way through it all, and he nodded, content to sit and hang out, knowing that she would talk when she was ready. They ate the appetizers Henry sent out for them in companionable silence, making comments about the game they were watching, and, sure enough, it was just after their dinners had been brought out to them–a Kobe beef cheeseburger with apple bacon, bleu cheese, and a sweet homemade barbeque sauce for him, and a Portobello mushroom burger topped with an absolutely heavenly basil-Dijon sauce for her–that Mac began to ramble.

"I think..." She began, her voice trailing off as she popped a perfectly seasoned french fry into her mouth. She chewed thoughtfully for a moment and sighed. "I fucked up."

Spencer stared at her wide-eyed and hurried to chew the bite in his mouth enough that he could ask, "What?"

"I fucked up," Mac repeated, picking up another fry and began drawing on the top of her burger with it.

"How?" Spencer mumbled around the same bite of food.

"Dude, smaller bites next time. I'm not gonna steal your food," Mac chuckled.

"What happened today after you talked with Liv?" he asked gently, having already been briefed on the student's situation.

"It just..." She sighed and licked her lips. "She explained what she had been thinking back then and...I never realized until today that part of it was my fault. That my absolute fear of being found out was what drove her away."

"She said that?"

"Not in so many words," Mac said, sighing as she put her beer down and picked up her burger. "She didn't blame me for anything, she just explained what she had been thinking back then. And, I mean..." Her voice trailed off thoughtfully and she took a bite as she tried to find the words she needed. "She was right. We could have acted like a couple when we were away from Wesleyan. My father didn't have spies in New Haven. I could have held her hand and yet I never did, because I..."

"Hmm?" Spencer hummed when it began to look like she was not going to finish the thought.

"I wasn't ready to come out to anyone but her." Mac shrugged. "I wasn't ready. And I know that my hiding also forced her to hide who she was and I just wish..."

"She'd waited?"

"Well, yeah. I mean, that's a given, right, considering the fact that I'm still hung up on her?" Mac arched a self-deprecating brow and shook her head. "But what I was going to say, was that I wish I had the guts back then that Liv showed by coming out to her parents last night. If I had, then–"

"I'm gonna stop you right there before you really get going on the *what ifs*," Spencer interrupted her. He set his burger back onto his plate and leaned forward. "It happened. It sucked. And neither of you are over it yet. But the real question is, what do you want now? Because I talked to her this morning after you took off with Liv, and she wants another chance with you."

"You talked to her about me?" she asked, her voice rising a little with disbelief. "Why would you do that?"

Spencer rolled his eyes. "It's my job as your best friend to grill any potential suitors and to make sure that any jerks from your past don't just magically reappear to fuck with you." His face softened and he asked in a gentler voice, "What do you want, Mac?"

"I don't want to get hurt again," Mac answered softly. "I don't want to let her back in and then have to watch her walk away again at the end of the school year when her contract is up and she goes back to New York." She looked at him and smiled sadly. "I know I'm not strong enough to do that again."

He gave her a look that said he disagreed with her assessment of herself, but didn't push her on it. "Okay. Do you want me to tell her that?"

"No," Mac muttered, rolling her eyes. "This isn't middle school."

"It's worse than middle school, it's real life," he argued playfully. "Seriously. What do you need me to do?"

"Just keep on keepin' on." She shrugged and reached for her drink. "Just be here for me to vent to when I need it, and let me deal with her. Please. Unless I'm two seconds from a breakdown, just let me deal with all of this on my own terms."

"And if she somehow convinces you to give her another chance?"

"She won't," Mac assured him, though her assurances sounded flat even to her own ears. She smiled at him and shrugged. "I'm a big girl, Spencer. I need to do this on my own."

He stared hard at her for a minute and nodded. He could tell that she was serious about wanting to protect her heart and wanting him to stay out of it all, but he could also see that there was a small part of her that hoped that Charlie would succeed in winning her over despite her misgivings. Whether she recognized that in herself yet or not, he didn't know, but he could see it plain as day in her eyes and he hoped she knew what she was doing. "Okeydokey. Lemme know if my orders change," he drawled. His eyes flicked back to the screen and he groaned. "And, we're back to being down by two. Great."

Chapter 9

After a long soak in the tub to help ease her aching muscles from running around campus all day helping wherever she could, Charlie padded barefoot onto her front porch in an old pair of soccer shorts and a t-shirt with a large glass of wine in her hand. The wood planks were cool beneath her feet and she sighed as she lowered herself into one of the Adirondack chairs that overlooked the street. The sun was just a thin sliver of golden light above the western mountain range that bordered Hampton, and there was a light breeze stirring the air, breaking up the lingering humidity that signaled summer was not quite over yet. She stretched her legs out in front of herself, wiggling her bare feet against the wind, and took a well-deserved sip of her wine. Hints of pomegranate and black cherry flooded her palate and she smiled as she rolled the smooth liquid around her tongue for a moment before swallowing.

"Perfection," she sighed. She leaned her head back and closed her eyes, savoring the peacefulness that surrounded her. The quiet chatter of leaves rustling overhead was the perfect soundtrack for a late summer evening, and Charlie smiled to herself as she took another sip of her wine, enjoying the simple sounds of nature that she would have never been able to enjoy in the city.

The longer she sat, the more her thoughts began to wander, and it didn't take long for them to turn to Mackayla. More often than not, it seemed, if there was nothing pressing on her mind to deal with, she would find herself thinking of her. The feeling of serenity that had filled her only moments before began to dissipate as she replayed her conversation with Mackayla in the blonde's office earlier that morning. The memory of the way Mackayla's expression had shifted as she explained her reasoning for her behavior all those years ago made her heart ache, and yet she could not think of a better way to express herself than she had. The truth of the matter was, they just weren't ready for each other when they were still in school.

But things had changed. They were older. Wiser. Each more experienced in the world with a better understanding and acceptance of themselves. She knew that things would be different if they tried again. That they would be better.

She replayed every second of their conversation from earlier over and over again in her mind, focusing time and again on Mackayla's quiet apology and the soft look in her eyes that, for the first time since her arrival in New Hampshire, held more affection than aversion.

Knowing that she needed to actually talk through all of the thoughts that were crashing around inside her mind, she reached for her phone and dialed the one person in the world she knew would be able to give her advice that she would actually be willing to listen to and use. He picked up on the second ring, sounding stressed and thoroughly distracted, and she grinned as she imagined him hunched over her old desk trying to get pages ready to submit for proof production. "Hey, it's me," she drawled, lifting her glass to her lips.

"How's it going, sexy?" Adam murmured, his smile evident in his tone. *"Miss you around here."*

"I'll bet you do. How's it coming?"

"Slow," Adam groaned. *"How's everything up there? Have you managed another non-vehicular run-in with your lady love yet?"*

Charlie nodded to herself and took another drink of wine before she answered. "I have. It's been a crazy twenty-four hours where Mackayla's concerned."

"Ooh, sounds like you have some juicy gossip to take my mind off of my work. Gimme!"

"Careful, Snow, your inner teenage girl is showing," she chuckled. Just the sound of his voice had a calming effect on her, and she relaxed in her chair as she looked out over her front lawn. She had expected to miss the hectic lifestyle she had grown accustomed to working at the magazine, and she was a little surprised to find that what she actually felt was relief that she was no longer trapped in the hustle and bustle of it all.

"Shut up. I've been looking over these layouts all day trying to find every possible mistake so that Davis doesn't call me up to scream at me later. Give a guy a break, huh?"

"Aww, you poor baby."

He laughed and blew a loud raspberry into the phone.

"Fine." She sighed dramatically, trying her best to sound put out when the entire reason she had called him was to talk about Mackayla anyways. "So, I saw her last night, which was epic in and of itself, and then we basically had to work together all day today."

"Meaning..."

"Well, last night was pretty much her screaming at me." Adam chuckled on the other end of the line and she rolled her eyes at him. "Shut up."

"What? I mean, you kinda had that coming, right? From what you've told me about the whole thing, you didn't exactly part ways on the best of terms."

"Oh, I knew I had it coming, especially after the way she reacted last week when I saw her in her office. Knowing that I was going to be hit with the full force of her ire—well deserved or not—didn't make taking it any easier, though."

"Why didn't you call me last night after it happened?"

She sighed and shook her head, reaching up with her free hand to massage the back of her neck. "I dunno. I guess I knew that you would be busy getting everything ready for the next issue to go to proof, and I really just needed some time to process it all. God, you have no idea how hard it was to see exactly how hurt she still is over it all. Although, there was one good thing to come out of it, at least."

"Angry sex?"

She laughed, easily picturing the playfully lecherous smirk he would always get whenever the topic of their conversation wandered into her bedroom. "No, you pervert. Not everything with me ends in sex."

"Bennett," Adam laughed. *"You know that's not true. You're a fucking god when it comes to women. Except when they start throwing shit."*

She rolled her eyes and took another drink of her wine. "You're never going to let that go, are you?"

"Nope. That story is an instant classic. But, I actually do need to submit these pages sometime today, so we can reminisce about that later."

"Well, because you're busy," she retorted, smiling as she swirled the wine in her glass and watched the way the fading sunlight set the crimson liquid aflame.

"Charlie," he whined. *"Just tell me what happened!"*

She sighed as she let her mind wander back to that culminating moment the night before, recalling the flashes of shock, hurt, and hope that had flickered across the blonde's face at her confession. "I pretty much told her that I still want her."

"You have a bigger set than anyone I know, Charlie-girl. How'd that go?"

"She seemed shocked."

He chuckled. *"I'll bet. And?"*

"Now she seems determined to stay away from me." She groaned as she remembered the way Mackayla would find something that needed to be done on the other side of campus every time she had rejoined the blonde and Spencer earlier.

"So what are you going to do?"

Charlie shrugged and took another sip of her wine. "I was kind of hoping you'd have some ideas for me. Because we did actually manage to sit down and talk about what had happened between us this morning without yelling at each other, and when I told her why I'd done what I'd done, I could swear that she actually began to understand. She's still hurt, but I think she might be past the whole wanting to eviscerate me thing."

He hummed understandingly. *"You want to win her back."*

"Ideally, yeah," she admitted, sighing softly and shaking her head. "But I don't think I can go from being her number one she-devil to her girlfriend in one fell swoop."

"How did you get her to date you the first time?"

"I..." Charlie's voice trailed off as she thought back to those early days of their relationship. "I was a total dork," she admitted with a quiet laugh. "I ambushed her after her classes and would walk her to her next one. Slipped little post-its with messages on them into her books. I brought her candy when she was studying in the library. I would leave a flower in the messages clip outside her dorm room. I basically badgered her into going out with me."

"Well, I'll be damned. Charlie Bennett is a closet romantic," Adam teased.

"Shut up. Just tell me what to do. You're my wingman, wingman for me."

"I can't wingman for you because you're in another fucking state. But I can tell you that you should stick with what works and, apparently, she likes that you're secretly a total dork."

"That's not much of a plan," she grumbled.

"Well, until you come up with something better, don't knock my feeble attempts to help," he retorted. *"Now, for as fun as this is, I just got handed a note that says I need to send these pages off for proof production, so I gotta jam. You cool for now, or do you want me to call you later?"*

Charlie smiled. "I think I'm good. Thanks for listening."

"That's what I'm here for," he replied gently. *"I was thinking I might try and come up sometime toward the end of October to visit. I was just handed the World Series so I can't really get away before then. Would that work?"*

"Of course. That would be great."

"Sweet. And I can check out this chick that has you all flummoxed too. I wanna see the girl who has you so hopelessly stuck on her."

Charlie laughed. "As long as you behave yourself around her."

"Who, me?" he retorted with a laugh. *"I'll catch you later, Charlie-girl. Be good. Don't do anything I would do."*

"I'll try," she chuckled as the line went dead. Left again to her own thoughts, she smiled as she remembered some of the things she had done to court Mackayla back when they had been in school. "God, I really was such a dork," she murmured as she took another sip of her wine.

Chapter 10

Mac looked up from her laptop at the sound of someone knocking on her open door. It was the first day of school, and she was waiting out the time between her only two classes of the day in the relative peace of her office in Sanborn. A small smile tweaked her lips as her eyes landed on Charlotte, who was standing in her doorway wearing a perfectly-tailored charcoal gray pencil skirt, an off-white blouse that was modestly unbuttoned at the neck and rolled at the sleeves, and a killer pair of black four-inch heels. The brunette looked amazing, elegant, and refined. Beautiful. Ready to take on Wall Street and the world, and completely out of place for a small private university in rural New Hampshire.

She realized as she looked at Charlotte, whom she had not seen since the week before, that the ache that had haunted her for so long where the brunette was concerned had lessened. It was still there, just muted, and she knew that it was because she had finally come to terms with everything that had happened. Finally understanding why Charlotte had left her gave her the feeling of closure that she had been missing for the last eight years.

Her gaze landed on the sly, self-satisfied smirk that tweaked Charlotte's lips, and she blushed, realizing she had been caught staring while lost in her thoughts. *Great, just great,* she thought, clearing her throat softly as she ran her hands through her hair. "Hey. How did your first class this morning go?"

"It went well, I think," Charlie said, smiling as she held up a cardboard tray with a couple of white paper coffee cups in it. "I stopped for a coffee, so I figured I would pick you up a tea as well. Just a splash of milk and four sugars, I hope that's still right?"

Touched that Charlie would remember such a trivial detail as how she liked her tea, Mac nodded. Granted, the last time she had a cup of tea was two years ago when she had the flu and had thrown-up a supersized cup of it. The lingering memory of the taste made even the thought of drinking tea now unappealing, but even her stomach had to admit that it was a sweet gesture on the brunette's part. "I…yeah. Thank you."

Though Mackayla's tone was genuine, her hesitation caught Charlie's attention, and she gave up trying to free the cup of tea from the tray as she looked at the blonde. "It's not how you take your tea any longer, is it?"

Not wanting to lie, Mac gave the brunette an apologetic smile as she shook her head. "I don't actually drink tea anymore. Stomach flu kind of ruined it for me a few years back," she explained. "But it was really nice of you to think of me, though. Really. Thank you."

Charlie rolled her eyes and gave Mackayla a look that quite clearly said thinking of her was neither a problem nor something she could ever stop doing, even if she wanted to. "You're welcome. So, for future reference then, what kind of coffee do you prefer?"

"You don't have to bring me coffee, Charlotte."

"I know I don't have to do it," Charlie said, grinning and arching a brow at the blonde that said she was not going to be deterred. "But, hypothetically speaking, if I were to spend good money on a cup of coffee to give to you to try and make you smile, which kind would be best for me to get?"

Mac laughed softly under her breath and shook her head. "Anything sweet," she said, smiling as she looked up at Charlotte.

"A caramel macchiato, mocha, anything like that. Or else a regular coffee with a lot of milk and sugar in it so that it doesn't actually taste like coffee."

"Duly noted," Charlie murmured, filing the information away for future reference. "Then, in the meantime, here," she said, pulling her cup of coffee from the tray and holding it out for the blonde. She chuckled at the way Mackayla eyed the cup warily and said, "It's a caramel macchiato."

"You don't have to give me your coffee," Mac argued.

"I'll drink the tea instead," Charlie said, shrugging as she waggled the cup in front of Mac's face. "I'll throw it away if you don't drink it, and that will anger the coffee gods."

Mac grinned. "It will, huh?"

"Indubitably," Charlie retorted. "And then, as penance for your egregious sin of refusing a heavenly brew such as this, you will be doomed to years of awful tasting coffee and stale scones."

Mac laughed and took the coffee cup Charlotte was still holding out for her. As always, it was impossible for her to turn the brunette down when she was being so adorably goofy. "Well, I can't have that, now can I?"

"Smart girl."

"I have my moments," Mac smiled as she took a sip of the coffee, a small sigh escaping her as the familiar taste of her favorite coffee drink filled her mouth. "This is great, Charlotte. Thank you."

"My pleasure," Charlie murmured.

"Just one question," Mac said, arching a brow at the brunette as she set her coffee down on her desk. "What would you have done if I wasn't here?"

Charlie shrugged. "Thrown the tea away. I mean, it's just tea, for god's sake."

"Okay, but by your logic, wouldn't that anger the tea gods?" Mac asked, grinning.

"Nah." Charlie shook her head. "It's what we Americans do. The tea gods expect us to chuck good tea. Boston Tea Party and all that. It's un-American to drink the stuff. Except, you know, when my hands are shaking from too much caffeine or I don't feel well. Then it's okay. But otherwise? Totally traitorous."

Mac laughed. "You're such a dork."

"Thank you, my dear," Charlie replied, grinning as she gave the blonde a short bow. "Now, I'm afraid I must get going. I have a senior seminar that begins in–" she checked her watch, an oversized stainless steel Michael Kors chronograph, "–ten minutes on the other side of the Green." She looked up at the blonde and grinned sheepishly. "Guess it's a good thing I'm in charge so I won't get in trouble for being a couple minutes late."

"If you had classes pretty much back-to-back in Reed, why in the world did you come back here?" Mac asked, shaking her head as she glanced at her own watch and realized that she, too, was going to have to get going in order to make it to her own class on time. Thankfully for her, Cregg Hall, home of the English Department, was practically next door to their offices.

Charlie shrugged. "Just because." She winked and began backing out of Mackayla's office. "Have a good rest of your day, Professor Thomas," she said, waving her cup of tea at the blonde as she turned and left.

"You too, Charlotte," Mac murmured, smiling as she shoved her phone into her satchel and slung the wide leather strap over her head. She picked up the coffee Charlotte had given her and her keys, and was not at all surprised to find herself smiling as she locked up. The brunette had always had that effect on her.

"Hey!" Spencer called out as she passed by his office.

Mac grinned and stopped in his doorway. "Hey yourself. What are you doing here? I thought you didn't have class until this afternoon?"

"I don't," Spencer said, nodding as he rocked back in his chair. He hooked his hands behind his head and shrugged. "Just figured I'd come in early in case Charlie needed help with anything since it's her first day and all. Was that her that I just saw leaving?"

Mac nodded. "Yeah. She, uh…just came by to bring me a coffee."

"I see," he drawled.

"Don't even go there, Walshy," Mac said, rolling her eyes.

"Where?"

"You know where. It's just coffee. Not a big deal. She's just being friendly and I'm fine with that. Besides, it would be best for everyone if we can find a way to get through the year without constantly being at each other's throats."

Spencer knew that, while it was just coffee, it *wasn't* just coffee; but he also knew that Mac wanted him to stay out of it, so he just nodded. "Of course it is. You have your master's seminar?"

"Yup. Last one for the day. It sucks having to get here so early, but at least I have the rest of the afternoon to do whatever I want."

"Got it. I'll see you at home later, then. Don't forget, it's your night to cook."

"I remember," Mac said, rolling her eyes. "Any requests?"

"Meat. Man food."

"Right. So I'll pick up a can of Alpo for you, and…"

He laughed and threw a pen at her. "Shut up. Whatever you wanna make is fine with me."

Mac grinned. "Good." She glanced at her watch and sighed. Even with the short walk to Cregg, she was going to be late. "I gotta go. I'll catch ya later, man."

Because she was in a hurry, Mac skipped the elevator and hurried down the stairs, the soles of her running shoes landing silently on the concrete steps. She speed walked across the lobby and jogged through the courtyard, glad that her "wannabe-Maddow" garb, as Spencer had dubbed her wardrobe of cords, oxfords, and blazers, made it easy to move quickly. Had she been wearing something as fancy as Charlotte, she would have been resigned to waiting for the elevator and actually walking to class. While she could appreciate the way a woman looked in a pair of high heels with the best of them, actually walking in them had never been her forte.

She slowed to a walk as she entered Cregg Hall, and ran a hand through her hair as she ducked through the open door to room 118. It was a small room, more of a meeting area than an actual classroom, but since the seminar had only four students, a larger space was not needed.

"Hello, Professor Thomas," Michael, a small, typically nerdy guy with a little boy haircut, glasses, and an abysmal taste in fashion greeted her.

"Hey, Michael. Everybody. Did you guys have a good summer?" Mac asked as she took her satchel off and set it down at the head of the conference table. When everybody nodded, she grinned and pulled the thin manila folder that contained the seminar's syllabi from her bag. "Good. So, let's get down to business then, shall we?"

Chapter 11

Saturday night found the aluminum bleachers at Blake Field awash in a sea of blue and black, the crowd's excitement for the Bears' first home game of the season was practically tangible, and Charlie smiled as she looked at the crowd around her. It had been years since she had last been to a college football game, and it was a spectacle she hadn't realized she missed until she was surrounded by the unbridled pomp and circumstance of it all. The vibe in the stands was electric. Horns, whistles, and blow-up "thunder sticks" were everywhere, and Charlie smiled as a couple of students she vaguely recognized from her 200-level Sports Journalism course waved hello as they took their seats a few rows in front of her.

"Hey, stranger," a familiar, laughing voice called out, and Charlie smiled as she turned to see Spencer standing in the aisle to her left. He was wearing a blue Blake hoodie that was an exact match to her own, though his looked more worn since she had only bought hers that afternoon.

"Hey yourself," she replied, running a hand through her hair as she automatically scanned the crowd for Mackayla.

The brunette's brief search for his roommate didn't escape Spencer's attention, and he grinned. Mac had actually been the one to spot Charlie sitting by herself in a surprisingly empty row at the thirty-five yard line, and he had been sent as an envoy to see if the brunette might like some company. It was like high school all over again, only this time the stakes were much, much higher. "You here by yourself?"

Charlie nodded. "Yeah."

"Cool, then would you mind some company?" Spencer asked, not bothering to wait for her response as he turned and waved at the rest of his group that was standing at the bottom of the stairs.

"Not at all," Charlie muttered, her brow furrowed as she turned to try and see who, exactly, he was beckoning toward them. Her eyes widened as she spied a familiar shock of blonde hair making its way up the stairs, and she cleared her throat softly as she scooted down the row a little to make room for the new arrivals. "You're sure she's okay with this?" she couldn't help asking as he dropped onto the bench beside her. While she had been actively scanning the crowd for Mackayla ever since she had arrived, she had not expected the blonde to come sit by her. The week had gone well, every day the tension between herself and Mackayla seemed to ease, but she was still terrified of making a wrong move that would send things between them spiraling back to where they had been when she'd first arrived in Hampton.

Spencer grinned. "Yeah. Someone, who shall remain nameless," he drawled, arching a playful brow at Charlie, "buttered her up with a week's worth of gourmet coffee deliveries."

"That was hardly gourmet coffee," Charlie chuckled, shaking her head. "It's passable, at best. There's a place by my apartment in New York that makes a caramel macchiato that's absolutely sinful." She took a deep breath as Mackayla and three people she didn't recognize started shuffling down the row. "But the company here is a million times better than anything I've found in New York," she added softly.

Spencer nodded knowingly and waved at the new arrivals. "Charlie Bennett, may I introduce Liam and Heather Griffin, and Jake Pearce," he said, pointing at each person in turn. Liam was tall and lean, built like a distance runner, with curly red hair and pale green eyes, and Heather was a few inches shorter than Mackayla with beautiful ebony skin and a smile that made Charlie feel instantly at ease. Jake Pearce was built like Spencer: tall, muscled, and obviously an athlete, with smiling brown eyes and his dark hair styled into a faux hawk that he somehow managed to pull off without looking foolish.

"Nice to meet you all," Charlie said, smiling a little self-consciously, feeling the sudden pressure of needing to make a good impression on Spencer and Mackayla's friends.

The Griffins waved and Jake grinned and leaned around the rest of the group to shake her hand. "The pleasure is mine," he assured her with a roguish smile and a playful wink.

"Put it back in your pants, Pearcy," Mac grumbled, smacking him in the stomach. She grinned as he *oomphed* dramatically and crossed her arms over her chest as she leaned back in her seat.

Charlie laughed as she shook his hand and turned her attention to Mackayla. "Hello, Mackayla," she said, her expression softening as she looked at the blonde who had taken a seat on the other side of Spencer.

"Charlotte," Mac murmured, nodding hello. She could feel Heather's eyes staring questioningly at her back, and she bit her lip as she turned back to the field to watch the teams line up for the kickoff. Only Spencer knew her entire history with Charlotte, and she had no interest in filling anyone else in on it all. She was making a conscious effort to leave the past in the past, and that meant she needed to strip away the hurt she had worn like armor for so many years and move on. It should have been an arduous task, and yet letting it all go, once she decided to do so, was easy as breathing.

The crowd around them jumped to their feet as the referee lifted his hand into the air and, following Spencer and Mackayla's cue, Charlie got to her feet and clapped as Blake's kicker sent the ball flying to the three yard line where one of the players from the Plymouth Panthers caught it and ran it back. The people in the stands stomped their feet and yelled as one of Blake's players took the returner down at the fifteen yard line, and Charlie smiled as she once again followed the cues of the crowd and retook her seat. She could hear Mackayla talking to somebody as Blake's defense ran out onto the field and she pursed her lips thoughtfully as she watched the teams line up.

"Oh my god, our left defensive end is huge," she said, brows lifting in surprise as the linemen dropped to a three-point stance.

Spencer chuckled. "That's Jimmy Gardner. Good kid. Senior. Could have gone D-1. He was being scouted by the Floridas and a few other big time programs, but he blew out both of his knees his senior year of high school, missed the entire season, and nobody was willing to take the risk on him."

"Their loss," Charlie muttered as she watched him do a textbook spin move around the kid trying to block him and sack Plymouth's quarterback seven yards behind the line of scrimmage. "I know this isn't the best competition or anything, but have any scouts been up to watch him?"

Spencer shrugged. "I dunno. Not that I've heard."

"He's how big?" Charlie asked.

"Six-eight, three twenty, something like that," Spencer said.

Charlie nodded thoughtfully and watched as Gardner fought through a double team to bat down the pass Plymouth's quarterback tried to sneak over his head. "Kid's good."

"Yeah, we'll be riding his coattails all the way to the Championship against Mount Union," Spencer said, nodding.

Well aware of the perennial Division III powerhouse from working at *SI*, Charlie pursed her lips thoughtfully and nodded. "Could very well be the case," she agreed as a weak side safety blitz brought Plymouth's quarterback down again because the

※ ※ ※

offensive line was so focused on trying to stop Gardner. "How's our offense stack up?"

Spencer grinned. "We're pretty good."

It didn't take long for Charlie to figure out that 'pretty good' was quite the understatement, as the Bears displayed a masterful use of the spread offense to easily work themselves to a three touchdown lead by the end of the first quarter.

"I'm going to go get something to eat," Mac announced. "Anybody want anything?"

"No thanks," Heather and Liam answered in unison.

Jake shook his head. "I'm cool."

"Can I come with you?" Charlie asked, pushing herself to her feet. Talking about the game with Spencer was fun, but she would prefer to spend her time with Mackayla.

"Of course," Mac murmured, her eyes sliding from the brunette to her roommate. "Spence?"

"I'm good," Spencer answered, smiling up at her. He was not going to spend the entire night holding her hand. He knew by the way she had come home smiling every night that she wanted to honestly forgive and forget everything that had happened between her and Charlie, and he also knew that it was something she needed to do on her own. He still thought there was a very high probability that the whole thing would end in heartbreak for both women, but he was determined to step back from it all and let them handle it like Mac had asked him to. "You two lovely ladies have fun."

"Thanks," Mac retorted, the word sounding more like a curse than a genuine thanks, rolling her eyes as she turned on her heel and started for the stairs without another word.

"I...um...excuse me," Charlie muttered, frowning as she squeezed past Spencer and his friends to catch up to Mackayla. She followed her down the stairs and under the bleachers to the small concession stand that was at the fifty-yard line. She chewed the inside of her cheek as they took their place at the end of the line. It had been her impression that things had been going well with blonde all week, and Spencer's comments about buttering her up seemed to reinforce that idea, but with the way Mackayla was all but ignoring her now, she was beginning to doubt her read on the situation.

Mac rolled her eyes, hating the fact that even with the progress they had made over the last week that things between them were still so tense. "So, you and Spence seem to be having fun," she drawled, finally breaking the uncomfortable silence that had surrounded them.

"Is that okay?" Charlie asked, frowning. "I didn't...I mean..."

Mac chuckled and shook her head as she turned to finally look at the brunette. "It's fine, Charlotte. I'm honestly surprised Jake didn't push his way down to you two to join the party. He and Spence usually spend the entire game talking Xs and Os like you guys were."

"Oh," Charlie muttered, nodding slowly. "Okay. Because if you don't want me to talk to him..."

Mac sighed and ran a hand through her hair as she turned to fully face Charlie. "It's okay, Charlotte. I know this is weird, but you don't need to be so afraid of making me mad."

"I do, though," Charlie said, shaking her head.

"And I appreciate it," Mac murmured. She turned so that she was fully facing the brunette and let her eyes sweep over her face, noting the anxiousness that was had dimmed Charlotte's normally bright green eyes. "But we won't be able to really move past everything if you're always walking on eggshells around me. The past is past, Charlotte. It's time we just leave it where it belongs."

A surge of hope swept through Charlie, and she licked her lips nervously. "Really? You want to move past it all?"

"Don't you?" Mac countered with a small smile. "I mean, I figured that was why you were bringing me coffees all week."

"Oh, I definitely want to," Charlie assured her.

Mac's smile faded a little at the unfettered hope she could see shining in Charlotte's eyes. "Good. But, just so we're on the same page, you need to understand that all I'm willing to offer you for now is friendship."

"I'll take what I can get," Charlie said, her heart fluttering at the 'for now' Mackayla had prefaced her statement with. "I've missed you."

Mac nodded, her eyes softening as she gave the brunette a wistful smile. "I've missed you too, Charlotte. I didn't even realize how much until you literally ran into me two weeks ago."

The urge to reach out and pull the blonde into her arms was nearly overwhelming, and Charlie sighed as she shoved her hands into the back pockets of her jeans to contain the impulse. "Yeah. Um, sorry about that."

The right side of Mac's mouth quirked up in a playful smirk and she shrugged. "It's fine. You can make it up to me by buying me a pretzel."

"A week's worth of coffee didn't get me out of that?" Charlie asked, smiling and holding a hand over her heart in feigned disbelief.

"Nope," Mac retorted playfully as she reached out to give the brunette's shoulder a light squeeze. "I'm going to be lording that one over your head all year, I think."

Though it wasn't the hug she really wanted, Charlie smiled at the friendliness of the gesture. "Great," she drawled. She sighed dramatically and added, "So, a pretzel, huh?"

"Mmm, with cheese sauce," Mac said, nodding as the person at the counter in front of them wandered off with their snacks and they were able to walk up to the register.

"Healthy," Charlie muttered under her breath.

* * *

"I ran today. I'm allowed some junk food," Mac retorted, bumping the brunette's shoulder with her arm.

Charlie rolled her eyes. "Like you even need to. You're gorgeous," she murmured.

Mac smiled, her cheeks flushing ever so slightly at the compliment that she was pretty sure she hadn't been meant to hear. "Thank you."

"You're welcome," Charlie answered softly. She cleared her throat and smiled at the kid working the register who was looking at them like they were nuts. "Two pretzels, one with cheese and one without." She looked at Mackayla and asked, "Drink?"

"Water," Mac answered.

"And two waters," Charlie told the kid as she pulled a twenty out of her back pocket.

"You really don't have to buy my food," Mac said, chuckling as she reached into her pocket for her money. "I was kidding."

"Hey. No, it's fine," Charlie replied, flashing a cheeky grin at the blonde as she handed the kid behind the counter her money. "I'm willing to do whatever it takes to atone for my sins. And, really, if you weren't here to tell me what you wanted, I would have bought one of everything and brought it back to the seats for you to pick what you liked, so in the end you're saving me money by being so demanding."

Mac laughed and shook her head. "I'm not being demanding!"

No, you're being absolutely adorable, Charlie thought to herself as she bit her lip and smiled at the blonde. "Whatever you say, Thomas. Whatever you say."

Chapter 12

A game of musical seats had taken place during halftime, ending with Charlie sitting in the middle of the guys, who were all too eager to ask her questions about athletes and events she had covered for *SI*. And while it was fun watching them fangirl over her stories, she was growing tired of recounting interviews she had done and describing the Yankees' locker room down to the most minute detail. So, even though it was still the middle of the fourth quarter, she stretched her arms up over her head and announced, "For as fun as this is, ladies and gents, I think I'm going to call it a night."

Mac looked up from the conversation she was having with Heather and frowned. She hadn't spent much time with Charlotte since their talk earlier because the boys had monopolized her attention, but she enjoyed watching her regale them with her stories. The brunette's mannerisms and speech patterns were the same as she remembered, but it was also like she was looking at somebody she had only just met. In school, Charlotte had always been confident, but the self-assuredness she exuded now was different. More mature. One born of excellence and success, rather than arrogance.

"It was really great to meet you all," Charlie continued, smiling at everybody in turn as she got to her feet.

"You too," Heather said, standing to give the brunette a light hug. "Thanks for entertaining the boys all night," she whispered in Charlie's ear.

Charlie laughed. "My pleasure."

"You're sure you want to go?" Jake asked as he glanced back at the field. "The game isn't even over yet."

"Yeah, it is," Charlie said, her eyes flicking over to the scoreboard. Blake was up 77-0 and their starters had been on the bench since the end of the second quarter.

"How are you getting home?" Spencer asked.

Charlie arched a questioning brow at him and shrugged. "I walked over. Not a big deal."

"Dude, no," Spencer said, shaking his head emphatically. "I know this is middle of frickin' nowhere, New Hampshire, but you can't just walk home alone."

Charlie rolled her eyes and set her hands on her hips as she smiled down at him. "Really? Because I do it all the time in New York. Which is, let's be honest here, a hell of a lot more dangerous than Hampton. My house is literally half a mile from here. I'll be fine."

"At least let me drive you," Spencer said, his hand automatically dropping to his pocket for his keys.

"That's sweet, really," Charlie said, smiling and shaking her head, "but I'm fine. You guys stay for the end of the game."

Mac looked at Spencer, who was looking from Charlie to the group of still clearly intoxicated frat boys that were shuffling out of the stadium hollering about an afterparty at their house. Memories of a dimly lit hospital room and somber voices speaking in hushed whispers flashed across her mind, and she sighed as she understood why he was so adamant that the brunette not walk home alone. "Walsh," she said, drawing his attention away from Charlotte, who was starting to look at him like he was crazy. "Relax. I'll walk home with her. You can pick me up at her place."

* * *

Spencer frowned. "I still..."

Mac flashed him a reassuring smile and gave a small nod to let him know that she would be careful. "We'll be fine."

Though it was obvious that he wasn't at all pleased with the idea of the two of them walking alone, Spencer nodded. "Okay. Charlie, what's your address?"

"Um, thirteen Cranbrook," Charlie muttered. "It's a little bungalow with sage green siding, about halfway down the block."

"I'll find it," Spencer assured her. "You two be careful."

"Yes, dad," Mac drawled. She ruffled his hair playfully as she edged past him to where Charlie was still looking at her with the most adorably confused expression. "Come on, Bennett," she said, tipping her head at the stairs.

They made their way quickly out of the stadium, as the majority of the crowd seemed content to sit through the remainder of the blowout in order to celebrate with their team at the final whistle. Charlie cleared her throat as they hit the sidewalk that looped around the stadium and cut across the practice fields and murmured, "You know, you really didn't have to do this."

"Yeah, well, it was either you stay for the end of the game and let us give you a ride home, or this," Mac said. She looked ahead to the group of students that had first drawn Spencer's attention when Charlotte had said she was going to leave. They were laughing and pushing each other around, typical boys being stupid behavior, and she shook her head. They were not a threat. In fact, she was pretty sure one of the guys was in GLOW, but she understood Spencer's caution.

"Don't get me wrong, I really don't mind," Charlie said quickly, shoving her hands into her pockets. Being alone with Mackayla, walking side-by-side with her like this, their shoulders bumping together every so often as their bodies naturally gravitated toward each other, it was just so tempting for her to reach out and take Mackayla's hand, and yet she knew that she could not do it. "I just..."

"Don't understand why he was so insistent that you not walk home alone," Mac finished for her.

Charlie nodded. "Yeah."

"His little sister was assaulted a few years ago. She was walking back to her dorm alone after a basketball game at Vassar and..." Her voice trailed off and she shrugged. "He's just extra protective now when it comes to stuff like this."

Charlie's stomach dropped. Suddenly, Spencer's overdramatic response to her walking home alone made perfect sense, and she couldn't help but feel a little touched that he would be so protective of her. "Oh."

"Yeah," Mac murmured. "It was pretty bad. She's okay now, but that's why he flipped out at the idea of you walking home alone."

There really wasn't a topic of conversation that could easily follow a revelation like *that*, and they drifted into silence as they wandered slowly across the practice fields toward Charlie's house. The bright lights from the stadium pretty much drowned out the stars that would normally be easily visible, and Mac's lips quirked up in a small smile as she heard Blake's band break out into another energetic rendition of the school's fight song.

"Eighty four," Charlie muttered.

"Yeah, well, at least we're on the positive end of that score," Mac replied, her smile growing wider at the soft chuckle the comment drew from Charlotte. "The guys seemed to enjoy your stories."

Charlie laughed and nodded. "I know, right?"

"You still know how to tell a good story," Mac said softly.

"Yeah, well..." Charlie shrugged and flashed Mackayla a self-deprecating smile. "Kind of my job, you know? How about you? Did you ever write that novel you always talked about wanting to write?"

Mac cleared her throat softly and nodded. "Yeah. I did."

"Good for you," Charlie murmured, her voice warm and sincere. "Did you ever publish?"

"I did, actually. It was a small printing, straight to paperback and it wasn't really carried in the big chains, but the response to it was pretty good. The follow-up novel will be coming out next year."

Charlie turned and grinned at the blonde. "Seriously? That's awesome. You'll have to give me the name of the first one so I can try and find a copy. And you'll definitely have to let me know when the sequel comes out. What genre?"

Mac blushed at Charlotte's obvious interest and said, "Crime procedural. Though it could be considered a romance too, I guess, but the main plotline follows a crime investigation."

"I guess all those Criminal Minds marathons paid off, huh?"

"Something like that," Mac murmured, nodding.

"Well, for what it's worth, I'm really proud of you, Mackayla," Charlie said softly.

"Thank you." Mac cleared her throat as her blush deepened, and she wracked her brain for a way to change the subject so that their conversation was no longer focused on her. "So, are you enjoying being at Blake?"

"Very much so," Charlie said, licking her lips as her eyes flicked up to briefly look at the blonde.

"Yeah?"

"Mmm," Charlie hummed, nodding. "I've always enjoyed lecturing when I got the chance, so, yeah."

"Where did you lecture before?" Mac asked, glancing over at her as they wandered beneath the heavy branches of an oak that hung over the sidewalk at the edge of the fields closest to Charlie's neighborhood.

"Just around Manhattan. NYU, Cornell, Columbia," Charlie said with a small shrug. "I started at NYU because that's where I got my master's, so the faculty there obviously knew me, but sports journalism is actually a pretty small world and it wasn't long before Columbia and Cornell started offering me lecture spots as well."

"So you did get your master's," Mac said, remembering that there had been a time that the brunette had considered skipping graduate school in deference to just jumping into the deep end and paying her dues at a magazine.

"Yeah. Almost went for my PhD, but…"

Mac arched a brow questioningly and glanced over at the brunette who was staring hard at the sidewalk in front of them, brow furrowed like she was trying to either forget or remember that part of her life. "But, what?"

Charlie sighed and shrugged. "I'd already gotten my foot in the door at *SI* and I didn't have the time to work my way up at the magazine and pursue a doctorate."

"Makes sense."

"Yeah, well, now I kinda wish I'd done it anyways." Charlie waved a hand at the houses that were across the street from them and said, "It's just down there."

"I'll follow you," Mac assured her. "Why do you wish you had the PhD?"

Charlie shrugged and looked up and down the street before stepping off the curb. "It would just give me more options."

"Options for what?" Mac pressed.

Charlie laughed. "Persistent little thing, aren't you?"

"You know it," Mac drawled, grinning as they walked across the street, their shadows stretching and blending together in front of them in the warm yellow glow of the streetlight. "You can tell me to drop it and I will, Charlotte. I don't want to make you uncomfortable."

"You're fine. It's just that ever since I got up here, I've been wondering if I really want to go back to the magazine or not. I mean, I should miss it and I don't. I…" Charlie's voice trailed off and she shrugged. "Besides my friend Adam, there isn't a whole lot about the city that I miss right now."

"I see," Mac murmured, nodding.

Charlie quirked a brow in surprise and asked, "Do you?"

"You like it here," Mac answered simply.

"There's a lot to like," Charlie agreed. It wasn't the whole truth, but it was better than telling Mackayla that what she truly loved about being at Blake was the blonde's company. "Just friends" did not make declarations like that, and Charlie was loathe to upset the delicate balance they had managed to establish. Her house came into view, and she swallowed thickly as she waved a hand at it. "There she is. Home sweet home. Such as it is, anyways."

"It's cute," Mac said, smiling as she looked at the little bungalow and its wide front porch. Her eyes swept over the flowerbeds full of hydrangeas and other perennials and she nodded to herself. "It suits you."

"It does?" Charlie looked at the house thoughtfully and tried to see what it was about it that made Mackayla think that she belonged there. "How?"

Mac smirked. "Well, it's small."

"Shut up," Charlie grumbled, daring to bump the blonde with her hip in response to the playful jab. "You're only like six inches taller than me," she added as she hopped up onto the porch.

Mac laughed and nodded. "Still touchy about your height, huh?"

"Not at all," Charlie retorted dryly as she unlocked the front door. She licked her lips nervously and looked back at Mackayla as she pushed it open. She wanted to invite her inside, but she wasn't sure how the blonde would react to such an invitation, despite the fact that there was nothing untoward about it. She sighed and rolled her eyes, silently chastising herself for making things between her and Mackayla more awkward than they really needed to be, and asked, "Would you like to come in?"

Mac nodded and purposefully ignored the way her stomach fluttered ever so slightly at Charlotte's invitation. "Sure. Thank you," she said as she walked through the open door.

Charlie cleared her throat softly as she closed the front door, and bit the inside of her cheek to keep from grinning as she watched Mackayla take in every detail of the small foyer and adjoining living room. "Would you like the nickel tour?"

"If you wouldn't mind," Mac replied, smiling as she turned to look at the brunette.

"Don't mind at all," Charlie said. She took a deep breath and, determined to keep things light between them, began, in the worst English accent she could muster, "What we have here is a cozy foyer slash entryway. Cozy is design-speak for small."

Mac laughed and shook her head, appropriately amused by Charlotte's antics. "I'll remember that."

"Yes, please do," Charlie replied, fake accent still firmly in place. "Now, if you'll follow me, we'll begin our tour with the private areas of the home. Here we have a small bedroom that is currently being utilized as an office, in as much as it contains a desk and a computer, neither of which are being put to much use at the moment."

Mac noted that the office was small but functional, with a large monitor and a smaller, wireless keyboard on the desk. There was a framed soccer jersey that she didn't recognize hanging on the wall beside the desk, along with a handful of awards. "Why aren't you using it?"

"I've been doing most of my work on my MacBook," Charlie explained. "I'm actually not sure why I even brought the desktop up with me. Anyways, moving on, we have the only bathroom in the house, which is important to remember in case you choose to honor me with your presence again."

The bathroom was predictably utilitarian, just a vanity, tub/shower, and toilet–and though the fixtures were nice, they were by no means extravagant. "I will keep that in mind."

Charlie grinned and waved a hand at the end of the hall. "And down here is what we'll call the master bedroom, if only because it's large enough to hold a queen-size bed and some other pieces of furniture."

The master bedroom at the end of the hall was certainly larger than the front bedroom, and Mac smiled as her eyes slid over the deep crimson comforter on the bed. It was pure Charlotte. Warm. Bold. Confident. "Very nice," Mac murmured as she turned to look at the brunette.

"Thank you," Charlie said, her accent disappearing for a moment as she offered the blonde a small, shy smile. She cleared her throat and spun on her heel toward the entryway, and when she spoke next, her fake accent was once again firmly in place. "If you'll follow me back this way, we can explore the more communal areas of the home."

Mac's eyes landed on the built-in bookshelves around the fireplace in the living room and she immediately gravitated toward them, curious as to what books Charlotte would have felt she needed to bring with her to New Hampshire.

"And, the bookworm loses interest in the tour," Charlie announced with a laugh, her accent slipping away for good. "Should have known."

"I'm sorry," Mac said, smiling bashfully over her shoulder at the brunette. "I just…"

"Peruse away," Charlie said, waving a hand at the books. "It's fine, Mackayla. Would you like something to drink? Water? Diet Coke? Beer? Wine?"

"Whatever you're having is fine with me," Mac said, her attention already drifting back to the books in front of her.

Charlie smiled and shook her head fondly at the blonde's back. It felt so right to have Mackayla here, snooping through her books, and she wished that she hadn't been so foolish to let all this slip through her fingers so many years ago. She cleared her throat softly as she left the room, and she hesitated for only a second in the kitchen before she pulled a bottle of Merlot out of the cupboard above the refrigerator.

When she returned to the living room with the drinks, she was not at all surprised to find that Mackayla had pulled a book from the shelf. "Which one did you find?" she asked as she walked over to the blonde hand handed her a glass. She smiled as she spotted the cover of one of her new favorites, the debut novel of a previously unknown author. "That one's actually really good."

"You think so?" Mac asked softly, glancing shyly up at the brunette.

Charlie nodded. "Yeah. I mean, for one–it has lesbians in it, which, let's be honest, is something I'm totally on board with."

Mac laughed and shook her head as she lifted her wine glass to her lips and took a small sip. "And?" she asked, genuinely curious about Charlotte's thoughts on the book.

"The author has a really engaging style. I don't know how to describe it, but you just feel every emotion she's trying to convey through the characters. By the end, I was literally in tears. Like, actually crying. It's beautiful and funny and sexy as fuck and real, god, so real, and just..." Her voice trailed off as she realized that Mackayla was blushing. "What?"

Mac cleared her throat and held the book up. "This is my book. The one I told you about as we were walking over here."

"You're fucking kidding me," Charlie muttered, eyes wide as she looked from the book to Mackayla and back again. "I mean, it's not that I don't...*you* wrote this? You're Lynn Turner? Oh my god, I've been pimping this out to anyone who would read it. My best friend Adam is like, totally in love with this book. Not even kidding."

"Thank you," Mac murmured, blushing so hard that her cheeks felt like they were actually on fire.

Charlie shook her head as she looked at Mackayla. The blonde was absolutely stunning with that shy, pleased smile tweaking her lips and an embarrassed blush tinting her cheeks; and it took every ounce of self-control she had to not lean in and kiss her because, god, she was just so proud of her. "You're welcome."

The emotion in the brunette's words made Mac's heart skip a beat and she nodded dumbly as she slipped the book back into its place on the shelf. "I..." She looked at the rest of the books and, seeing one she didn't recognize, pulled it from the shelf, desperate for some kind of distraction to draw Charlotte's attention away from her. Everything was just too raw at the moment, and she was determined to keep things between them simple. And the things her heart was quietly wishing for weren't either of those things. "*The Iron Druid Chronicles.* I've never heard of this one. Any good?"

Charlie glanced at the novel and nodded. "That's actually the fourth book in the series. But, yeah. He's good. No lesbians in it, which sucks, but he writes a good story. Fun dialogue and the main character can communicate telepathically with his dog, which leads to some really funny conversations. Here," she said, pulling a different paperback from the shelf and handing it to Mackayla. "This is the first one in the series. I think you'd like it."

"Thank you," Mac murmured, flipping the book over in her hands to peruse the back cover. It did look interesting and she smiled sheepishly at Charlotte as her phone rang and she was forced to put her wine glass down so she could answer it. "Hey, Spence. You're on your way now? ... Okay. ... Yeah, no, I'll be out front. See you soon."

Second Chances

"Game over?" Charlie asked quietly as she watched Mackayla slip her phone back into her pocket.

Mac nodded and held up the paperback Charlie had given her. "He's heading over now. Are you sure you're okay with me borrowing this?"

"Of course. Here, take the rest of the series too," Charlie said, quickly pulling the other books from the shelf and holding them out to Mackayla in a neat stack. She smiled at the blonde and tipped her head at the front door. "Ready?"

"Yeah." The cool night air felt nice against her cheeks, which still felt warm from her earlier blush as she stepped out onto the porch. She cleared her throat softly as she looked out toward the street. Charlotte's glowing praise of her writing was still echoing inside her mind, and she was surprised at how much the brunette's opinion mattered to her. She bit her lower lip as her eyes swept over the brunette's face, tracing familiar planes she had long ago committed to memory. It was so easy to be with her, even with the lingering tension that simmered between them, and she had to look away before the urge to reach out and trace the delicate line of Charlotte's jaw became too much to resist.

Charlie sighed and tried to figure out a way to break through the awkwardness that had fallen between them, but nothing came to mind. Inane conversation would have worked, but she didn't want to fill the silence with cheap words. She wanted to fill it with warmth and affection, with soft touches and even softer kisses. And as neither of those were an option, she instead sat on the arm of one of the Adirondack chairs and sipped at her wine that she had brought out with her, content to let the absence of words attempt to convey everything she was thinking.

She got to her feet as a car pulled into her driveway and looked at Mackayla. The blonde was obviously lost in her own thoughts and conflicted about something; and even though she wished she knew what it was that was going on inside that brilliant mind of hers, she knew that it was not her place to ask. "Thank you for walking me home."

Mac nodded and her eyes darted over to Charlotte as her body rocked forward toward the path that led to the driveway where Spencer's SUV idled quietly, and she swallowed thickly at the emotion evident in the brunette's gaze. An overwhelming urge to take the smaller woman into her arms shot through her, and she swallowed thickly as she shook her head, forcing herself to remain where she was. "My pleasure," she whispered. "Thanks for the books. I'll, um, see you Monday," she added somewhat lamely, flashing Charlotte a quick smile as she stepped off the porch and hurried down the walk to the safety of Spencer's car.

Chapter 13

A month had passed since the night Mackayla had walked her home from the football game and, though random moments of awkwardness would inevitably crop up whenever they were together, Charlie was hopeful that someday soon Mackayla wouldn't run away from her whenever those moments arose. Charlie bit her lip as she stepped off the elevator on the third floor of Sanborn, her body relaxing as silence and stillness swept over. It was what she liked to think of as the twilight of the academic day, where the majority of the students were gone for the day, while those who took classes at night had yet to arrive. It was the most peaceful time on campus, and Charlie had grown to savor the late afternoons where she could decompress and get her work done with minimal interference from her students, who seemed to enjoy stopping by her office to just sit and chat.

She hummed softly under her breath as she dug in her satchel for her keys, and a small smile quirked her lips when she saw that Mackayla's office door was open. It was unusual for her to be at school so late on a Thursday, and Charlie wandered toward the blonde's office, drawn like a moth to a flame. She could no more stop herself from gravitating toward Mackayla than she could stop herself from breathing, and she had no interest in doing either.

Mackayla's desk was predictably clean, notebooks stacked in neat piles along one edge, and Charlie's heart fluttered into her throat as she saw the "broquet" she had given the blonde the day before sitting atop the tallest stack of notebooks. She knew that flowers would have been too much, but had wanted to give Mackayla something other than coffee, so she settled on a bunch of the blonde's favorite candies taped to wooden cooking skewers and arranged in a vase like they were the most precious of blooms. It was just dorky enough to be endearing without treading on the fine line between friendship and something more that she had been tiptoeing along, and the smile she got from Mackayla was enough to make her grin uncontrollably all day long.

For as happy as the sight of her gift holding a place of such prominence on Mackayla's desk made her, Charlie's smile fell as her gaze finally landed on the blonde herself. Mackayla was hunched over her desk, lips pursed in what Charlie recognized as thoughtful frustration as she flipped her phone back and forth between her hands. Something was obviously wrong.

Completely unaware of Charlotte's presence, Mac swore softly under her breath as she leaned forward to lightly bang her forehead on her desk. She hooked her hands behind her neck and closed her eyes, her mind racing to figure out how she was going to keep the kids in check on her own. If it were any other night, Spencer needing to run down to Albany to help his sister move into her new apartment wouldn't be a big deal at all. But it was the second-to-last GLOW planning meeting for the club's annual Mish-Mash Fashion Show fundraiser, and harnessing the energy of over a hundred kids who were generally very opinionated, and who would, no doubt, be feeling more than a little stressed about the impending show, was a headache waiting to happen.

She jumped at the sound of a light knock on her door and smiled in spite of herself when she saw Charlie leaning casually against her doorframe, looking as beautiful as ever in a pair of tailored black slacks, a fitted maroon blouse that was open at the neck, and yet another pair of killer stilettos. She had her suit coat draped over her arm and a soft, concerned look in her eyes that made Mac's heart skip a beat. "Hey," Mac said, running a hand through her hair as she leaned back in her chair.

"Everything okay?" Charlie asked.

Mac nodded. "Just peachy."

Charlie flashed the blonde a lopsided smile that did nothing to chase the worry from her gaze, and shook her head. "Not buying it, Thomas. What's up?"

"Nothing." Mac sighed as the brunette gave her a disbelieving look and shrugged. "Spence is down in Albany for the rest of the week to help his sister move, so I'm stuck managing the GLOW meeting tonight on my own."

"I see," Charlie drawled, glancing at her watch and noting that it was a little after five o'clock. "And what time is the meeting?"

"Five thirty."

Charlie nodded. "Okay. Where?"

"Where, what?" Mac frowned.

Charlie shook her head and chuckled softly under her breath. "Where's the meeting? As I'm sure you know, I have nothing to do up here besides teach, which I'm done with for the day, so I'll help."

Mac shook her head and smiled appreciatively at Charlotte. "You really don't have to do that."

"I know I don't *have* to do it. I want to. Let me help you." Charlie grinned as she was hit with a burst of inspiration. "And, maybe we can grab a late dinner afterwards? My treat, of course."

Touched by the earnestness in Charlotte's tone, Mac smiled and nodded. "Okay. But I think the very least I could do is buy you dinner for helping me out. Never mind all the coffee and candy you've been bringing me. I'm going to have to start running again to burn off all the extra calories."

Charlie laughed and resisted the urge to fist pump in celebration. "Like you ever stopped running. You forget that I know you, Mackayla Thomas. Worst case scenario is that you've backed your routine down to every other day, but you wouldn't ever actually stop running."

"Fine," Mac muttered, purposefully ignoring the way her stomach fluttered ever so slightly with butterflies at the sound of Charlotte's laughter. "I'll have to start running more often."

Charlie nodded, trying her best to not look as thrilled about her changed evening plans as she actually was. She hooked a thumb over her shoulder at her office and said, "Just let me put my satchel away and we can walk over to wherever the meeting is."

"You're sure?"

"Positive," Charlie assured her. "I can think of no better way to spend the rest of my night."

It was impossible to miss the faint hint of longing in Charlotte's voice, and a small shiver rolled down Mac's spine as it slid over her like a caress. That was the problem with being around Charlotte. The more time she spent in the brunette's company, the harder it was to remember why she was so determined to keep her at an emotional distance. "Great," she said, her voice far breathier than she would have liked.

Charlie nodded. She could have continued with the flirty banter, but she knew that she was already dancing dangerously close to the line where Mackayla would shut down on her. And, with the promise of an entire evening with the beautiful blonde in front of her, she wasn't about to push.

She unlocked her office quickly and tossed her satchel onto her desk, where it landed with a quiet thud, and bit her lip to try and contain the ear-splitting grin that was threatening to break free as she slipped her coat back on. Her eyes lingered for only a moment on her satchel that was laying open on her blotter, she had some papers she needed to go over, short, timed essays she had assigned that afternoon, but she rationalized that she could always do that later. Spending some one-on-one time with Mackayla trumped everything else she could or should be doing.

"Ready?" Mac asked, licking her lips nervously as she watched the brunette lock up.

"Always," Charlie replied, smiling warmly as she turned to look at Mackayla. "So, where are we going?"

"The meeting is over in the Student Union."

"Okay. What about dinner?"

Mac sighed, hating the way her heart raced with anticipation at the idea of going out with the brunette. "Um, I dunno. Is there anything you're in the mood for?"

"Nope," Charlie said, shaking her head as they stopped in front of the elevators. "I'm game for anything."

"How did I know you'd say that?" Mac muttered, the corners of her lips quirking up by a fraction as she rolled her eyes.

Charlie just laughed and shook her head. She was not about to point out that, despite Mackayla's current misgivings, Mackayla knew her just as well as she knew the blonde. "No clue."

"You always were a smartass," Mac grumbled. She looked over at Charlotte and swallowed thickly as the air between them seemed to crackle with electricity. The elevator dinged as the car arrived and the doors in front of them opened, and she sighed softly under her breath as she gratefully stepped into the car.

Chapter 14

Dusk had fallen by the time Charlie followed Mackayla out of Sanborn, blanketing Blake's campus in shades of charcoal and gray. The air had grown noticeably colder with the setting sun, making it impossible to ignore the fact that fall had arrived, bringing cooler temperatures in on the backs of the changing leaves.

As they wandered beneath the changing boughs that overhung the walkways of the Green, Charlie shivered at the chill that had worked its way to her skin. "It's getting cold."

"Well, it is the first week of October," Mac drawled, smirking as she looked over at the brunette. "Why didn't you bring a warmer coat?"

"I haven't broken out my winter suits yet." Charlie rolled her eyes. "Guess I'll be needing them a little earlier than I normally would, huh?"

"Probably, yeah."

"So, what's going on at this meeting tonight that you needed help? Not that I'm complaining, of course. This gives me an excellent excuse to miss out on a Lean Cuisine dinner and some quality time with my DVR."

Mac shot the brunette a surprised look. "You still haven't learned to cook?"

Charlie shook her head. "I learned a little bit. I can cook chicken, so long as there's a broiler pan I can just spray with Pam and whack it on, mac 'n cheese from a box, and I pour a mean bowl of cereal. Oh, and I have totally mastered how to make Rice a Roni."

"You're a culinary genius," Mac chuckled.

"I know, right? But, really, why would I waste my time learning to cook when New York is filled with restaurants that are all too happy to deliver food to my doorstep?"

Mac's heart sank a little at the reminder that Charlotte's life was in New York and not New Hampshire, and she forced a small smile as she replied, "Well, I guess you have a point there."

It wasn't hard for Charlie to pick up on the sudden shift in Mackayla's mood, and she nodded as she hurried to change the subject. "So, this meeting tonight. What do you need me to do to make your life easier?"

"I just need you to help me make sure that the kids have everything planned for the Mish-Mash."

"Okay." Charlie waved her left hand in a circle in front of herself. "And a Mish-Mash is what, exactly?"

"A fashion show that GLOW puts on every year on the day before Halloween," Mac explained as they walked up the front steps of the Student Union.

"Okay. Could you maybe tell me what, exactly, a Mish-Mash Fashion Show is?" Charlie asked as she hurried to open the door to the Union open for Mackayla.

"It's just a mish-mash of everything. Some kids do the show in drag, some don't, it's one of those anything goes type of things that fits with the club's philosophy of 'who cares, do and be what you like'."

Charlie pursed her lips thoughtfully and nodded. "Sounds cool."

"We always get a good turnout. The student body is incredibly accepting and supportive. We even have fraternities and sororities send chapter members to do the show, and whoever garners the most applause wins their house points for Greek Week, which always coincides with our show. It's actually turned into a pretty big deal."

Charlie reached for the door that had a neon green paper that read "GLOW" taped to it and pulled it open. "Now it really sounds like a good time."

"It is," Mac assured her with a smile as she walked through the door. She looked over the crowd of students gathered in the room and nodded as she saw that the majority of the group was there already. "Hey guys," she greeted the room as she walked to the front and stood beside a long folding table to face the group. She caught Charlotte's eye and waved the brunette forward. "This is Charlie Bennett."

"Hey, Ms. Bennett!" a flamboyant junior Charlie recognized from her Intro to Sports Journalism class yelled from the middle of the room.

Charlie grinned and waved at him. "Hey, John."

"Hi, Charlie," Liv, the brunette who Charlie had met when she had come to Mackayla for help before school started, called out.

Charlie noticed that Liv looked much more relaxed than the last time she had seen her, and she smiled and waved at her. "Hiya."

"Charlie is going to help out with the meeting because Spence couldn't make it tonight," Mac shared. She pushed herself up onto the table and looked over the room. "So, Mish-Mash. What do we have left to do?"

Charlie eased off to the side to watch as Mackayla ushered the group through the initial planning of the event, and she couldn't help but smile at the way the kids all responded to her.

Mackayla was never completely at ease around her, especially when it was just the two of them, but she was now. Her posture was relaxed, and her smile was both unguarded and entirely infectious. Charlie watched her in awe, her eyes tracking each wave of Mackayla's hands and her stomach fluttering uncontrollably at the sound of her laughter. She had known, of course, that the blonde would have grown and matured over the years, but witnessing it firsthand, actually seeing the warm, confident woman she had become, had Charlie falling even further in love with her.

"All right, break into your groups and make sure you have everything either done or in the process of being done," Mac told the group, snapping Charlie out of her thoughts. "Charlotte and I will come around and help out where needed. Remember, we only have three and a half weeks or so until the show, so we don't have a lot of time left."

Mac smiled as she watched the kids break into smaller groups, moving chairs to form small conversation clusters. Once they seemed settled, she turned to look at Charlotte and her heart leapt into her throat at the unfettered affection she could see shining in the brunette's bright green eyes. She swallowed thickly as she crossed the room to where Charlotte was standing, and she flashed a shaky smile as she stopped in front of her. "Hey."

"Hey," Charlie murmured, her eyes locking onto the blonde's. Her heart raced as Mackayla's gaze held her own, and the hairs on the back of her neck stood on end as time seemed to stop around them. Before she could control the urge, she was reaching for the blonde, her hand open and ready to cradle the sweet curve of the taller woman's jaw, and she flinched when Mackayla took a step away from her. "Sorry," she whispered, her eyes dropping to the ground as she mentally kicked her own ass for losing control like that. She knew she was walking a tightrope where Mackayla was concerned, and Mackayla was not ready for any gesture that wasn't entirely platonic. Her eyes had just been so warm, her smile so soft and reminiscent of the times she *had* been able to reach out and pull the blonde into a kiss, that the instinct to do so had overridden her common sense. "I don't know…"

"It's fine," Mac said, her gaze darting around the room to see if any of the kids had seen what had almost just happened. She ran a hand through her hair in relief when it was obvious that none of them had been paying any attention to her, and sighed as she dared look back at the brunette.

"No, it's not," Charlie insisted softly, shaking her head. Her stomach twisted unpleasantly at the way Mackayla's eyes darkened ever so slightly as the blonde's walls were thrown firmly back in place, and she licked her lips nervously as she added, "I shouldn't have done that."

Mac honestly couldn't disagree with that sentiment. The gesture had been entirely too familiar and intimate for their tenuous friendship, but the little voice in the back of her head that was shouting that she liked it was enough to make her offer Charlotte a small smile as she said, "It's fine," she repeated, adding, "don't worry about it."

Relieved that Mackayla seemed content to let the whole thing slide, Charlie nodded. "Okay." She cleared her throat and looked around the room, noticing for the first time how the students had rearranged themselves into smaller groups. "Um, what do you need me to do?"

Mac noticed a few groups looking at them with their hands in the air. "Just go around and try to offer suggestions where you can. If you don't know, wave me over and I'll come help out."

When the meeting ended a little over an hour later, the group had made decisions on everything that needed to be finalized that night and identified quite a few issues that would be addressed later on. Charlie stood at the front of the room and watched as Mackayla said goodbye to every student. Liv was the last to leave,

Second Chances

and Charlie bit her lip as she watched Mackayla pull a check from her pocket and hand it to the brunette, waving off whatever protestations the amount elicited from the girl. Liv left with a grateful smile and Charlie pushed herself off the wall as Mackayla's gaze landed on her. "All done?"

"All done," Mac confirmed with a small nod. "Thanks so much for helping tonight. I didn't realize you knew so much about fashion shows."

"Just picked up a few things over the years," Charlie deflected, not wanting to admit that everything she knew was from having attended last year's Fashion Week in New York with her at-the-time girl of the month who wrote for *Vogue*.

"Well, it was a big help. So, thank you. The kids seemed to really appreciate it as well."

Charlie smiled. The kids were a safe topic and she had really enjoyed working with them. "They're a good group."

"They are. Liv and John both asked if you were going to help out some more."

"I would love to. Would it be okay if I came to the next meeting?"

"Of course," Mac agreed softly.

"Great." Charlie ran a hand through her hair and asked the question that had been eating away at her since her earlier slipup, "So, do you still want to go grab a bite to eat?"

It would be easy to say no, Mac knew. All she had to do was bow out gracefully and Charlotte would accept the rejection without argument, but she couldn't do it. Yes, she had been half a heartbeat away from melting into the brunette's touch. No, she did not want to go down that road. Yes, it had caused the tension between them to grow. But she still selfishly enjoyed Charlotte's company and was not ready to let her go just yet, even if it was the kindest thing she could have done for the brunette considering the fact that they wanted such very different things. "Of course I do.

And I know the perfect place. Did you want to follow me over there?"

A relieved smile tweaked Charlie's lips and she shook her head. "I don't have a car. I walked to school today."

Mac nodded. "Okay then. I'll drive and bring you home afterwards."

Chapter 15

Charlie whistled softly as her eyes ran down the menu at Shenanigans. The pub was about half full, which Mackayla had told her was pretty standard for a Thursday night, and they were seated at a booth near the center of the room. Charlie had no doubt that Mackayla had chosen it because it was in the middle of everything. The tables of people around them guaranteed that they would have little-to-no privacy, and though she wished she were sitting closer to the blonde, she had to admit that the distance the booth forced between them was probably a good thing. It was just too easy to fall into old habits when she was alone with Mackayla, and at least this way she wouldn't be as tempted to do something stupid.

"Hmm?" Mac looked up from her menu, which she was using as a distraction so that she wouldn't stare at Charlotte.

Charlie shook her head. "This is insane. Can the chef actually make all of this?"

"Indeed I can." Henry laughed as he approached the table. "Lovely to see you, as always, Mac. And with much more beautiful company than Spencer. I approve."

Charlie blushed as she looked at the man standing beside their table. He was pretty average in height, build, and appearance, but his smile was warm and welcoming. "Sorry."

Henry held his hand out to Charlie as he introduced himself. "Henry Miller."

"Charlie Bennett."

"Pleased to meet you, Charlie Bennett," Henry drawled, winking at her as he shook her hand.

Charlie laughed and glanced over at Mackayla, who was rolling her eyes at Henry.

"Down boy," Mac chuckled. "Charlotte, Henry is the chef and owner of Shenanigans."

"Pleased to meet you," Charlie told him sincerely. "So, if you're the chef, what do you recommend?"

Henry pursed his lips thoughtfully as he pulled the menu from Charlie's hands and set it back behind the silverware at the end of the booth. "How hungry are you?"

"Starving, actually," Charlie admitted with a small laugh.

"Excellent." Henry clapped his hands eagerly. "I love hungry people. Do you like spicy food?"

Charlie grinned and nodded. "I love it."

"Any dietary restrictions?"

Charlie shook her head. "None."

"Right. Then I'll whip something up for you, don't you worry. Mac, darling, do you want your usual?"

"Sounds good, thanks," Mac said, smiling as she laid her menu down on the table.

"Drinks?"

"A glass of the house red is fine," Charlie said.

"Make that two," Mac added.

Henry grinned and threw a conspiratorial wink in Charlie's direction. "Ah, I like this one, Mac. She makes you change things up at least a little bit."

Mac laughed, her cheeks flushing with embarrassment as she shook her head. "Shut up. Shouldn't you be in the kitchen or something?"

"Or something," Henry retorted, turning on his heel and heading for the kitchen. He gave the bartender their drink orders as he passed the bar, and he looked back at them as he pushed the swinging door to the kitchen open. "I'll send out some appetizers for you in a minute," he hollered with a grin and one last roguish wink before he disappeared.

"We didn't order any appetizers," Charlie said, frowning.

"He's always trying new recipes out on me and Spence," Mac explained with a shrug as she watched the bartender, a man she didn't recognize, pour their wine up at the bar.

"I see," Charlie murmured, nodding slowly as her gaze swept over the pub. She noticed a wide doorway at the back of the bar and tipped her head at it as she asked, "What's back there?"

"The closest thing to a night out you can find in Hampton," Mac said, folding her hands on her lap as their server made his way toward them with their wine. "Henry bought the space behind the restaurant last year and put in a handful of pool tables and dart boards for those of us who don't want to hang out with the college kids over at Pulse," she explained, referring to the popular bar and hangout that sat just off the western edge of campus, within stumbling distance of Greek row.

"Good to know," Charlie murmured, licking her lips as she turned back to face the blonde. "So is this were you guys come after football games and stuff?"

"Either here or someone's house, yeah," Mac said, leaning back in her seat as their server stopped at the end of their table.

"Here you go, ladies," their waiter announced as he set the glasses down in front of them. "Anything else?"

"I think we're good for now," Mac said with a small smile. "Thanks."

"No problem. Henry says your appetizers will be out in just a minute."

Their conversation stalled as he walked away, and Charlie rolled her eyes as she reached for her glass, knowing that the awkwardness that had crept up between them was entirely her own fault. "So, any plans for a third book?" she asked, figuring that was as safe a topic as she could get.

Mac smiled wryly and shrugged. "Not yet, though my agent and publisher are bugging me for an outline for a new project. *Convergence*, my second novel, wrapped up all the loose ends from *Divergence*, so I don't know if I'll go back to that world or not. May have to come up with something new."

"Wait!" Charlie exclaimed, bouncing in her seat as she leaned forward excitedly. "So does that mean you fixed the whole Mia-Rachel relationship debacle? Because they are obviously soulmates and you totally screwed them over at the end of *Divergence*."

Mac laughed and shrugged. "I dunno. Guess you'll have to wait until you get the book to find out."

"That's not fair," Charlie grumbled playfully, grinning and shaking her head. "Why won't you tell me what happens? Did I tell you that I literally cried reading *Divergence*? I haven't cried over a book since *Old Yeller*, by the way. So that's huge." She batted her lashes playfully and flashed the blonde a hopeful smile. "Pwease?"

"Here we go," their waiter interrupted as he set a plate of the stuffed mushrooms Henry beta-tested on Spencer and Mac a couple weeks ago as well as a plate of fried mozzarella sticks down on the table. "Enjoy."

Mac reached for a stuffed mushroom and popped it into her mouth. "I am so glad he put these on the menu. So good," she practically moaned after she swallowed.

Charlie licked her lips as the sound of Mackayla's moan did wonderfully inappropriate things to her body, and shook her head. "I still think you should tell me what happens," she said, giving the blonde a pointed stare as she reached for one of the moan-inducing mushrooms.

"You always were impatient when you wanted something," Mac chuckled.

Charlie shrugged. "There are worse character flaws to have."

Mac arched a brow questioningly as she picked up a mozzarella stick. "Like what?"

"Wouldn't you like to know," Charlie retorted, grabbing another mushroom. "These really are amazing."

"Everything Henry makes is out of this world."

"I believe it," Charlie murmured. "Are you really not going to tell me what happens with Mia and Rachel?"

Mac shook her head. "Nope. So, new topic. What was your best interview, Ms. Famous Sports Writer?"

"Does Spencer know how it ends?" Charlie asked, ignoring her question.

"He does not," Mac chuckled. "Come on, Charlotte. I actually do want to know about your life since we left Wesleyan."

There was a softness to the blonde's voice that made Charlie's stomach flutter, and she sighed as she popped another mushroom into her mouth and chewed it thoughtfully. She had done many interviews over the years that had been incredible and it was hard to pinpoint one as her favorite. "I dunno. There were a lot that were good for different reasons, but if I had to pick one as my absolute favorite, it would probably be when I interviewed the women's national team after the gold medal game in London."

Mac grinned. "I knew it would be a soccer one."

"Yeah, well..." Charlie shrugged.

"Did you ask them for any autographs?"

Charlie blushed and nodded. "I did. It was perhaps the least professional moment of my career, but I did. I fangirled like nobody's business and got the whole team to sign a jersey for me. It's hanging on the wall beside my desk at home. I actually got a call this morning from Billy, my boss at the magazine, asking me to do a freelance story about the controversy revolving around the next Women's World Cup because of that article after the Olympics."

"What controversy?"

Charlie shrugged and picked up a mozzarella stick. "Pretty much the entire tournament is currently scheduled to be played on artificial turf instead of grass, and a lot of the big name players are understandably upset about it."

"Why are they upset?" Mac asked, reaching for her wine.

"Soccer is a different game on artificial turf. It's faster, the ball bounces more. It favors teams that are bigger and stronger because the game becomes less technical and more physical as teams tend to rely more on the long ball than shorter passes. Players bemoan increased injury risks, though there isn't enough quantifiable data to support that argument. The biggest argument, for me, is that playing the biggest, most important tournament in soccer on artificial turf is completely sexist."

"How?"

Charlie shrugged. "Because FIFA would never dare schedule a men's World Cup on anything but grass. I mean, I get that Canada doesn't necessarily have the number of outdoor stadiums needed to host an event like this. And sure, they may have a harder time than most getting fields into shape for an international competition like the World Cup considering their climate and everything, but there is no way the men would ever be asked to play a tournament of that magnitude on an artificial surface. Hell, most of the top men's players refuse to play even single matches on turf with their club teams."

Mac couldn't help but smile at the passion in the brunette's voice and she nodded. "So that's why they asked you to do it, then."

Charlie frowned. "What do you mean?"

"Well, you're incredibly knowledgeable about the subject, passionate, and if anyone is going to write an article smacking FIFA in the face for blatant sexism, I doubt there is anyone who could do it more justice than you."

Charlie blushed and reached for her wine. It was embarrassing exactly how much that little bit of praise from Mackayla affected her, but she couldn't deny that it didn't. "Thank you," she murmured, holding the blonde's gaze for an extended moment to let her know exactly how much she appreciated her kind words.

"Dinner is served," their waiter announced, drawing the women's attention away from each other. "Grilled Portobello burger–" he set Mac's plate down in front of her with a flourish, "– and a buffalo chicken sandwich with homemade bleu cheese dressing and applewood smoked bacon," he said as he slid Charlie's plate in front of her. "Enjoy."

Mac chuckled and shook her head as their waiter disappeared. "You may want to ask for a glass of milk," she told Charlotte.

"Why?" Charlie asked as she inspected her sandwich. The chicken was shredded and tinted the familiar shade of Frank's Red Hot Sauce, the bacon was thick and crisped to perfection, and the bleu cheese dressing looked chunky and absolutely divine.

"Whenever Spence gets it, he's sweating buckets by the time he's done."

Charlie grinned and picked up the sandwich. "Really? Well, challenge accepted, then."

Chapter 16

"Spencer is a wuss," Charlie declared as she climbed into Mackayla's Jeep after dinner. It was total bravado on her part, her tongue was still burning and she was pretty sure she was sweating, but she was not about to admit defeat.

"Really," Mac drawled, her eyes twinkling with laughter. "So that sheen of perspiration on your forehead is from what, exactly?"

"The heater was turned up too high in there."

"If you say so, Bennett," Mac murmured, rolling her eyes as she smiled and slid her key into the ignition.

Charlie smirked. "I do say so."

"Well, you sure showed me, then," Mac retorted, flashing Charlotte a grin as she pulled away from the curb.

Charlie hummed and nodded, feeling suddenly sad that the night was coming to an end. This was the first time since she had arrived in New Hampshire that she had spent some real, quality time with Mackayla, and she was not ready for it to end. There had been moments of awkwardness, of course, but, by and large, the night had been entirely enjoyable and she'd had fun just spending time with the blonde.

A comfortable silence filled the car as Mac drove, and she was surprised at the way her heart felt suddenly heavier as the brunette's house came into view. She had enjoyed spending time with her, trading barbs and listening to her talk about her career,

Second Chances

and even though she knew that she would undoubtedly see Charlotte again the following day, she could not help but feel a little disappointed.

Mac licked her lips as she turned into Charlotte's drive and sighed as she pulled to a stop near the walkway that lead to the front porch. "I had fun tonight," she murmured, rolling her eyes at the cliché line that usually marked the end of a date. This hadn't been a date, of course, but the sentiment was the same. She really did have a good time.

Charlie smiled and nodded. "Me too. Thanks for dinner."

"My pleasure. Thanks for helping with GLOW."

"My pleasure," Charlie assured her with a small laugh. Her hand hovered over the door handle, unwilling to open it and officially call the evening complete.

"Are you planning on coming to the game this weekend?" Mac asked.

Charlie smiled sadly and shook her head. "I'm leaving tomorrow afternoon after my last class to fly down to Miami for that article I was telling you about. There's a doubleheader friendly Saturday night, Canada versus Japan, and the US versus France, so I'll be able to talk to quite a few players about it all."

"Is the magazine at least paying for your airfare?" Mac asked.

Charlie nodded. "Of course. The cost for a hotel room and transportation are factored into my fee."

"And you get to watch a couple of games."

"That is an added perk, yes," Charlie admitted with a grin. "It will be fun. And warm."

"Don't forget to pack your bikini," Mac drawled.

Charlie laughed and shook her head. "If only I had time for that in my schedule. Unfortunately, this will be a working vacation, short as it is, and I will be back on a plane Sunday morning to fly home so that I don't miss my Monday morning class."

"Your dedication is impressive, Ms. Bennett," Mac teased.

"It is. I should get a raise or something for it."

"Of course you should, but you won't. You'll just have to suck it up like the rest of us poor, underappreciated souls."

Charlie chuckled and nodded. "Duly noted. When is the next GLOW meeting, by the way? I want to put it in my calendar."

"Two weeks."

"And the Mish-Mash is on the thirtieth?"

"You got it," Mac said, smiling. "Thanks again for your help with it all. The kids seemed to love you."

"That would be because I am incredibly lovable." Charlie grinned and winked at the blonde. "Right, well, I guess I should be going."

Mac nodded. "Okay."

"I'll see you tomorrow?"

"Of course. I'll be waiting for my coffee," Mac said with a smile.

"As the lady commands." Charlie tipped her head in a small bow. "Then, I shall say good night 'til it be morrow."

Mac laughed. "I'll see you tomorrow, Shakespeare."

"Goodnight, Mackayla," Charlie murmured as she finally opened her door. She sighed as she slid out of the car and couldn't resist leaning back in and adding, "Sleep well," before she closed the door and hurried up her front walk to the porch to get out of the cold.

Mac watched Charlotte unlock her front door and slip inside, and she smiled at the way the brunette waved at her before closing the door. It was impossible for her to ignore the way her heart was beating erratically, and she sighed as she backed out of Charlotte's driveway to head home.

Chapter 17

Though eighty degree weather, sunshine, quality soccer, and interviewing her favorite female athletes had all made Charlie's weekend in Miami enjoyable, the brunette was glad to be back in New Hampshire, shivering as she walked into the campus coffee shop. Her nine a.m. lecture had ended only moments before, and she was eager to see Mackayla. She waved at the baristas as they looked up at the jingle of the bell above the door that announced her arrival, and smiled as Jared, one of the kids who always worked the morning shift, pointed at two cups on the side counter and motioned that they were hers. In little more than the time it took Jared to run her card, she was back out the door, coffee in hand, with an energetic bounce in her step.

Campus was quiet as she made her way across the Green toward Sanborn, and the faculty office building was not much more alive as she stepped into the elevator. That serene stillness, the quiet, the feeling of being one of the few people awake was what made mornings such as this enjoyable. The sight of Mackayla smiling as she strode into the blonde's office with their hot drinks was what made her love them.

"Coffee, milady."

Though she would never admit it aloud, let alone to herself, Mac had been looking forward to this moment from the very second she had said goodbye to Charlotte the Friday before, and she grinned as she reached for the familiar white paper cup the brunette offered her. "Thank you. How was your trip?"

Charlie smiled and lowered herself to her usual chair across from Mackayla. "It was good. Warm. I got a nice run in on the beach Saturday morning."

"I'm jealous. Did you get what you wanted for that article?"

"I did." Charlie nodded and took a sip of her coffee, sighing contentedly as the hot drink worked its way down her throat and chased away the chill that had settled into her bones as she walked across campus. "The Canadians wouldn't go on record, they couldn't, because it's their federation hosting the tournament, but everyone else did, so I got some good stuff for it. I did a lot of my background research on the plane, so now I just gotta sit down and pound it all out."

"When is the article due?"

Charlie shrugged and relaxed in her chair. "I told Billy I'd have it to him by the end of the week. It only needs to be fifteen hundred words or so, so it won't take long to write it out. It'll probably take me longer to edit it down to get to that word count. I can be a bit of a longwinded bastard," she added with a smirk.

"Oh, I believe it," Mac laughed.

Charlie gave the blonde a wounded look and shook her head. "Wow. Such love. And to think that I spent *hours* wandering around Miami trying to find the perfect souvenir to bring home for you."

"Yeah right," Mac muttered, taking a drink of her coffee to distract herself from the way her stomach flip-flopped at the underlying meaning behind Charlotte's playful retort. She wasn't blind. Or stupid. She knew that the brunette had been courting her from the very first day of the semester, but coffees and candies were simple, easy treats to give. The idea that Charlotte would spend any time at all thinking about her when she was so far away was both flattering and frightening. She liked the idea of being on the brunette's mind and yet, at the same time, that very idea scared her half to death.

Charlie pulled a bright pink plastic bag from her satchel and grinned as she set it onto her lap. "I'm serious. Coming up with something that I thought you'd like was incredibly difficult, but I'm sure I ended up with just the right thing."

The sight of the bright bag emblazoned with *South Beach Collectables* piqued Mac's interest and she bit her lip as she looked at it. "I'm a little afraid right now."

"I don't know why," Charlie drawled, her eyes twinkling mischievously. "TSA wouldn't let me bring any of the really good stuff through security."

"Thank god for small favors," Mac muttered, playing along.

"Yeah, well," Charlie sighed, offering Mackayla the bag. "Anyways, here. These are for you."

"I actually am worried about this," Mac mumbled as she opened the top of the bag.

Charlie smiled around the rim of her coffee cup as she watched Mackayla paw through the collection of cliché souvenirs she had bought at the airport before she boarded her plane to fly home. The blonde's real present was tucked safely inside her satchel, but she wasn't ready to hand that one over just yet.

"An alligator in a snow globe." Mac shook her head as she pulled one of the ridiculous prizes from the bag.

Charlie grinned. "I named him Chomper."

"Of course you did," Mac chuckled as she gave the snow globe a shake and set it down on her desk. She reached back into the bag and arched a brow at Charlotte as she pulled a second kitschy souvenir out and gave it a jiggle. "A dashboard hula girl. I thought these were a Hawaii thing."

"They're a tropical vacation spot thing," Charlie explained, rolling her eyes. "And besides, it's not like you get to see those every day up here. Plus, she's hot. Cut little haircut, nice rack, what else could you want?"

"I have no idea," Mac murmured as she set the doll onto her desk besides Chomper. "Does she have a name?"

"I'll let you name her," Charlie replied with an imperious wave of her hand. "Keep going. There's more."

"You really didn't have to do this," Mac said as she obediently reached into the bag again.

"I know. But I wanted to. Enough stalling, Thomas. Pull out the next one."

Mac smiled as she pulled out an eight oz. bottle of rum. "You brought me alcohol."

"Oh, don't be like that," Charlie laughed. "Well, I mean, it is from the Mount Gay distillery. It was just too good of a name to pass up, never mind the fact that they make great rum. I would have brought a bigger bottle back, but the stupid liquid carry-on rule made it impossible. Like anyone would dare turn a bottle of really good alcohol into a bomb or something. Besides, if memory serves, rum and coke used to be a favorite of yours."

Mac bit her lip and gave the brunette a surprised look. "You remember that?"

"I remember a lot of things," Charlie said, her voice softening even as she brushed the question off with a wave her of her hand, knowing that Mackayla was not ready for that particular discussion. "So, there's one awesomely fantastic souvenir left."

"Right," Mac said, setting the little bottle onto her desk beside the alligator snow globe and the hula girl that actually reminded her a little of Charlotte with its shorter hairstyle. "One more." She reached into the bag one last time and pulled out… "A shirt. How original."

"Open it up," Charlie urged with a grin. She had purposefully folded the shirt so that the front couldn't be seen when it was pulled from the bag.

"Oh my god," Mac laughed as she unfurled the shirt to find an airbrushed woman's torso with bikini bottoms and a bedazzled coconut shell bra. "That's..."

"Hideously amazing?"

Mac bit her lip and nodded. Spencer was going to laugh his ass off when he saw this one. And then he would probably steal it. "Something like that." She sighed and smiled at Charlotte. "Thank you for my souvenirs."

"Not a problem," Charlie murmured. She reached into her bag and pulled out a wrapped package. "But there is actually one more. Now, this is your real souvenir, but I couldn't resist the little touristy things. So, I hope you like it."

It was impossible to miss the seriousness in Charlotte's tone and Mackayla's heart beat double-time in her chest as she took the package from her. She worked at the paper slowly, careful to not damage whatever was inside, and when the last piece of paper was dropped into the trashcan beside her desk, she couldn't help but smile. "How did you...?" Her voice trailed off as she looked at the framed note from her favorite author.

Dear Mackayla,

*I am a **huge** fan of your work, and I am so excited to hear that you will be sharing more of Mia and Rachel with us, your loyal readers. Keep writing, you have an amazing gift.*

Most sincerely yours,
Helena Wells

Charlie smiled. "She was in South Beach for a book signing, and was staying at my hotel. I ran into her in the lobby Saturday afternoon when I was leaving for the stadium. I know she used to be one of your favorite authors, so I introduced myself, told her a little about you, and she was nice enough to give me that."

Mac bit her lip as she looked back down at the note, her eyes stinging with tears even as she smiled uncontrollably. This was, without a doubt, the single best present she had ever received, and she had to clear her throat three times before she found the voice to tell Charlotte that. "Seriously, Charlotte, this is amazing. Thank you so much."

"I'm glad you like it," Charlie murmured. She took a deep breath and let it out slowly as she glanced at her watch.

"Do you need to go?"

"Yeah." Charlie gave the blonde a small smile. "I'm already late for my 10:30."

"Okay, yeah," Mac said, nodding understandingly as she got to her feet.

Charlie pushed herself to her feet as well and slung the strap of her satchel over her left shoulder. "I'm glad you liked your presents."

Even though Mac knew that doing so was dangerous to her resolve to keep things with Charlotte platonic, she couldn't resist walking around the side of her desk to pull the brunette into a hug. "Thank you," she whispered as she embraced her. The hug was light and tentative, but it made Mac's entire body come alive in a way that it hadn't done in years. She knew that she should let go, but she couldn't find the power to actually do it.

Charlie's heart swooped into her throat as she wrapped her arms around Mackayla. It was painfully perfect, and she bit her lip as she closed her eyes and savored the feeling of being in the blonde's arms again. "You're welcome."

Chapter 18

The night of the Mish-Mash was perfect. It was chilly, but not so cold that it was unpleasant, and the cloudless sky was hung with bright, twinkling stars. The heavy bass beats pumping inside the Student Union could be felt on the sidewalk outside the building, and Charlie arched a brow in surprise as she wound her way through the small crowd that had gathered, waiting for the doors to open.

She smiled at the sight of a muscular redhead in a little black dress on the other side of the locked doors. Wide shoulders and muscular arms told her that it was a man in drag, and she laughed when she knocked on the door and Spencer turned around. His dress was a classically conservative A-line that landed just above the knee and had a high neckline, his wig made her think of Milla Jovovich in *The Fifth Element*, and she couldn't help but chuckle when she saw that he had gone all-out when it came to stuffing his bra. He even had a little eye shadow and lipstick on.

"Damn, Walsh," Charlie drawled when he opened the door. "If I didn't know you were packing under that dress, I'd totally hit on you." She smirked as she shrugged out of her coat and hung it on the rack beside the front door.

Spencer laughed and gave her a once-over as well. The brunette's outfit wasn't flashy, but it was undeniably sexy. The pale cream and black dress was simple yet stunning, with what looked like one-inch bands of black satin around the hem, shoulder caps, and neckline. The collar dipped low in the front, slit to just below the sternum, and by the flash of side-boob that he got, it was obvious that Charlie wasn't wearing a bra. Her makeup was smoky, drawing attention to her cheekbones and eyes, and her hair was done in such a way that it made him think of wrinkled sheets and flushed, sated bodies. "Thank you, ma'am. You're looking rather luscious yourself."

Charlie grinned and tipped her head. "Thank you." She bit her lip nervously as her eyes darted over the familiar faces that were surrounding the runway that ran down the center of the Union. She had known that Spencer and Mackayla always dressed in drag for the show, which was why she chose to go her more traditional, feminine route. While it was fun to butch it up every now and again, she wanted to wow Mackayla, and she knew that a dress and heels was the way to do it.

What Charlie hadn't been expecting was to find herself rendered completely speechless by Mackayla's outfit for the evening. She had always had a thing for women in suits, there was something about the blend of femininity and masculinity that never failed to drive her wild, and Mackayla in one was no different. If anything, her response was magnified because of the fact it *was* Mackayla wearing the suit. Tailored tuxedo pants sat low on the blonde's trim hips, the smooth fabric hugging the curve of her ass perfectly. Charlie watched as Mackayla turned to gesture at something near the front doors, and she saw that the blonde's white shirt was open at the neck. Though the open shirt didn't show as much skin as her dress, she still licked her lips at the flash of black bra that she could see in the gap. A black bow tie hung limply around Mackayla's neck, begging to be grabbed onto, and Charlie whimpered softly at the thought of using that hold to pull the blonde into a kiss. Mackayla's playful pixie cut was slicked back, making her patrician features stand out even more than they usually did, and Charlie startled when Spencer chuckled beside her.

"You're drooling."

She wouldn't be at all surprised if she actually was, and she ran a discreet hand over her chin as she turned to look at him. "Can you blame me?"

He grinned and shook his head. "Not at all. But, hey, if it makes you feel any better, she's going to have that same reaction when she sees you."

Though she was pleased by his assessment, Charlie still flashed him a surprised look. "I thought you were staying out of this whole thing?"

Spencer shrugged. "I am. But I can still state the obvious. She is going to swallow her goddamn tongue." He grinned and added, "Of course, you don't look as good as me, but still. You clean up nice, Charlie Bennett."

"Well, we mortals must do what we can," Charlie retorted, rolling her eyes.

Spencer laughed. "Yes. You poor girl you. You have it so rough."

"You're too much, Walsh," Charlie chuckled, smiling warmly at him. "What do you need me to do tonight?"

"I'm going to be up here for a bit making sure the ticket stuff goes smoothly. Can you go back and help Mac with the kids? They're going to need help getting any last-minute wardrobe issues taken care of, and then they're going to need to be lined up according to the order of appearance so that the MC gives the right people, designers, whatever credit."

Charlie nodded. "Okay."

"Get on with your fine self, now, Ms. Bennett," Spencer said, tilting his head in Mackayla's direction. "I know I'm not the one you really came to spend time with anyways."

"Well, you know. You're cute, but just not my type," Charlie apologized with a playful shrug. She laughed at the dramatic pout he threw her, and grinned as she started for the end of the runway where Mackayla was talking with John and Liv. She slowed as she approached the small group, not wanting to interrupt in case the blonde was giving instructions to her charges, but, before she could do anything to announce her presence, she was spotted.

"Wow! You look hot, Ms. Bennett!" John yelled. He was, surprisingly, Charlie thought, not in drag, but instead wore a tailored pale gray suit, white shirt, and a sky blue skinny tie.

"Thank you, John. You look quite dashing, yourself," Charlie told him with a sincere smile as she sidled up to the group.

He grinned and ran his hands down his suit. "I designed and made this myself. Do you really like it?"

Charlie gaped. "You made it? Wow. Seriously, man. You look good. And, I'm sorry, hello, Liv. The leather jacket thing really works for you," she said, smiling at the girl as she looked at her. Though she was not technically in drag, she had definitely gone more butch for the evening than was her usual style, with black biker boots, jeans, a tight t-shirt, and leather jacket.

The younger brunette blushed. "Thank you."

"You're welcome," Charlie murmured as she turned her attention to Mackayla. "Hello, Mackayla. You look..." She swallowed thickly and nodded. "Yeah. Amazing."

Mac cleared her throat and nodded dumbly, her eyes locked onto the daring neckline of Charlotte's dress. The strip of skin between the brunette's breasts was hypnotic, and she had to force herself to look away. "You too," she husked, blushing as she cleared her throat again. "Positively stunning," she added softly. Her stomach fluttered at the pleased smile and slight blush that tinted Charlotte's cheeks at the compliment, and she couldn't help but smile in return.

Ever since she had hugged Charlotte in her office after the brunette had returned from her trip, their relationship had grown even more awkwardly familiar. Quick touches that had been considered out-of-bounds began happening more and more frequently, and it was rare that she left an encounter with Charlotte without some kind of physical contact. The little touches in and of themselves didn't bother her, but the way she had started to crave them was incredibly disconcerting.

Liv grinned and elbowed John. When he shot her a questioning look, she just shook her head and hiked a thumb over her shoulder, silently telling him that they should give the two professors a moment alone.

Neither Charlie nor Mac saw the two students leave, and both were too lost in each other to particularly care that they were staring much longer than was platonically acceptable.

"Jesus, Mackayla," Charlie said, licking her lips as she reached out to lightly finger one end of the blonde's tie. She knew she shouldn't, but she couldn't help herself. She needed to touch. The fabric was cool against her fingertip, and she felt the familiar stirrings of desire coil low in her hips as she rubbed the smooth material between her thumb and forefinger. "You really do look amazing. Not that you don't usually, it's just…"

"Thank you," Mac whispered. Because she was wearing flats and Charlotte was wearing four-inch heels, they were almost the same height, and she was surprised by how strongly her body reacted to the emotion she could see burning in Charlotte's eyes. She knew that Charlotte wanted her, but the depth of that longing had never been more evident in the brunette's gaze than it was in that moment. It was as if Charlotte's soul was bared to her, all of the brunette's wants and desires on display for her to see. It made her heart beat erratically as it soared into her throat and, even had she wanted to, she was completely powerless to look away.

The sound of the DJ's voice echoed through the Union, announcing that it was time for the fashion show participants to head backstage, and Charlie swallowed thickly as the intrusion brought her back to the present. "Yeah," she muttered, feeling her cheeks flame as she released the tie she had been playing with. "I'm sorry," she apologized as she took a quick step away from Mackayla.

Disappointment shot through Mac at the loss of Charlotte's touch. "Nothing to be sorry for," she said. She could hear exactly how low and rough her voice was, and she shook her head as she forced herself to look away from the beautiful brunette. "Um…we should probably go backstage with the kids." She waved a distracted hand at the towering black drapes that had been erected over the end of the runway opposite the front doors of the union. "Would you help the non-GLOW kids get ready and I'll go through our kids?"

Charlie nodded. "Of course."

"Perfect," Mac murmured, licking her lips as her eyes danced over Charlotte's face one last time. "Thank you."

Before Charlie could respond, Mackayla was gone, striding toward the backstage area with long, purposeful steps that showed how anxious she was to get away. Charlie sighed as she followed at a more leisurely pace, more than willing to allow Mackayla the space the blonde so clearly needed to recover from the intensity of the moment they had just shared.

It didn't take much to make sure the participants were ready to go, and, before long, it was show time. Mackayla looked over at Charlotte, who was standing on the left side of the runway while she manned the right, and she smiled at the brunette as Spencer announced the beginning of the show. It was his insistence to also dress in drag that had brought in the fraternities for Greek week–getting the girls involved hadn't been nearly as hard a sell–and she knew that it was his comfort at walking around in a dress that made the fraternity boys taking part in the show comfortable as well. She bit her lip as she watched Charlotte give the guys at the front of her line one last quick pep talk, complete with fist bumps and manly pats on the shoulders, and, as the boys laughed, she knew that whatever nerves they had been feeling had been put to rest.

Up on stage, Spencer grabbed the microphone and announced, "Let's do it!" as he handed the mic off to the Mish-Mash's M.C., a girl from the A.V. Club named Tina. The music swelled as Tina called for Liv, who was starting the show off, and Mac was forced to look away from Charlie as she directed Liv, who was standing at the front of her line, up the stairs to the runway.

"Knock 'em dead!" Mac hollered, grinning at Liv as the girl walked past her.

Liv rolled her eyes and pasted on a smile as she started down the runway, determined to start the show off right, despite her nerves about being asked to lead things off.

Charlie sent Will, a guy from Sig Ep who was wearing a red evening gown and looked unapologetically excited about being in the show, up to wait just offstage until Liv made it to the end of the runway. She smiled and nodded at him when Liv made her turn-around, and she laughed at the excited *whoop* he let loose as he started strutting down the runway. Mackayla got her next participant ready as Will did his thing, and it wasn't long until they fell into an easy pattern, each line filing in after the other until Charlie and Mackayla were basically able to resort to being bystanders and enjoying the show.

"And, last, but certainly not least, we have John Larson!"

Charlie grinned as she watched John jog up the stairs and smooth his hands over his hair before he slipped between the curtains and took his turn on the runway. He was a natural, bringing the show home with an infectious grin and an energetic hop-step that had the crowd applauding louder than they had all night. When he reached the end of the runway, he did a little spin, holding his coat open for extra flair, and laughed as he took an extra microphone from one of the A.V. students who were helping with the show.

"Thank you guys for coming tonight!" John yelled, beaming as the crowd erupted with catcalls and cheers. "But, before we can call this thing done, there are three more people who need to take their turn on the runway. Please put your hands together for our awesome advisors, Spencer Walsh, Mac Thomas, and Charlie Bennett!"

The crowd cheered as Spencer jumped up onto the runway and started to do an exaggerated sashay down the runway, smiling at the crowd and doing a frighteningly spot-on princess wave.

Charlie shot John a surprised look as he beckoned her out onto the runway. "Seriously?"

He grinned and nodded. "Seriously, Ms. Bennett," he said into the mic, his laughing voice echoing through the room and drawing a wave of echoing laughter from the crowd. "Get up here!"

"Come on, Charlotte. It's not that bad, I promise," Mac murmured as she gallantly held her arm out for the brunette.

Even if Charlie had wanted to bow out of the curtain call, she couldn't. Not with Mackayla smiling at her like that. "If you say so, Thomas," Charlie murmured, licking her lips as she slipped her hand into the crook of the blonde's arm. It was impossible to ignore how right it felt to walk like this with Mackayla, and Charlie kept stealing glances at the blonde as they made their way down the runway together.

"I think you have a few fans," Mac observed as she caught sight of an entire row of frat boys blowing kisses at Charlotte.

"I think you're right," Charlie agreed, waving at the boys even as she squeezed Mackayla's arm gently. "Too bad for them, they don't stand a chance."

Spencer smiled at Mac and Charlie as they stopped beside him, and pulled the microphone from John's hand. "Let's get everybody up here one last time!"

Charlie slipped her hand from Mackayla's arm turned beside the blonde to applaud as the kids who had taken part in the show made their way back out onto the runway. The night had been a colossal success, and as Charlie watched the crowd get to their feet to give the participants a standing ovation, she felt so proud of Mackayla that she could have sworn her heart was going to burst.

Chapter 19

"I come bearing gifts," Charlie announced with a grin as she strode into Mackayla's office just before midday on Friday with a confident swagger and two Styrofoam take-out boxes in her hands. The swagger was forced, it was hard to be purposefully nonchalant whenever she was around the blonde, but she was determined to keep things between herself and Mackayla moving forward. "Food, milady," she drawled as she set one of the boxes onto Mackayla's desk.

Mac looked up as Charlotte pulled a bottled water from her satchel and set it on her desk beside the take-out box, and grinned. She had not seen Charlotte since they had parted ways after the Mish-Mash, and she purposefully ignored the way her stomach flip-flopped at the sight of the brunette. "And to what do I owe this pleasure?"

"I don't know what you mean," Charlie argued playfully as she dropped into an empty chair across from Mackayla. "I'm just bringing you actual food because I haven't seen you since Tuesday night and this way you'll eat more than a peanut butter Cliff bar for lunch."

"I don't know what you mean," Mac retorted, sweeping the energy bar she had been planning to call lunch off her desk and into an open drawer.

"Of course you don't," Charlie laughed, opening her own lunch and pulling out half a sandwich. "Just eat, Thomas."

Mac's stomach growled at the sight of food, and she smiled as she reached for the box Charlotte had set onto her desk. "What is it?"

"Rat poison," Charlie drawled sarcastically, rolling her eyes. "It's a Panini. And no, I didn't make it myself, so it's completely edible."

"Good to know." Mac smiled as she looked at the pressed sandwich that was sitting on top of a bed of golden crinkle fries. "What's in it?"

Charlie's brow furrowed as she quickly chewed the bite of food in her mouth so she could answer. "Um, grilled marinated tofu, zucchini, red bell pepper, provolone cheese, and some basil."

"You remembered," Mac said, a soft smile tweaking her lips as she picked up half of the sandwich.

"That you're vegetarian?" Charlie asked, frowning.

"Yeah."

Charlie shrugged. "As I've told you before, Mackayla, there isn't a whole lot about you that I don't remember."

"I'm learning that," Mac murmured, nodding to herself as she took a bite of the sandwich. The flavors of the grilled vegetables and tofu combined perfectly on her tongue and she moaned softly as she chewed. "Oh my god, this is so good."

Charlie cleared her throat softly and shook her head. "I'm actually kind of jealous of that sandwich right now," she muttered, chuckling under her breath at the way Mackayla's face flushed ever so slightly at her words.

"Yeah right," Mac muttered, her eyes darting to her lap as she felt her ears begin to burn with embarrassment.

"I'm serious!" Charlie argued playfully. "I mean, goddamn, woman. Do you have any idea how sexy that little moan of yours was? I am totally jealous of your food right now. In fact, mine isn't nearly as orgasmic as yours apparently is, so I think you should trade with me."

Mac laughed and shook her head even as her stomach fluttered at the sound of Charlotte's honeyed alto saying the word orgasmic. "I'm not trading with you!"

"I bought the damn food," Charlie grumbled, enjoying the sound of Mackayla's laughter as she made a mock grab for the blonde's lunch. "What about half?"

"Well, that depends," Mac drawled, smiling as she wrapped a protective arm around her food. "What's in yours?"

Charlie laughed and shook her head as she leaned back in her seat. "It's the same as yours," she admitted. "But, to be fair, mine isn't nearly as moan-inducing as that one." She nodded at the half of a sandwich clasped in the blonde's hand. "I think the sandwich guy likes you better."

"I wasn't even there when you ordered," Mac pointed out.

"Yeah, but still," Charlie replied, nonplussed. "Guy totally likes you better. I mean, I can't blame him at all, but it still sucks."

Mac shook her head. "You're such a dork."

"All part of my charm," Charlie retorted with a smirk, knowing exactly how true that statement was when it came to the blonde.

"Ah," Mac chuckled, "so that's what the kids are calling it nowadays. Good to know."

Charlie nodded and waved a confident hand up and down her body. "All this magnificence totally brings the chicks running."

"Is that so?" Mac teased, arching a brow challengingly as she took another bite of her sandwich. She smirked as she purposefully remained silent as she chewed.

"Absolutely." Charlie grinned and added, "I gotta admit, I missed the moan that time. Think you could fake it just for me?"

Mac choked on the bite she was swallowing and shook her head. Before she could censor herself, she retorted, "I never had to fake it for you, Charlotte." Her face flamed as she realized exactly what she had said, and she shook her head. "Don't go there," she added with a stiff warning finger.

Charlie smirked and nodded. "As you wish."

"And no *Princess Bride*."

"But that's my favorite movie!" Charlie argued, looking utterly appalled that Mackayla would dare ban *The Princess Bride*.

Mac nodded. There wasn't much she didn't remember about Charlotte either, and she had many fond memories of being curled up around the brunette in her dorm room as they watched that particular film. "I know. You like to think you're Wesley," she said, smiling as she remembered the way Charlotte would mouth his lines throughout the movie and the way the muscles in her arms would twitch as she just barely held herself back from acting out the sword fighting scenes.

"I'm totally Wesley," Charlie argued, pouting. "I'm brilliant and funny, I would make a kick-ass pirate, and I look damn good in a pair of tight black pants."

"And you're modest, too," Mac drawled, shaking her head.

Charlie grinned and, sensing that she had pushed the blonde as far as she should for the day, said, "Yeah, well, there's no point in trying to downplay this much awesomeness."

"If you say so, Bennett," Mac muttered, rolling her eyes as she took another bite of her sandwich.

"I do," Charlie announced. She tilted her head at the stack of *Iron Druid* books on the corner of the blonde's desk and asked, "Where are you at in them?"

"I actually brought them in to give back to you. Spencer just finished the last one last night."

Charlie nodded. She knew that he had picked up the first book not long after Mackayla had finished it, and she had caught them both with their noses stuck in one book or another for the series at various times since she loaned them to Mackayla. "And your conclusion?"

"I liked them," Mac said, smiling.

"Which part did you like the best?" Charlie asked. She had always enjoyed the little insights that the blonde would interject into a text, and she was genuinely curious as to what she thought of the series that was one of her current favorites.

That was all the leading Mac needed to get started talking about the books, discussing what parts of the plots she thought worked well and what didn't, and she went on for quite some time talking about way the author blended myths and legends with his own take on them all. In fact, they traded observations and thoughts on the books for so long that Charlie was honestly surprised when the alarm on her phone beeped to warn her that it was time to get to her next class.

"Shit. I'm sorry," she apologized as she hurried to clean up after herself. Not that there was a lot, just a few crumpled napkins that she tossed into her empty container and a half-empty bottle of water that she slipped into her satchel. "I didn't realize it'd gotten so late." She smiled at Mackayla as she got to her feet, and offered the blonde a small bow. "Thank you for allowing me to buy you lunch today."

"Well, I'm not sure you should really be thanking me for it," Mac chuckled, "but you're welcome. Thank you for thinking of me."

"Thinking of you is never a problem," Charlie murmured, her voice sincere and her eyes warm with emotions she knew she could not express. She glanced at her watch and groaned as she ran a hand through her hair. "I gotta go."

Mac smiled. "Go, then. I'll see you later. Are you planning on coming to the game tomorrow?"

"Um…" Charlie shrugged. "Maybe? Adam gets into town tonight for a short weekend visit, and we haven't really decided what we're doing yet."

The idea of meeting the man Charlotte considered her best friend was intriguing, and Mac impulsively offered, "You should bring him, too. We can all sit together again."

Charlie nodded. After the first game, it had become something of a routine for her to sit with Mackayla, Spencer, and their friends. "I'll ask him and see what he says."

"Yeah, and then we can all go out for drinks afterwards," Mac added.

Charlie tipped her head and flashed Mackayla a small smile. "I'll shoot you a text tomorrow and let you know if we're going to go to the game or not."

"Okay," Mac murmured. "And, thanks again for lunch. Really."

"My pleasure," Charlie assured her with another short bow. "I shall talk to you soon, Ms. Thomas."

"You know you two are total dorks, right?" a new voice chimed in.

Charlie grinned and turned to look at Spencer, who was leaning against Mackayla's doorframe. "I'll tell you the same thing I told her earlier: it's all part of my charm."

Spencer nodded in agreement. "It does seem to work wonders."

"It does not!" Mac argued, shooting Spencer an incredulous look.

"It so does," Charlie mock whispered to Spencer with a grin as she gathered her things and started for the door. She laughed at the quiet huff the comment got from Mackayla, and added, "I got a freshman seminar in ten across the Green. I'll see you guys later."

"Later, Bennett," Spencer drawled, smirking as he allowed the petite brunette to pass. Once she was out of earshot, he tilted his head at Mac and grinned. "It totally works."

"Ugh, I know," Mac admitted, throwing her hands up in defeat. "But it doesn't matter, because I'm so no going there."

Chapter 20

Though it was the first weekend of November, the trees were desperately clinging to the last vestiges of their autumnal magnificence that was growing thinner and thinner by the day as leaf after leaf fell, blanketing the ground beneath their branches in shades of red, orange, and yellow. The days had grown shorter, the temperature cooler, though it was still tolerable enough to be outside with a coat on, and Charlie took full advantage of the pleasant fall weather as she wandered beneath the portico that stretched along the tracks outside the small train station that served as the terminus for the general Hampton area. The station itself was no larger than a moderately sized two-story house, but the portico she sat under was much larger because it also covered an old, meticulously maintained steam engine.

The telltale rumble of an incoming train cascaded down the track, and Charlie smiled when she caught sight of the gleaming silver Amtrak train slowing down as it approached the platform. She had been looking forward to Adam's visit ever since the details for it were finalized, but she had not realized exactly how much she missed him until she saw him make his way down the train's stairs with a small black duffel slung over his left shoulder. Tall and lean, with wide shoulders and a trim waist that she knew he maintained by working out in the pool every morning before work, he always turned more than his fair share of heads. She was both impressed and jealous that his olive-toned skin still held some of its summer tan and, as he loped across the platform toward her, she could see that his warm brown eyes were twinkling with delight.

"Hey sexy," he drawled, grinning as he dropped the bag and swept her up into a bone-crushing hug.

"Hey yourself," Charlie laughed, wrapping her arms around his neck as he picked her up and spun her in a circle. "I've missed you."

He pressed a quick kiss to her cheek and set her back onto her feet. "Me too, Charlie-girl," he murmured.

"You changed your hair," she noted as she reached up to lightly touch it.

"Yeah." He bit his lip nervously. "I did it last week. Do you like it?"

Charlie smiled and nodded as she looked at him. It really wasn't *that* different from the conservative left-part style he had worn since she met him seven years ago; it was just a little shorter on top and combed forward. The front was swept up and to the side, and the combined effect made him look distinguished and yet simultaneously younger than his old hairstyle. "You look hot. I'd do you…you know, if you were a chick."

"I'll take that as a compliment," he laughed, winking at her as he leaned down to pick up his bag.

"You do that," she chuckled, slipping her hand into the crook of his arm. She lead them down the platform toward the small parking lot that sat in front of the station. "How was the ride?"

"A train ride. Though I did have a bubbly little brunette talking my ear off from Penn all the way to New Haven."

"It's because you're just so approachable," Charlie teased.

"It's because I'm a fucking magnet for stunning little lesbians," he retorted. "She was going to visit her girlfriend at Yale."

Charlie laughed and shook her head as she popped the hatch on her little SUV. "Sucks to be you, huh?"

"Like you wouldn't believe," he muttered, tossing his bag into the back of her car. "But, enough about me and my glaring lack of a social life. How're things going for you, Romeo?"

Charlie rolled her eyes at his newest nickname for her as she watched him slam the hatch shut. "It's going."

He turned to her and frowned. "What's up? I thought things were going well where Mackayla was concerned. You two looked fucking hot together in those pictures you sent me from that fashion show thing the other night, by the way."

"Thank you. And, they are," Charlie murmured. "It's just hard because I want so much more than playful flirty banter and unresolved sexual tension."

He nodded and pulled her into a hug, pressing a quick kiss to her forehead. "You know what you need?"

Charlie bit her lip and pulled away to look him in the eye. "What do I need, oh wise one?" she asked, expecting his answer to either be 'get laid' or 'strip club'.

"Our patented bros before hos night. Enough alcohol to make us shit-faced and goofy, and a bunch of movies with gorgeous girls we can drool over."

Charlie laughed and nodded. "That sounds great."

"And, because you need this night more than I do, I'll even let you pick the first movie."

Charlie arched a brow in surprise and asked, "Even *D.E.B.S.*?"

He bit his lip and nodded. "Yeah. Even *D.E.B.S.* Again. Because you totally have a thing for Amy, and I think Janet's cute."

"You're too sweet," Charlie cooed, smiling as she pulled away from him.

"Yeah, well, that's just the kind of guy I am," he retorted with a wink. "Come on, Charlie-girl, let's get out of here."

Once they were in the car and on the highway headed for Blake, Adam cleared his throat loudly, breaking the comfortable silence that had fallen between them. "So, are you going to let me meet Mackayla sometime this weekend?"

"She, ah–" Charlie licked her lips nervously, "–actually wants us to go to the football game tomorrow night with her and some of her friends."

Adam grinned and nodded eagerly. "Sounds good to me. Let's do it."

Still not entirely sold on the idea of allowing the two of them to meet, Charlie hedged, "Are you sure? I mean, you're only here until noon on Sunday…"

"Oh, I'm sure. I want nothing more than to meet her."

"You better not do anything to embarrass me."

Adam laughed and smirked at Charlie. "Do you really think I would do something like that?"

"Of course I do." Charlie said, rolling her eyes and nodding.

"So, will there be sorority girls there? How hot are the cheerleaders?"

"You're incorrigible," Charlie groaned. "You do know that you're entirely too old for them, right? Like, I can't in good conscience let you do more than ogle."

"I'm good with ogling. I mean, unless they just can't keep from begging for some of this–" he waved a hand up and down his body, "–because, who am I to say no?"

Charlie laughed and shook her head. "I love you, Snow, but I don't have a guest room, and there's no way I'm letting you bang some random co-ed in my bed."

"Fine," Adam sighed dramatically. "Be like that."

"Oh, I will," Charlie assured him.

"You're lucky I love you."

"I know," Charlie murmured, glancing over at him.

He reached out and gave her knee a gentle squeeze. "Me too. But, I'm not the only one. Billy sends his love."

"Yeah right," Charlie scoffed. "What did he really say?"

"To tell you hello and that he hopes you're enjoying your sabbatical. I swear, he's a fucking tyrant with the rest of us, but you're like the daughter he never had or something."

Charlie nodded. She had long suspected the senior editor thought of her that way as well. "It's just because I'm so fucking awesome."

"Totally," Adam laughed.

Charlie grinned. "Yeah, well…fill me in on all the sordid office gossip that I've missed. Is Renee still dating the guy from accounting?"

"She is," Adam confirmed. "He sent her an obscenely gaudy bouquet the other day that has everybody trying to figure out what it was that he did wrong that he needed to suck up to her so badly. And Brian is maybe possibly going to find the courage to nut up and ask the security guard Hank out sometime soon."

Charlie glanced at him and arched a brow questioningly. When Adam confirmed with a nod that he wasn't kidding, she hummed softly under her breath. "Well, if he does, try and follow him down and get it on video for me. I wanna see how that goes."

"You got it," Adam said, grinning.

"Anything else exciting happening?"

Adam shook his head and looked out the window at the passing scenery as Charlie merged into the right-hand lane to exit the highway. "Not really. Same ol', same ol'. You know how it is, same shit, different day, most of the time."

"Yeah, I know how that goes," Charlie murmured as she eased onto the ramp to exit the highway.

By the time Charlie turned into her driveway and killed the engine, she had caught up on all the comings and goings of things that had happened at the magazine in her absence. And, while hearing about it all made her miss some of the people involved, she couldn't say that she wished she were back in the city either. If anything, hearing Adam talk about who was doing what and who was dating whom only made her realize how much she had grown to love the life she managed to carve out for herself in New Hampshire.

"It's cute," Adam said as he looked at the house. He grinned and added, "It's small, just like you."

Charlie rolled her eyes. "Shut up."

He jumped out of the car as she took a swipe at him and laughed. "What?"

"I can put your ass back on that train."

"Yeah, tomorrow afternoon," he retorted as he sauntered around the car to the hatch and retrieved his bag. "Hate to break it to you, Smalls, but you're stuck with me."

"Fuck you, Snow," Charlie grumbled, slamming her car door shut. "If you don't play nice…"

"What?"

Charlie grinned. "I'll make you sleep on the couch."

"No you wouldn't," Adam said, slamming the hatch shut and following Charlie up the path to the front porch. "You love me too much to make me sleep on the couch."

"That's debatable," Charlie pointed out as she unlocked the door.

"So do I get to be the big spoon this time?"

Charlie laughed and shook her head as she pushed the door open. "No way. I don't want to wake up with little you poking me in the ass. I'm the big spoon."

"Spoilsport," he grumbled playfully as he entered the house and gave the foyer a quick once-over. "Fine. Where is this bed you'll be taking advantage of me in?"

"Back that way." Charlie waved at the hallway on the left. "Do you want Chinese or pizza?" she called after him as he disappeared down the hall with his bag.

"Pizza! I don't trust Chinese food unless it's from Flaming Wok!" he hollered, referring to the restaurant that was just down the block from his apartment.

Charlie rolled her eyes and nodded. "Should have known."

Chapter 21

"Come on!" Adam paused the movie he had chosen and jumped to his feet excitedly. He swayed a little as he found his equilibrium, the four beers he had consumed while they ate dinner and watched *D.E.B.S.* were still raging in his bloodstream. "You gotta do this with me!" he pleaded as he held his hands out to Charlie, palms up and fingers waggling beseechingly.

Charlie laughed and shook her head. "No, man. Just, no."

"But, Charlie-girl, this is how you're gonna get into Mackayla's pants. I just know it. We need to choreograph you a musical number like this and…"

"Choreograph a musical number?" Charlie repeated, her lips quirked up in an amused smile. "You're really drunk right now, aren't you?"

He grinned and shook his head. "I'm not drunk at all. You're just blurry."

"Nicely played, Snow," Charlie chuckled, rolling her eyes as she gave him her hands and allowed him to haul her up off of the sofa. "Okay. Fine. Grab that end of the table," she instructed with a wave of her hand as she bent down to grab the edge of the coffee table. "If we're doing this, we're doing it right."

Once the table was moved safely out of the way, Adam grabbed the clicker and took his position beside Charlie. "You ready, Bennett?"

"Just try and keep up, Boy Wonder," Charlie retorted.

Adam just grinned and pointed the remote at the DVD player. "Oh, I got this," he assured her as he hit play.

Up on the television, the Barden Bellas took the stage in Lincoln Center and Charlie couldn't contain her grin when she glanced over at Adam. This was why she loved him. He was silly and spontaneous, and he always knew how to make her smile.

"Focus," he whispered. "Don't make me go all Aubrey on your ass."

"Like you ever could," Charlie muttered, biting back the rest of her retort as Beca blew on the pitch pipe. She knew that she actually did have to focus because he was actually a really good singer and, even being decidedly "blurry" herself, she was competitive enough to want to show him up if at all possible.

"Seems like everybody's got a price," Adam sang in an impressive falsetto, and Charlie bit the inside of her cheek to keep from laughing as they both began mimicking the choreography of the Bellas.

Step for step, they moved with the women on the television, singing giddily along with the mash-up. Charlie handled the little beatbox section of the arrangement while Adam took care of the rap, and then he stepped aside and let her take center rug to handle Beca's solo. Though the arrangement was fun and upbeat, but some of Charlie's enthusiasm dimmed as she realized that the lyrics she was singing were eerily fitting for her own love life at the moment.

Adam noticed that the exuberance in Charlie's voice had dimmed by a fraction, and when he glanced over at her, he saw that the smile that had been lighting up her face had fallen just a little. He knew why that was, and it killed him to see that crack in her armor. He also knew that she wouldn't appreciate him pointing it out, so instead of stopping and asking her about it, he jumped in and sang with her so that she wouldn't lose steam. Her wrist was positively tiny in his hand as he grabbed it and punched both of their arms into the air, and he smiled as he heard her laugh. She needed this night of stupid fun, and he was determined to give it to her.

They finished the song with a flourish, and as they fell back onto the couch, laughing and slightly out of breath, Adam looped his arm around Charlie's shoulders and pulled her into his side. "That was aca-awesome."

Charlie chuckled. "Whatever you say, Aubrey."

"Aubrey is my spirit animal," Adam retorted, only half-jokingly.

Charlie grabbed the remote, stopping the movie before Bellas left the stage. "Yeah, well, that doesn't really surprise me."

"I know, right? Why do you always stop the movie there?" Adam asked, not bothered enough to make a grab for the clicker to turn it back on.

"Because I prefer to think that after they take that final bow, Chloe grabbed Beca, dragged her offstage, and fucked her up against a wall somewhere in celebration of their epic win," Charlie replied matter-of-factly as she turned off the television.

"They do have some killer chemistry," Adam agreed. He leaned his head on her shoulder and asked, "If you had to pick between Beca and Chloe, who would you choose?"

Charlie didn't hesitate. "Chloe."

He laughed. "The blue eyes, right?"

"Yeah," Charlie groaned. "We both know that I'm a sucker for the baby blues."

"That you do, my predictable friend. And her boobs looked fucking great in that last scene."

"I know, right?" Charlie nodded. "I miss boobs," she added wistfully.

Adam laughed. "What do you mean, you miss boobs? You have a killer rack."

"Yeah, but mine aren't fun to play with," Charlie whined, looking down at her chest like it had betrayed her somehow. "I miss other girls' boobs."

"You miss Mackayla's boobs," Adam corrected.

Charlie groaned, grabbed a pillow, and smacked him in the head with it. "Don't remind me."

He chuckled as he took the pillow from her and set it on his lap. "Do you want to vent?"

Charlie shook her head. "No. I just…"

When she didn't finish her thought, he turned to face her and his heart dropped at the utterly broken expression on her face. "You just, what?" he prodded gently.

She sighed. "What if she doesn't give me another chance?" She bit her lip as her eyes stung with tears. The combination of the alcohol in her system and Adam's sympathetic gaze were more than enough to bring down the walls she had constructed around her heart to protect herself from such crushing thoughts. It was much easier to proceed with feigned confidence than it was to submit to the raging doubt that was always coursing just below the surface where the beautiful blonde was concerned. "I am so fucking in love with her, and I can see that she feels something for me too. I can see how good we could be together, and it kills me that she is so determined to not let it happen."

"Oh, sweetie," Adam murmured. He reached out and pulled her into him so that her head was nestled in the crook of his neck. "It'll work out how it's meant to," he murmured, running a comforting hand up and down her back. "I know that's not what you want to hear, but you can't make her give you another chance. And, even though I know I might end up sleeping on the couch for this, I can understand where she's coming from. You *are* only here for the school year. Another seven months or so and then you'll be back in New York. The distance isn't insurmountable, but it's big."

Charlie nodded. Nothing he said was anything she hadn't thought herself. "I would stay here, for her." Her stomach fluttered with butterflies as the words she had just whispered sank in. It was the first time she had actually said them aloud.

Adam sighed. "Would you really torpedo your career for her? You know you're going to be made Senior Editor when Billy retires."

"If she actually took me back, I would do it in a heartbeat."

He pursed his lips thoughtfully as he pulled back to look at her. The determined glint in her eye told him that she meant it. She would give up her dream job for Mackayla. "Say you did that. Say you walked away from *SI* and moved up here permanently. What would you do?"

Charlie shrugged. "I mean, I'm sure I could always freelance or something. I *am* actually good at what I do, you know. Or maybe Blake would let me continue to lecture as I worked for a PhD. I dunno. Whatever it was, if I had her, I'd be happy. And we both know that happy is the one thing I wasn't before."

"And if she doesn't change her mind?" he asked. "Are you going to come home?"

"I don't know," Charlie sighed, closing her eyes as she shook her head. "I actually do like it here. You're the only thing I miss about New York, to be honest. You wanna move to New Hampshire?"

Adam shook his head. "Sorry, babe, but I'm a city boy at heart. It's fun to visit places like this, but I need traffic and crowds and strangers flipping me off because they're in a pissy mood and I had the audacity to make eye contact with them."

"I miss flipping people off when they had the audacity to make eye contact with me," Charlie muttered, smiling in spite of the weight that had settled itself on her heart.

"I'm sure you do," Adam laughed. "You were always crazy fast on the draw." He swallowed thickly as Charlie leaned back into him, resting her head on his shoulder, and he sighed as he pressed a soft kiss to her forehead. "Can I beat some sense into this girl when I see her?"

"No," Charlie whispered, shaking her head.

"Can I not-so-subtly point out that she's being an idiot?"

"No," Charlie yawned.

"Damn. Fine, can I subtly point out that she's being an idiot?"

"You don't know how to do subtle, Snow," Charlie chuckled.

Adam grinned. "I can if I need to."

Charlie shook her head and wrapped an arm around her waist as she snuggled into him. "Just be my best friend. That's all you need to do. Like you said, things will work out like they're supposed to."

"I can do that," Adam murmured, pressing another kiss to her forehead. "Come on, Bennett. It's getting late and we're both too tired to do another movie. Take me to bed, you sexy woman, you."

Charlie pulled away from him and smiled. "Flattery will get you nowhere."

"Yeah, yeah, whatever," Adam grumbled playfully as he pushed himself off the couch. "Just no groping the goodies while we sleep."

Charlie grinned and rolled her eyes. "I'll try and contain myself. Same rules go for you."

"Like I can grope anything when I'm the little spoon," he muttered, smiling as he pulled her into another quick hug. "I love you, Charlie-girl. We'll get you through this, okay?"

She smiled as she sank into his embrace. "Okay."

Chapter 22

The night was cool enough that everybody entering Blake stadium carried blankets with them to cover up with, and Charlie smiled as she took the blanket Adam shoved in her arms so he could pull his wallet out of his back pocket to pay for their tickets.

"Mah hero," she teased in a horrendous southern accent.

He looked over at her and grinned. "Whatever, Bennett. This is nothing. Tonight, my hopeless friend, I am going to wingman for you, and we are going to get you that much closer to winning the heart of your lady love."

"Oh really?" Charlie scoffed, rolling her eyes.

"Indeed, oh smitten one," Adam retorted. He shoved his wallet back into his pocket and took his blanket from her. "It's a shame we didn't choreograph anything, though," he added as he followed her through the gate and under the bleachers.

Charlie laughed. "I'm sure you'll tell me why that is."

"Of course I will. One, chicks love grand romantic gestures like that. And two, you know as well as I do that we kill it when we go to karaoke together."

"Yeah right," Charlie muttered.

He grinned and looped an arm over her shoulder. "I am right. We get standing ovations every time. Never mind the fact that an Off-Off director tried and get us to come audition for his musical last year. And," he added loudly, holding a finger in the air importantly before she could argue that the director only really wanted him, "I also know that you would do anything, even a ridiculously cheesy song and dance number, if it meant you'd get a sweet lady-kiss from the fair Mackayla."

Charlie sighed in defeat and nodded, knowing that she really would do pretty much anything to get a kiss from Mackayla at this point. She scanned the crowd for their group as they exited from beneath the bleachers onto the sidewalk that ran between them and the track, eager despite Adam's promised interference to see Mackayla again. When she had called the blonde earlier to let her know that she and Adam would, in fact, be going to the game, Mackayla had told her they would be sitting in their usual spot at the thirty-yard line. Mackayla had seemed genuinely excited that they were going to go, and Charlie hoped it was a sign that she was slowly but surely coming around. Her heart swooped into her throat when she spotted Mackayla about halfway up the bleachers, and she giggled when Adam made kissy sounds in her ear. "Knock it off, you jerk!"

He laughed and pressed a wet kiss to her cheek. "Whatever. You love it. Now, where's this woman of yours?"

Resigned to her fate, Charlie pointed up at Mackayla, who was now standing up and waving to get their attention. "Please try and behave," she begged as she waved back at the blonde. It was impossible to miss the way Mackayla smiled in response to her, and Charlie leveled a serious look at Adam. "Seriously, man. I've finally gotten her to legitimately enjoy my company. If you fuck that up…"

"Psht. Like I would ever do anything to hurt you," Adam brushed her off as he started up the stairs, waving enthusiastically at Mackayla like they were old friends. He looked over his shoulder at Charlie and hollered, "Get that ridiculously sexy ass of yours moving, Bennett!"

The little voice of reason in the back of Charlie's head warned her that this was a train wreck waiting to happen, and she groaned as she watched Adam stop at the end of Mackayla's row. He offered Mackayla a small bow as he dropped a gallant kiss to the back of her hand, and Charlie shook her head as she started up the steps after him. "What in the world was I thinking letting him meet her?"

Charlie smiled apologetically at Mackayla as she stopped at the end of the row, and shook her head at Adam, who was now introducing himself to Spencer. "I swear, I can't take him anywhere."

Mac laughed and shook her head. "I'm glad you guys could come," she said, giving Charlie a soft smile as she reached out and pulled the brunette into a quick hug.

"You say that now," Charlie murmured, lightly wrapping her arms around Mackayla's waist and savoring the few seconds of contact before Mackayla pulled away from her. She didn't have the guts to warn Mackayla that Adam had promised to wingman for her that night. She knew *that* would only serve to scare the blonde off. Her only hope was that he would behave himself, but she wasn't especially optimistic that he would. If his sudden obsession with choreography and musical numbers was any indication, he was determined to help her be as goofy and awkward as she could possibly be. "Just wait. He's the consummate class clown."

"Then he and Spencer will get along famously," Mac replied with a small laugh as she retook her seat. She looked down the line of her friends to where the two guys were doing a complicated high five, fist bump, handshake thing and shook her head. "Do all guys just inherently know that handshake?"

Charlie laughed. "I'm beginning to think so, yeah."

Mac nodded her agreement and turned her attention back to Charlotte. She had been interested to meet the man the brunette considered her best friend, but, more than anything, she just wanted to spend some more time with her. She knew that it was a dangerous game she was playing, but with Charlotte so close, she just couldn't resist the allure of her company. Nobody, even Spencer, had ever understood her as well as the brunette did. "So, what did you two do today? Anything exciting?"

"Hardly," Charlie chuckled, shaking her head. "We just hung out at my place and watched movies all day. Didn't even get out of our pajamas until it was time to shower and get ready to come here. It was a perfect lazy day."

Mac smiled and nodded, even as the feeling of happiness that had filled her when Charlotte had sat down beside her twisted into something that she knew was dangerously close to jealousy. Had she been honest with herself, she would have admitted that it absolutely was jealousy that she was experiencing. She remembered all too well what Charlotte considered a perfect lazy day, and her heart swooped up into her throat as the memory of the brunette stretched out on the small loveseat in her one-bedroom apartment in Middletown flashed across her mind. Her stomach fluttered as she remembered how fond Charlotte was of laying on the couch in nothing but a pair of bikini briefs and a tight little t-shirt that rode up to expose her toned stomach. They had more often than not ended up in bed on those days, losing themselves in each other, and she hated the idea that anyone else might share them with the brunette. Even when that someone was a man who she knew Charlotte was not at all sexually attracted to. "That sounds like fun," she muttered, looking away and desperately trying to squash that memory before it could bring up any more just like it.

Charlie frowned. "You okay?"

"Fine," Mac assured her. She licked her lips and met Charlotte's questioning gaze. "I'm fine, Charlotte. Just..."

"Charlie-girl!" Adam yelled, interrupting whatever it was Mackayla was going to say. He winked at the brunette as he shimmied past her and then sat down practically on her lap, forcing her to scoot toward Mackayla so that she was pressed up against the blonde.

"Well, hello to you too. Why don't you go ahead and make yourself comfortable," Charlie muttered.

"I will, thanks," Adam assured her, wiggling on the bench to prove his point. He winked at Charlie before he turned his full attention to Mac. "So, Professor Thomas, Charlie tells me that you are the author of my all-time favorite lesbian novel."

Mac laughed and nodded, remembering how Charlotte had mentioned that her best friend had enjoyed the book. "If you mean *Divergence,* then yeah. That's me."

Adam grinned. "I know this will make me sound like a pervert, but I don't care. Damn, girl. That was so freakin' hot."

"Um, thank you. I think," Mac mumbled, blushing. She couldn't help but think that this conversation was why she wrote under a pen name.

"No, thank you," Adam drawled, waggling his eyebrows suggestively.

"Oh my god," Mac muttered.

"Knock it off, you ass," Charlie groaned, smacking Adam in the stomach with the back of her hand as she shot Mackayla an apologetic look.

Adam laughed and grinned, looking entirely unrepentant even as he apologized. "Sorry."

"No you're not," Charlie said.

"No, it's fine," Mac assured them, licking her lips as she looked at Charlotte. "It's fine. There's just a reason I write under a pen name."

"You know what you should put in your next book?" Adam piped up.

Charlie looked at Mackayla and shook her head. "Please don't encourage him."

"It's fine," Mac assured her. She turned her attention to Adam and added, "I'm afraid I've already submitted the final manuscript for it to my publisher."

"Damn, too bad," Adam grumbled, feigning disappointment. "Because less plot and more porn would have been awesome."

"Oh my god! Snow!" Charlie smacked him in the stomach again. "Damn it, you said you'd behave!"

"This is me behaving," Adam argued. He caught Mackayla's eye and grinned. "I'm just messing with you. The book was amazing, I eagerly await the sequel, and if I could maybe get a signed copy of *Divergence* from you before I leave tomorrow, you would make me the happiest perverted straight guy in the world."

Mac bit her lip and looked from Adam to Charlotte, who was staring at him like he had grown a second head, and nodded. "I'll drop a signed copy off at Charlotte's house tomorrow morning. I'm assuming you're taking the 1:15 train back to New York?"

Adam nodded. "Yup. That would be awesome, thanks."

"Not a problem," Mac assured him. Wanting to move past the fact that she did, in fact, write lesbian porn, as he called it, she asked, "So, you work with Charlotte at *Sports Illustrated*, huh?"

"That I do," he drawled, wrapping an affectionate arm the brunette's shoulders.

"Were you an athlete in college too?" Mac asked.

"Yeah. I swam."

"He's being modest," Charlie said. "He actually just missed out on making the Athens team."

"Damn," Mac whistled.

"Damn, what?" Spencer asked as he sat down on the other side Mac.

"Adam almost went to Athens," Mac shared.

"Dude. Nice," Spencer drawled. "What sport?"

"Swimming," Adam answered with a shrug. The P.A. system roared to life as the players took the field at a sprint, and he grinned as he watched them line up. "This is the first college game I've been to since I was at Princeton," he announced to nobody in particular as they all got to their feet.

Charlie sighed with relief, knowing that he would put a lid on his antics so long as the game was on. She just prayed that it wouldn't be a blowout like every other game this season.

"Hey, Charlie-girl!" Adam said, turning to grin at her. "You should tell Mackayla that joke you told me this morning!"

Charlie laughed and shook her head. They had been trying to one-up each other with stupid jokes over breakfast, and she won. "I don't think she wants to hear it," she told him, raising her voice to be heard over the crowd that was now yelling as Blake's kicker sent the ball flying into the end zone for a touchback.

"Sure she does!" he argued, his eyes twinkling with playful mischief.

Mac laughed and Spencer leaned forward to hear as well. "What's the joke?" they asked in unison.

Charlie groaned as Adam shot her an 'I told you so' look. "Fine," she said as she retook her seat. "Two lesbians were out playing golf. They tee off, and one drive goes to the right and one drive goes to the left. One of them finds her ball in a patch of buttercups. She grabs a club and takes a big ass swing at the ball. The shot is fucking perfect, rolling right up onto the green, but in the process she hacks the hell out of the buttercups. Suddenly, a woman appears out of nowhere. She blocks her path to her golf bag and looks at her and says, 'I'm Mother Nature, and I don't like the way you treated my buttercups. From now on, you won't be able to stand the taste of butter. Each time you eat butter you will become physically ill to the point of total nausea.' The mystery woman then disappeared as quickly as she appeared. Shaken, the woman calls out to her girlfriend, 'Hey, where's your ball?' Her girlfriend answers, 'It's over here in the pussy willows.' She screams back, 'DON'T HIT THE BALL!!!! DON'T HIT THE BALL!!!!'"

"Oh my god, that's hilarious," Mac chuckled.

Spencer laughed and nodded his agreement. "That's awesome. I'm so stealing that."

"I know, right?" Adam replied.

"Totally," Spencer agreed.

"Validation tastes so sweet!" Adam declared, throwing his hands up into the air. He winked conspiratorially at Charlie and tilted his head at Mackayla, who had turned back to the game.

"You're such a dork.".

"But I'm your dork," he retorted, mussing her hair playfully. "And you made her laugh," he whispered in her ear.

Charlie sighed and nodded, hating to admit that he was right. "Yeah."

"Told ya I was going to wingman for ya," he whispered, bumping her with his shoulder as he turned his attention back to the game.

"Still not sure if that's a good thing or not," Charlie muttered under her breath, smiling in spite of herself.

Chapter 23

"Right, so, here's another one," Adam said, grinning as he hooked his arm through Mackayla's and started leading the blonde out of the stadium. The game was over, ending in yet another spectacular blowout victory for Blake, and he had given up watching the game in favor of telling stories sometime around the middle of the second quarter. The night was cold enough that the rest of the group left during the middle fourth quarter to go home and get warm, and only Mac and Spencer had stayed with Charlie and Adam until the end of the game. "So, first year at the magazine, we're both grunts doing the interviews nobody else wants. Writing Ellie-worthy articles that would later be chopped to three paragraphs and fit into whatever corner of the layout they needed to fill, the usual. And Charlie-girl gets handed Dante Jones."

"The baseball player?" Spencer asked, looking intrigued.

Adam nodded. "Yeah. Guy is a colossal dick. Like, seriously. Everybody knows it, and it's kind of a rite of passage for female reporters to have to deal with him because if they can survive a run-in with him, they can handle any interview."

"Why only female reporters?" Mac asked, looking over at Charlotte who was shaking her head at his story.

"Because he's a misogynistic asshole," Adam explained. "He's just a regular asshole to male reporters, but he reaches a whole new level of 'you have got to be fucking kidding me' with the women."

Mac's eyebrows shot up on her forehead. "And your bosses sent you to interview this guy?"

Charlie nodded. "Yeah."

"That they did," Adam confirmed. "But, Heather Young, one of the senior reporters at the magazine–"

"She's awesome," Spencer interrupted.

Adam nodded. "Very awesome. Anyways, Young grabs Charlie by the arm as she's leaving for the interview, warns her about what she's walking into, and then she grabs me and tells me to go with her."

"Why?" Mac asked.

"Just in case." Adam shrugged. "The interview was scheduled to happen at the stadium after practice, and she wanted to make sure Charlie would be safe. Jones had never physically attacked anyone, but he was enough of a dick that it was better to be safe than sorry."

"Sounds like a real charmer," Mac muttered.

"Oh, he isn't," Adam assured her. "Anyways, as we're leaving the building, I can tell that Charlie is thinking hard about what Young had told her. Then, as we're climbing into the cab, she tells me that we need to make a stop before we get over to Yankee Stadium."

"Where?" Mac asked, looking at Charlotte who had just caught up to them.

"Can't tell you that, it'll ruin the rest of the story," Adam chuckled. "So, we get to the stadium, security lets us in, and the team's PR guy tells us that Jones is waiting for us in the locker room for the interview."

"That can't be good," Mac interjected, shaking her head.

"It was perfect," Adam laughed. "So, we go in there, dude totally ignores me and focuses all of his pervy attention on Charlie here. Of course, he's lounging in a chair wearing nothing but a towel around his waist."

"Which I was expecting, because Young had warned me that he loved to do this," Charlie piped up.

Adam nodded. "Exactly. So, Charlie pulls out her recorder and starts asking him the typical bullshit questions, how he felt about his season so far, yada, yada, yada, and the whole time he's inching his towel higher and higher up his legs."

"Fuck," Spencer drawled.

"Like I said, asshole," Adam brushed him off. "So, Charlie's getting ready to ask him another question when, oops, his towel falls open."

"I'd have pressed charges," Mac muttered.

"Normally, I would have too," Charlie agreed. "But, unfortunately, to make it in the business, I needed to just ignore it. Which wasn't hard, because the steroids he's been rumored to be taking had done their job on his boys, if you know what I mean."

Adam guffawed and nodded vigorously. "Right, so the team's PR guy jumps in, yells at Jones and gets him to put some goddamn pants on. And then he starts apologizing to Charlie."

"As he should," Spencer and Mac said in unison.

"Indeed. But, the best part was that Charlie completely ignored the PR guy, who was stammering out a lame-ass apology, looked Jones dead in the eye, and pulled a giant fucking dildo out of her purse. I'm talking, like, horse-sized, there's no way anyone would actually be able to use this thing. Anyways, she tossed it onto his lap and said, 'Mine's bigger.' He flung it onto the floor, screaming like a little girl–which was fucking hilarious–and Charlie here just nonchalantly picked it back up, slid it into her purse, and proceeded to politely thank them both for their time before she literally sashayed out of the room. It. Was. Epic."

Mac laughed softly under her breath and shook her head as she shot an amused smile at Charlotte.

"Oh my god," Spencer chuckled. He held a hand out to Charlie and said, "High five. That's awesome."

Charlie grinned and slapped his hand. "Thank you, sir."

"So, what's the plan now?" Adam asked. "Rumor has it that you guys have some kind of after-party thing you usually do?"

"We just go to Shenanigans for a few drinks and play a little pool. It's nothing fancy, just a handful a tables, but it's about the best you can do around here," Spencer said. "You game?"

"Oh yeah," Adam drawled, nodding.

Charlie rolled her eyes. "Just so you know, he's a bit of a pool shark. Don't let him talk you into playing for money. We walked over, so we'll meet you guys there."

"Why? We can all fit in my car," Spence said, pulling his keys out of his pocket and unlocking the SUV they had been standing in front of as Adam finished his story. "I'll just drive."

Adam looked over at Charlie and winked. "I call shotgun!"

"What are you, twelve?" Charlie laughed.

"Whatever. You're just a sore loser," he retorted as he jumped into the passenger's seat.

Mac chuckled and shook her head. It was impossible to not like Adam. Fun stories aside, he brought out some of the old Charlotte she remembered. Not that she didn't enjoy the brunette's company now, she did, but everything between them was always just that little bit strained. But with Adam, Charlotte's walls were down completely, and she couldn't help but wish that she could have that relationship with the brunette. No walls. No tension.

She watched Charlotte out of the corner of her eye as they made the short drive from the stadium to the bar, hating the way her heart would beat double-time whenever she caught the brunette looking at her. Charlotte's left hand was laying on the middle of the seat, palm up and just waiting for her to take it, and Mac fisted her hands in her lap as the urge to do just that surged through her. It would be so easy to just reach out and twine their fingers together. She remembered with stunning clarity exactly how well the brunette's hand fit in her own. But she meant what she had told Spencer the day before. She wasn't going to go there. No matter how beautiful Charlotte looked, how funny she was, or how much she wanted it, she was not going to let her heart get broken again.

Shenanigans was predictably busy when they arrived, and Mac felt herself relax as they walked into the bar. The noise and the crowd was the perfect distraction from Charlotte's presence. "I'll get the first round if you guys want to go grab a table."

"You want some help?" Charlie asked.

Mac shook her head. "I got it. You guys go and get one of the pool tables before they're all taken."

"This way, guys," Spencer said, tipping his head toward a doorway at the back of the bar.

By the time Mac walked into the back room carrying a small tray with four pints on it, Spencer and Adam were already halfway through their first game. Charlie smiled at the blonde as she put the tray down onto a small square table that was pushed up against the wall, and gratefully reached for one of the beers. "Thanks."

"No problem," Mac assured her with a small smile as she picked up a pint. "How's it going?"

"Snow's going easy on him," Charlie said, rolling her eyes.

"Why?"

"Because he likes to spot whoever he's playing a few balls before he actually starts playing for real."

"Do you two do this often?"

Charlie shook her head. "No. Well, yeah, but I don't play against him. I suck at pool and he teases me about it the whole time we're playing." She grinned as she saw a familiar flash of amusement in her friend's eyes and pointed at the guys. "Watch. He's about to go for the jugular."

Spencer didn't know what hit him as Adam cleared the table without missing another shot. "Damn."

"Sorry dude," Adam laughed. The music that filled the small back room of the bar changed, and he grinned as he looked up at Charlie. "Bennett! This is my jam!"

Mac shot Charlotte a disbelieving look. "*Call Me Maybe* is his jam?"

"Um, I guess so," Charlie muttered with a small shrug. Last time they went out, his "jam" was some clubby whatever song that was popular.

Adam smiled at Mac as he took the pint from Charlie's hand and set it on the table. "I'm just gonna borrow her for a minute," he explained as he pulled the brunette with him into a small area between the tables where they could actually move.

Charlie stood, arms crossed over her chest, and stared at Adam as he started dancing. "What are you doing?"

"Wingmanning for you," Adam replied with a grin. He reached out and grabbed her hips. "Dance with me."

"Why?" Charlie asked, even as she allowed him to guide her into motion.

"Because whether she wants to admit it or not, I have caught Ms. Thomas shooting daggers at me on several different occasions this evening."

Charlie shook her head. "Yeah right. You're imagining things, Snow. Everybody knows there's no way we're going to sleep together, so I sincerely doubt that anything you're doing is making her jealous."

"Think so, huh?" Adam asked, grinning and looking over at Mac, who was glowering at him and Charlie. "I call bullshit. She's jealous. Maybe not of me sleeping in your bed, but of this."

"Of what?" Charlie scoffed.

"Us. Face it, Charlie-girl, besides the lack of sex, we have a fucking awesome relationship. So, dance with me, you lovesick fool. Not only will it push her buttons, she will also get to see how well you move that luscious body of yours, and you get to goof it up a bit because, seriously, it's Carly Rae-fucking-Jepson. Win-win-win."

"I don't think you're right," Charlie told him, glancing over her shoulder at Mackayla. She was surprised to see that the blonde was, indeed, watching them with a furrowed brow and a slightly annoyed expression on her face. "Or, maybe you are."

"Of course I am," he retorted. "Now, dance with me!" He threw his hands up in time with the chorus and bobbed his head with the beat.

He looked so ridiculous that Charlie had no choice but to follow his lead, laughing as she threw her hands up in the air and started singing along with him as they danced.

At the table, Spencer pushed himself up onto a stool and grabbed a beer. "I know that this is a stupid song and everything, but they can really dance," he said, sounding impressed.

Mac lifted her glass to her lips and nodded, humming in agreement. Her eyes were glued to the way Charlotte's hips moved. She had vague memories of how well the brunette could dance, but the moves she was pulling on the floor now were miles above anything she had been able to do in college. The song was stupid and the pair's dancing was borderline ridiculous, but the smile on Charlotte's face, combined with the seductive sway of her hips, had Mac's stomach fluttering with desire, and she groaned as she took another long drink of her beer.

Her glass was empty by the time the song ended, and she shook her head as she set it back onto the tray. "Thank god," she muttered.

Spencer laughed as *Hot N Cold* began playing and Charlie and Adam showed no sign of stopping. They moved closer, their bodies grinding together with the beat. "If you say so."

Mac clenched her jaw and reached for Adam's still untouched beer as she watched Charlotte spin in front of him so that he was pressed against her back. She bit her lip hard enough to almost draw blood as she watched his hands wrap possessively around Charlotte's hips, and she had to look away when he whispered something in Charlotte's ear that made her throw her head back and laugh. There was nothing about their dancing that was improper or anything more than two friends having fun, but she just couldn't stomach watching it.

"Breathe, Thomas," Spencer murmured, easily reading her emotions. "You can't murder the guy for dancing with her."

"Shut up," Mac muttered, shaking her head and lifting her glass to her lips. "I don't want to murder him."

"You don't want him dancing with her like that, though." Spencer glanced at her out of the corner of his eye and added, "You could always go cut-in."

"It's not like that." Mac shook her head. "Besides, we both know that I can't dance like *that*," she added, waving an irritated hand at Adam.

Spencer scoffed and shook his head. "Psht. Like Charlie would care. She'd just be happy you were out there with her."

Mac's heart swooped up into her throat at the idea of taking Adam's place with the brunette, her imagination having no problem picturing how it would feel to have Charlotte moving like that against her, but she forced herself to ignore it. "No."

"Why the hell not?" Spencer pushed. "Friends can dance together. We do it all the time."

"As do they, apparently," Mac muttered.

Spencer cleared his throat loudly and, when Mac looked at him, said, "You know, jealousy doesn't look good on you."

"Fuck you," Mac grumbled petulantly.

Spencer grinned. He had expected that response from her, and he couldn't resist giving her another little push toward the one thing she wanted, but wouldn't allow herself to have. "We tried that once, remember? Orientation weekend for our master's. We got totally shitfaced after having to sit through that god-awful opening lecture that went on for-fucking-*ever* and somehow ended up in bed together. Still not sure how that happened." He shook his head. "Anyways, you ended up in tears before we really got anywhere, I ended up in a cold shower, and thus, our epic bromance was born."

Mac laughed in spite of herself at the memory of that particular train wreck, and shook her head. "Well, you know…"

"I know," Spencer assured her, his smile softening as he set his glass onto table. He sighed, wrapped an arm around her shoulders, and pressed a soft kiss to her temple as he pulled her into his side. "Can I tell you something?"

"Of course."

"I don't know why you're fighting her so hard," he said, his eyes trailing over to Charlie. "It's obvious that you want her."

"I do," Mac admitted quietly. She took a deep breath and added, "But it doesn't matter."

"Why? You're not a scared closeted kid anymore. Why not give it another try?"

Mac's heart swooped up into her throat, and she shook her head. "She's only here until the end of the school year." She took a long drink of her beer and forced herself to look away from Charlotte. "It doesn't matter how charming she is, or how much I want her, because she'll be back in New York by June and I'll be here with a broken heart; and I know I won't be able to bounce back from that again."

"She's going to keep doing her adorable wooing thing. You know that, right?"

"I know." Charlie laughed loudly and Mac automatically turned to look at the brunette, who was now doing the Cabbage Patch with Adam. "God, Spence. Just…why? Why did she have to come back into my life just when it was getting good?"

Spencer took a sip of his beer and shrugged. He knew that she was close to the point where she would shut down and run, but she had been the happiest he had ever seen her these last few months and he liked seeing her that way. She had been through so much, had come so far, and she deserved to be happy. And it killed him to watch her try her damndest to run away from the person who made her feel that good. Thankfully, Charlie seemed just as determined to chase after her as Mac was determined to run away. "Do you really want me to answer that?"

Mac shrugged and took another long drink, almost draining the glass. "Sure."

"Because she'll make it better. She makes you better. I get that you don't want to hear that, and I understand that you don't want to have your heart broken again. But I've watched her work her way past your walls these last few months, and I can promise you that that girl would move mountains for you. She won't do anything to hurt you."

Mac caught Charlotte's eye across the room, and her heart told her that he was right. That things were different. But her head wasn't ready to listen. "I'm gonna go get another round of drinks. I'll be back in a few."

Chapter 24

"Shit," Mac hissed as she accidentally knocked the eight ball into the side pocket. She had been beyond relieved to find that Charlotte and Adam had given up dancing by the time she returned with a second round of drinks, and had gladly accepted the cue Spencer held out for her to join their game. That was three games ago, however, and she groaned as she watched Adam and Charlotte trade celebratory high fives at the win she just handed them.

"That's three games to one," Adam said, grinning at Spencer. "You guys wanna go again?"

Mac shook her head. "I'm done."

"Yeah, me too," Charlie said, patting Adam on the shoulder as she squeezed by him to put her cue back on the rack on the wall. "You boys have fun."

"I pass too, man. My ego needs a few minutes to recover," Spencer laughed, shaking his head in response to the challenging look Adam gave him.

"All right, fine," Adam grumbled playfully. "How about one last round before we call it a night? I'm buying."

Charlie nodded and lifted herself onto one of the barstools at their table. "Sounds good."

"I'll go with you," Spencer said, ignoring the glare Mac shot him as he followed Adam to the bar.

Alone with Mackayla for the first time that night, Charlie sighed and leaned back against the wall. After a few minutes of companionable silence, she turned to smile lazily at the blonde. Her eyes roamed slowly over Mackayla's features, tracing the slope of her jaw and the plump curve of her lips, and she swallowed thickly as the urge to lean over and kiss Mackayla swept through her. "Are you having fun?"

Mac propped her right foot on the edge of her stool and looped her arm around her knee as she turned to look at Charlotte. Her heart skipped a beat that the depth of emotion she found staring back at her, and she bit her lip as she looked away. The little voice of reason in the back of her mind was muted by the alcohol in her system, and in the absence of that persistent reminder to keep her distance, a quieter, more hopeful thought took its place.

What if?

What if Spencer was right? What if letting Charlotte back in didn't have to end in heartbreak? What if she stopped fighting so goddamn hard?

The longer Mackayla stared into space without answering her, the more worried Charlie became, and she reached across the table to give the blonde's arm a gentle squeeze. "You okay?"

Mac cleared her throat and nodded. "Absolutely." It was impossible to miss the concern in Charlotte's gaze, and she forced herself to smile as she added, "I'm having a great time. Are you?"

"Of course," Charlie murmured, not at all convinced by the fake smile Mackayla was giving her. She gave her arm one more light squeeze as she saw Adam and Spencer returning with their beers, and sighed as she pulled her hand away.

"Here you go," Spencer drawled as he handed Mac a beer. There was something off about her expression, and he frowned. "Everything okay?"

"Fine," Mac assured him, her smile too bright and not coming close to reaching her eyes. "Thanks."

Adam set Charlie's beer down on the table in front of her. He smiled when the song that had been playing ended and a new one began, the opening chords instantly recognizable and much slower than anything that had played while they had been in the bar. It wasn't clubby. Or even that upbeat. But it was his and Charlie's drinking song, the one they inevitably sang whenever they went to karaoke together, and he laughed when he saw her recognize it too. "Sing it with me, Charlie-girl."

Charlie laughed and shook her head, more than content to let him serenade them all on his own. "No way, man. But you go on ahead."

"Yes way," Adam retorted, reaching out and swiping Charlie's drink away from her before she could pick it up. "Give me a second I, I need to get my story straight," he sang, grinning as he lifted the glass out of her reach. "You gotta earn it, Charlie Bennett."

Charlie shot him an incredulous look that he met with a defiant one of his own. He was not going to back down. "Fine," she grumbled, rolling her eyes and nodding. "Okay, fine."

He started singing again, grinning at her as the song reached the chorus.

"Tonight, we are young," Charlie sang, shaking her head at Adam as he did a celebratory fist pump for getting her to cave and join in. "So let's set the world on fire, we can burn brighter, than the sun," she belted, her shoulders bouncing with silent laughter as she allowed him to pull her from her chair.

Mac found herself completely captivated by the way Charlotte moved as she sang, hips swaying seductively from side to side with the beat of the music. Though the brunette had put up a small fight when Adam had first asked her to sing with him, it was obvious that she was enjoying herself. The duo's voices blended together perfectly. Smoky and strong, deep and full of emotion, fading in and out as one or the other took the lead before picking the song back up together. Mac swallowed thickly when Charlotte started crooning for somebody to carry her home, and she cleared her throat softly as she looked away from the brunette to look for her beer, needing something cold to counteract the heat that was spreading through her body.

"Come on, you two!" Adam said, beckoning for Spencer and Mac to join them for the final chorus as Charlie sang about angels arriving.

Mac looked up in surprise when Spencer started singing, his voice nowhere near as good as Adam or Charlotte's, and she smiled, shaking her head when he looked at her expectantly. She was not about to embarrass herself by trying to sing. Undeterred by her refusal to sing along, the trio formed a half-circle around her, each of their faces split in wide smiles as they serenaded her, and she laughed when they looped their arms around each other and started swaying with the beat. It was a ridiculous ending to what had been an incredibly strong performance until that point, and Mac found herself both relieved and disappointed when it was over.

"That was awesome!" Adam declared as he traded high fives with Charlotte and Spencer.

"It was fun," Charlie conceded, smiling as she slid back onto her stool. "So, are you happy now, Snow?"

Adam grinned and handed her back her drink. "Absolutely. I can go back to New York a happy man."

Spencer laughed and reached for his beer. "That was actually fun. You two can really sing."

"Thank you," Charlie murmured, biting her lip and looking over at Mackayla. "What did you think?"

Mac smiled and, this time, it did reach her eyes. "You guys were great."

"Why didn't you join us too?" Spencer asked, bumping her with his hip for emphasis.

"Yeah right," Mac muttered, lifting her glass to her lips. "You know damn well I can't sing."

"You sing better than I do," Spencer retorted.

"Well, yeah," Mac allowed with a smirk, finally tearing her eyes away from Charlotte. "But that's not really saying much, is it?"

"It would have been fun," Charlie murmured, smiling shyly at the blonde.

Mac cleared her throat softly and nodded, unable to resist the quiet allure of the brunette's gaze. "Maybe next time."

Chapter 25

Mac knew that she wasn't at the top of her game when she walked up the path to Charlotte's house with the copy of *Divergence* she had promised Adam. She had gotten only a couple of hours of sleep, at most, after crawling into bed at a little before two that morning because her mind was stuck on an infinite loop, replaying the seductive sway of Charlotte's hips as she danced, the enchanting sound of her laughter, and the smoky sexiness of her voice when she sang. But, even had she been fully rested, she would have never expected to have a shirt thrown at her the moment she stepped foot onto Charlotte's front porch.

And yet, that was exactly what happened.

She was still a few feet from the front door when it opened just far enough for Adam's arm to reach through the gap, and before she knew what was happening, a red and black plaid flannel was flying at her face. She instinctively reached out and caught the shirt before it could hit her but, before she could do anything else, the door slammed shut and she could hear Adam laughing uproariously on the other side.

"What the hell?" she muttered, shaking her head and looking at the door in utter confusion.

She was answered by the sound of Charlie's indignant, "You did not just do that!", and before she could react in any way, the door was thrown open and she found herself face-to-face with the brunette.

Mac froze as she greedily drank in the sight of Charlotte standing in front of her wearing nothing but a pair of running shoes, faded low-slung jeans, and a red and white polka dot patterned demi-cup bra. If the shirt flying at her had been unexpected, it had nothing on the reality of Charlotte opening the door to her only half-dressed. It was like the beginning of a bad porno, except it was actually happening to her in real life, and she swallowed thickly as her gaze landed on Charlotte's chest. Her eyes traced the supple curve where the brunette's breasts and the fabric of her bra met, and she licked her lips at the way Charlotte's breasts moved when she breathed.

If Mackayla was surprised to have Charlie open the door topless, it was nothing compared to the surprise Charlie felt at seeing somebody standing on her front porch. Her heart leapt into her throat before she realized that it was Mackayla. *Oh well. At least it's somebody who's seen me naked before*, she thought wryly. She grinned as she realized that Mackayla's attention was focused on her chest, and couldn't resist pushing her breasts forward just a little. "Hey, you," she chuckled, stepping away from the door so that she wasn't putting on a show for the entire neighborhood.

The sound of Charlotte's laughter snapped Mac out of her haze, and she felt her cheeks flame with embarrassment as she forced herself to meet the brunette's gaze. Her blush deepened at the knowing sparkle in Charlotte's eyes, and she stammered an apology as she held the shirt out to her. "I wasn't...I just..." She huffed a breath and shrugged. "Sorry. Um...here you go," she muttered, her attention dropping back to the brunette's chest. She didn't want to look, but she just couldn't seem to help herself.

Amused by how flustered Mackayla was acting, Charlie grinned and took her shirt from the blonde. It was endearing, considering the fact that this certainly wasn't the first time Mackayla had seen her undressed. "Thanks." It was obvious that she still didn't have Mackayla's attention as she flipped the shirt over her shoulders and slid her arms into the sleeves, and she had to bite the inside of her cheek to keep from laughing. "You wanna come in?"

Mac honestly wasn't sure if she should, but she nodded and stepped into to foyer anyways. She could not look away as Charlotte begin doing up her shirt, and groaned softly as the sight of the brunette's fingers working at the opalescent buttons made her stomach clench. She really didn't get enough sleep to have to try and deal with all this. "Um…" She cleared her throat softly when she realized that Charlotte was not going to close those final three buttons, and looked away, trying to force herself to focus on something other than Charlotte's breasts. "I'm afraid to ask, but why, exactly, did Adam throw your shirt out onto the front porch?"

Charlie smirked and dragged her hands through her hair, scratching her scalp and making the strands stick up in a million different directions. "I may have insulted his manhood."

"There was no 'may have' about it," Adam argued as he sauntered out of the kitchen with a can of Diet Coke. "You totally did."

Charlie laughed and pointed a finger at him. "Yeah, well, you deserved it, mister 'I made Quiche Lorraine for breakfast and sewed a button onto your shirt for you'."

"I should have thrown that damn thing away instead of fixing it," Adam retorted.

Charlie rolled her eyes. "Why? It's soft and comfortable, and if all I'm doing today is driving your ass to the train station and grading papers, there's no reason to dress up!"

"Charlie-girl, it's flannel!" Adam groaned, looking like it pained him to even think about the fact that he touched the shirt.

"So?"

"Should I go?" Mac asked, her eyes darting back and forth between the bickering friends.

"You're fine," Charlie assured her with a gentle smile. "Mr. Drama Queen will stop with the hysterics now."

"See, shit like that is why I threw your fucking shirt out the door," Adam retorted, pointing an accusing finger at Charlie. "I poked myself in the finger three times with the needle sewing that goddamn button on, and do I get any thanks for my suffering?" He shook his head. "No!"

"D'aww, you poor wittle guy," Charlie cooed, laughing as she kissed the tip of the finger he was still pointing at her. "Better?"

He grinned and nodded. "Much."

Charlie laughed. "Good. Now, behave. We have company."

"Hello, company," Adam drawled, winking at Mac.

"You two are insane," Mac chuckled, shaking her head.

"Yeah, but it's a loveable kind of insanity," Adam quipped, giving Charlie an affectionate bump with his hip.

"If you say so," Mac retorted, her grin giving away the fact that she didn't necessarily disagree with him. "Anyways, I just came over to bring you this."

Adam whooped excitedly and pulled his hands out of his pockets to take the book she held out for him. "Awesome," he enthused as he opened the cover. "*To Adam, I'll try and keep your suggestion of 'less plot, more porn' in mind when I sit down to write my next novel. It was great to meet you, and hopefully we can find a time to hang out again soon. Love, Lynn Turner (Mac Thomas). P.S. If you tell anyone my real name, the porn stops.*"

Charlie laughed as Adam grinned and swept Mackayla up into a bear hug.

"You're the best, Lynn Turner parentheses Mac Thomas," Adam crowed as he spun the blonde in a circle.

"Oh my god," Mac laughed, looping her arms around his neck and holding on for dear life as he twirled faster and faster, sending her legs flying out behind her.

Charlie took a step back so that she wouldn't get kicked, and bit her lip as she watched her two friends, her heart swelling with affection for the both of them. The alarm on her phone went off just then, warning that Adam would miss his train if they didn't leave soon, and she sighed. "Sorry to break up the love fest, but that's our cue," she said, waggling her phone at Adam.

"Aww, come on!" Adam whined as he set Mackayla back onto her feet. "You're just jealous that we were having fun without you."

Charlie smiled and nodded. "Maybe a little," she admitted. "But we really do need to get going."

"Fine," Adam groaned. He smirked at Charlie as he offered Mac a gentlemanly bow and pressed a chaste kiss to the back of her hand. "Lynn Turner parentheses Mac Thomas, it has been an absolute pleasure meeting you. You are just as smart and beautiful as Charlie said you were."

"Christ, Snow. Knock it off," Charlie laughed as she aimed a kick at his ass. "Go get your bag."

"It's already in the car," Adam said, laughing as he hopped away from her. He pulled the front door open with a dramatic huff, strode imperiously through it, and called over his shoulder, "If you don't stop dawdling, we're gonna be late. Get a move on, Bennett!"

"I really am sorry about all that," Charlie apologized as she followed Mackayla out onto the porch.

"No reason to apologize," Mac assured her, smiling as she watched Charlotte lock the front door. Her breath hitched when Charlotte turned to face her, the brunette's shirt flaring open to reveal a tantalizing hint of smooth skin and patterned fabric. "Drive safely."

Charlie nodded and tucked her hair behind her ears. "Of course. You too. Thank you for bringing Adam that book. He will be talking about that non-stop for the next month, at least."

"It wasn't a big deal," Mac demurred, shaking her head.

"Yeah, well, still," Charlie murmured, sighing as she reached out and pulled Mackayla into a light embrace. "Thank you anyways."

Mac swallowed thickly as her body reacted to the press of Charlotte's against her, warmth spreading through her as her stomach swooped and soared with butterflies. After the utter craziness of everything that had happened from the moment she stepped onto Charlotte's front porch, the feeling of the brunette's arms around her made all that madness disappear, leaving her feeling safe, protected, and content. "No problem," she muttered, giving Charlotte a gentle squeeze before she forced herself to pull away. "You guys should probably get going."

"Yeah, probably," Charlie agreed. She smiled and added, "I'll see you tomorrow."

Mac nodded. "See you then."

Chapter 26

Mac's head wouldn't stop spinning. The serenity she had found in Charlotte's arms earlier had left her the moment she got in her car, and now all she could think about was the brunette. The way she looked when she opened the front door without a shirt on. Her smile. The sound of her laughter. The seductive sway of her hips as she danced. How right it felt whenever she held her.

She had tried to keep busy so that her mind didn't have time to wander, but nothing worked, and she was slowly beginning to lose it. Even the Patriots game she was watching with Spencer did little to keep her mind from drifting to thoughts of Charlotte, because every time the television panned to Houston's cheerleaders, she saw Charlotte standing in front of her in her bra. It didn't matter that the women on the television were wearing navy blue halter tops, her mind replaced all of them with a smiling brunette in a red and white polka-dot patterned bra.

Well aware of the fact that *something* was definitely bothering Mac, Spencer cleared his throat softly and asked, "So, are you going to tell me what's going on?"

"Charlotte stuff," Mac muttered, shaking her head and pressing her hands to her eyes to try and force the image of the bra-clad brunette from them. It didn't work. Instead, it made the Charlottes blurring her vision splinter into multiple sexy, smirking brunettes in patterned bras. "Shit!"

He was only mildly concerned about Mac before, but he frowned at her outburst. "Seriously, Mac, you okay?"

Mac sighed and shook her head. "Yeah. No. I dunno. I'm gonna go for a run."

"Are you sure that's a good idea?"

The game came back on with the cameraman still tracking the dance moves of Houston's cheerleaders, and Mac nodded. "Yeah. I'll have my phone on me. I'll be fine."

"If you say so," he muttered, shaking his head. "Remember, I have a basketball game tonight at eight, and me and the guys are all going out for drinks afterwards. So, depending on how long you're out, I may not be here when you get back."

"Okay. Have fun," Mac said, pushing herself up off of the couch and heading for the stairs. "I'll see you tomorrow."

Ten minutes later, she was hitting the sidewalk in a pair of running shorts and a long-sleeved compression shirt, phone strapped to her left arm and earbuds firmly in place. She ran like a woman possessed, eyes burning holes in the sidewalk as she tried to forget about the way Charlotte had looked earlier.

It didn't work.

She counted her steps, focused on her breathing until she felt lightheaded, and still, nothing helped. Every step was a different memory. The surprised look on Charlotte's face the day they had literally crashed into each other in downtown Hampton. The way Charlotte would smile whenever she complimented her. The way Charlotte looked at the Mish-Mash. High heels and impossibly long legs, smooth skin, and a seductively sexy smirk. Every step reminded Mac of Charlotte. Hips swaying with the beat of the music in the bar. A rich, smoky, soulful voice crooning for somebody to carry her home.

She ran harder, faster, eventually working her way out onto the track at Blake where she ripped off lap after lap, each blending into the next as her mind continued to race, flitting faster and faster from one memory to the next. Teasing smiles and expressive eyes full of affection. A deft tongue sweeping slowly over plump lips. The sound of Charlotte's laughter, so unguarded and free, full of joy and promises of happiness.

She ran faster. Trying to forget, but unable to do anything but remember.

The first time she saw Charlotte across the room at the Tri-Delt house. An absolute vision in hip-hugging jeans and a skin tight sequined tank top. Their first kiss, shy and sweet, pop music that was way too loud filtering up from the first floor of the party providing the soundtrack to the moment that changed her life forever. Their first Christmas, presents exchanged in front of a two-foot tall artificial tree. The way Charlotte would look to her every time she scored a goal, lips quirked up in a secretive smile, two fingers pressed to her chest above her heart. The first time they made love. Bumbling and awkward and perfect. The first time Charlotte had said she loved her. They were tucked away in the brunette's dorm room, and there were strings of multi-colored Christmas tree lights hanging from the ceiling in mess of a pattern that was the most beautiful thing ever created. Post-it notes stuck to her door, with snippets of sonnets Charlotte thought she would like scribbled onto the squares. Fingers playing with opalescent buttons. Strong arms sliding around her neck, pulling her in close. The soft press of Charlotte's body against hers. The faint scent of sandalwood that would envelop her whenever she dared to hold the brunette close.

She ran harder, trying to escape the slippery slope of her thoughts, but only managed to become lost deeper in them. Her legs burned and still she pressed on, chased by the ghosts of her memories until her mind echoed the same thought with every step. What if?

What if?

What if?

"No," she groaned, shaking her head as she somehow managed to run even faster than she had been running before. She didn't want to get hurt again. She had sworn to herself that she wouldn't get hurt like that again.

What if?

A gentle embrace that made her feel so loved and cherished.

What if?

A smoky voice that made her name sound better than it had ever sounded in her life.

What if?

A polka-dot patterned bra and a plaid flannel shirt.

What if?

Green eyes that were simultaneously dark and the brightest she had ever seen. Shining with need. Love. Want. Desire. Hope.

What if?

Her vision blurred as she ran harder, faster, her thoughts growing more and more chaotic with every step. She ran, not paying any attention to where she was going, just trying to get away. From her thoughts. From her memories. From the things she wanted and wouldn't let herself have.

She ran.

And then she stopped. She stared at the black door with its pewter knocker that shone in the light illuminating the porch. Her breath hitched even as her pulse raced, and she couldn't stop herself from reaching out and ringing the doorbell.

She wanted to run, but she couldn't. Not any longer.

The door opened, and she saw the utter confusion and worry on Charlotte's face as the brunette looked at her.

She was tired of running.

Green eyes stared at her, searching for answers as she tenderly cradled Charlotte's jaw in the palm of her hand. She saw Charlotte's lips move, no doubt asking what was going on, but she couldn't hear anything beyond the sound of her pulse pounding in her ears. She licked her lips as she stepped in closer, and her heart soared at the understanding and acceptance she saw dawn in Charlotte's expression.

She was tired of running.

"My god, Charlotte," she breathed as the last of her walls came down.

Warmth surged through her as she captured Charlotte's lips with her own and finally, finally her mind stopped spinning. The pulse that had been pounding in her ears went silent, and she was aware of nothing but the feeling of Charlotte's lips against her own.

Chapter 27

Charlie knew that they had been building to this moment for quite some time now, but she still froze in surprise as Mackayla's lips landed lightly, almost hesitantly on top of her own. It was shockingly reminiscent of their first kiss, and she sighed as she melted into it. She reached up and tenderly cupped Mackayla's face in her hands as she lifted herself up onto her toes, and she smiled as she lightly sucked the blonde's lower lip between her own. Like that first time so many years ago, she didn't know if Mackayla would run away from her when the kiss broke, and she was determined to take everything she could from the moment. Every ragged breath. Every swoop of her heart into her throat. Every flutter of butterflies in her stomach. It was a feeling that was simultaneously new and familiar, and as Mackayla's hands finally wrapped around her hips, strong fingers digging into her sides and pulling her into the blonde's body, a slow rolling tremor of anticipation tumbled down her spine.

God, she had missed this.

The need for air eventually forced them apart, and Charlie swallowed thickly as she savored the lingering feeling of Mackayla's kiss, reveling in the way her heart beat an irregular staccato in her chest. It was perfect and everything she wanted, and she knew that when she opened her eyes, she would have to face the reality of their situation that was, at the moment, anything but perfect.

Mac licked her lips as warm, questioning green eyes finally locked onto hers, and she wrapped her arms around Charlotte's waist and held her close. The sound of her pulse pounding in her ears made it hard to think, and she sighed as she pressed her lips to the petite brunette's forehead. "What are we doing?"

The quiet confusion in Mackayla's voice made Charlie's eyes flutter shut, and she swallowed thickly as the very real fear that she would soon hear her front door slam shut made her stomach clench. She wanted this—oh, how she wanted this—but it was not just her decision to make. "That depends on you, Mackayla," she whispered. She smoothed her thumbs over the blonde's cheeks and added, "I'm sure you know where I stand on this."

Mac shook her head. "It's not that easy."

"Yes, it is," Charlie murmured. "What do you want?"

When put that simply, there was no way Mac could avoid the truth that was evident in the way her arms were still wrapped possessively around the brunette, or the way she continued to brush the softest of kisses across the smaller woman's forehead. "You."

Charlie smiled. "Then have me."

"It's not that simple. You're only here until the end of the year."

"The future isn't set in stone, Mackayla," Charlie whispered gently. "The only thing guaranteed to any of us is the here and now."

Mac nodded as the backs of her eyes stung with tears. "I can't," she breathed, her voice cracking with emotion.

Even though it felt like her heart had just been ripped out of her chest, Charlie nodded. "Okay. It's okay, sweetie."

"No, it's not," Mac said, shaking her head sadly as she pulled back, her hands sliding around the soft curve of Charlie's sides until she was holding onto the brunette's hips, unable and unwilling to let her go just yet. Her heart thudded heavily in her chest as she looked into green eyed dulled by rejection, and shook her head. Now that she had admitted it to them both, there was no way she could go back to the awkward friendship they'd rebuilt.

She didn't want to go back to that. She didn't want to go back to coffee dates that weren't dates, and lunches that ended entirely too quickly.

"It's not okay," Mac whispered as she leaned in and recaptured Charlotte's lips in a slow, sweet kiss. She sighed as she felt the brunette melt into her, soft curves fitting so perfectly against her own, and she knew that she would never forgive herself if she let this perfection slip through her fingers. Because this time, it would be her walking away. Not the other way around. She would be breaking her own goddamn heart.

"Mackayla?" Charlie whispered hesitantly when the hands on her hips began guiding her backwards. Her breath hitched in her throat when her back came into contact with the wall, and she moaned softly as Mackayla's lips crushed against her own.

This time, the kiss wasn't hesitant. It wasn't soft. It was hard and desperate and hungry, full of conflicting emotions too strong to put into words. It spoke of need and want and desire. Of fear and anger and desperation. And yet, even as their hands roamed with frantic urgency over each other's bodies, grasping, squeezing, kneading, pulling, there was an undeniable tenderness underlying each and every touch that said this wouldn't be a one-time thing. That if they did this, there would be no going back for either of them.

Mac groaned as she felt Charlotte's hands slide under her shirt, and she licked her lips when she pulled back to look into emerald eyes that were dark with desire. "I want you." She swallowed thickly as she watched the brunette's lips quirk up in a small smile, and she felt compelled to add, "I don't want to let you go."

"So don't let me go," Charlie whispered, her smile growing wider as she pressed a light kiss to the blonde's lips. "Take me to bed."

A soft, unintelligible whimper escaped Mac as she leaned in and recaptured the brunette's mouth with her own, and she felt her heart skip a beat as she finally allowed herself to slip her hands beneath Charlotte's shirt and press her palms to the soft, warm skin of the smaller woman's back. Though they both knew that Charlotte's bedroom was their inevitable destination, neither felt compelled to move from their spot in the foyer as they gave in to the desire they'd each been holding at bay for what seemed like forever.

Clothes were removed between heated, languid kisses, tossed aside and forgotten as fingers wandered over newly revealed skin, tracing familiar planes as memories of curves and valleys were adjusted to allow for time and maturity. They made their way down the hall to Charlie's bedroom in staggered, halting strides that came to frequent stops as the need to touch, to taste, to kiss, to fondle overcame them. When they eventually tumbled into bed, they came together with a practiced familiarity that was simultaneously comforting and surprising.

Too many years had passed for this to be so simple, and yet it was as easy as breathing.

"My god," Charlie moaned, her eyes rolling back in her head as Mackayla's thigh pressed against her. The light from the hall was enough to let her see the hunger burning in the blonde's eyes, and she whimpered with need. "Mackayla."

"Charlotte," Mac whispered, her voice rough with emotion as she dipped her head and claimed Charlotte's lips in a kiss that was slow and deep, tongues stroking lazily together in the space between their parted lips.

Their bodies fell into a familiar tempo as they kissed, hips rocking slowly together in a dance that had always been uniquely theirs. Hard then soft, fast then slow, bodies arching together, gasping breaths drawn between kisses that stole the air from their lungs.

It was perfect, and Mac's heart sped as she pulled back, a slow, sly smile tweaking her lips as she ground her hips down into Charlotte. "Hi."

"Hey," Charlie chuckled. She swallowed thickly at the way Mackayla's pupils seemed to dilate as she stared into the baby blue eyes she loved to lose herself in, and she had to remind herself that this was not a dream. That this was actually real. She moaned at the feeling of Mackayla's hand covering her right breast, and she couldn't contain the whimper that escaped her as long fingers closed around her nipple.

Mac hummed softly as she began trailing a line of kisses down Charlotte's throat, licking, nipping, and sucking at the sensitive column as her fingers continued to tweak and massage the brunette's nipple. She smiled against the hollow of Charlotte's throat as she traced the indentation with her tongue, enjoying the way the brunette's breath seemed to catch at the touch before she moved lower, over the plane of her chest and up the gentle slope of her left breast.

A feeling of déjà vu swept over her as she brushed her lips around the sweet curve of Charlotte's breast, letting her tongue drag over the sensitive underside of the mound and making the brunette squirm. All of it was so familiar, and yet, somehow, it managed to still feel like it was the first time she had touched her like this. The feeling of Charlotte's blunt nails scratching lightly at her scalp as she sucked lightly on her nipple made her stomach twist in the most wonderful way, and the quiet gasp that escaped the brunette when she gently pinched the bud between her teeth made her stomach clench.

She switched sides, taking Charlotte's other nipple into her mouth and covering the one she had been attending to with her hand. A long, low, trembling moan rumbled in Charlotte's chest, and Mac finally realized what was so different about their situation. And it had nothing to do with Charlotte. It was her. She was comfortable with herself in a way that she hadn't been all those years ago, and though sex with the brunette had always been good, this was the first time they were really meeting as equals. As two women who fully embraced their sexuality and their desires. She was no longer hiding who she was, and there was no denying how badly she wanted the woman who was spread beneath her.

Charlotte looked down along her own body, smiling at the top of Mackayla's head. She watched as the blonde slowly worked her way lower, leaving behind a trail of kisses. "Oh god."

Keen blue eyes flashed up to lock onto green, and Mac smiled as she flicked her tongue in the brunette's navel. "Is this okay?"

"Yes," Charlie croaked, her hips bucking of their own accord as if to punctuate her consent.

"Good," Mac murmured, stroking her hands up and down Charlotte's sides as she moved lower, running her tongue back and forth between the brunette's hipbones. She hummed quietly as she pressed a string of light kisses down the line where the brunette's leg and torso hinged. The scent of Charlotte's arousal was intoxicating as she settled herself fully between the brunette's thighs, and she licked her lips as she leaned in to deliver that first intimate kiss.

The feeling of Mackayla's tongue running through her made Charlie cry out, and her hands scrabbled across the sheets, searching something to hang onto as a light lick danced over her clit. She fisted the covers as strong hands wrapped around her thighs and pulled her open wider, and she was helpless to contain the drawn-out moan that tumbled from her lips when she felt the blonde's tongue push into her. Mackayla had never been a bad lover, but there was an assuredness to her touch now that made Charlie's toes curl. The woman making love to her now was not the same scared girl that she had made love to in the past. Time, it seemed, had done wonders for Mackayla's confidence in more ways than one.

"Oh fuck," Charlie gasped, her hips rocking hard toward Mackayla's mouth, which had pulled away from her so that the blonde's tongue was just lightly flicking back and forth over her clit. "Mackayla!"

Mac smiled and blew softly over the swollen bud she had been toying with, delighting in the way it pulsed and jumped as her breath cascaded over it. "Yes?"

"Oh my god, you're a tease now," Charlie groaned, her head dropping heavily back to the pillows even as her hips strained toward the blonde's mouth. "Great."

Mac chuckled softly under her breath as she leaned in and laid a heavy lick over the bud before swirling her tongue around it. "Better?" She laughed at the way Charlotte grunted in response to her question, and sighed as she dipped her head lower, all thoughts of teasing the brunette disappearing as the heavenly taste of Charlotte's arousal coated her tongue, and the feeling of a strong hand fisting itself in her hair.

"Fuck yes," Charlie whimpered as the force and speed of the touch against her increased. Mackayla was suddenly everywhere, her hot mouth absolutely ravenous as she touched and tasted and teased every part of her.

The sounds of Charlotte's moans and gasps spurred Mac onward, and she hummed approvingly as she began alternating fucking the brunette with her tongue and lapping lightly at her clit. She knew that the disjointed rhythm was the only thing keeping

Charlotte from finding her release, and she smiled as the hand in her hair tightened and the hips in front of her lifted almost desperately off the bed. It was a powerful feeling, to know that she was the one making Charlotte feel like this, and she sighed as she wrapped her lips around the brunette's clit and began sucking lightly against it, flicking the bud with the tip of her tongue in a tempo that she was sure would send her flying.

Charlie was lost to the pleasure coursing through her, only vaguely aware of the almost incoherent words that were spilling from her lips. The tingling heat that had been building low in her hips began to spread outward, up through her torso and down her legs until it seemed to consume her. Her grip on Mackayla's hair tightened as her body primed itself for release, and the moan that tore itself from her throat as she climaxed shook the rafters.

Mac whimpered as her body spasmed sympathetically at the sound of Charlotte's pleasure, and she sighed as she swept up the brunette's body to capture her lips in a deep, desperate kiss. She ran her right hand between Charlotte's legs and began rubbing light circles against her to ease her through her release. She groaned at the way Charlotte's tongue pushed boldly into her mouth to taste herself, and the feeling of strong, small hands covering her breasts, nimble fingers pinching and rolling her nipples made her gasp. "God, Charlotte."

"My turn," Charlie murmured, smiling. She reached down to pull Mackayla's hand from between her legs and used her body to flip their positions so that she was hovering above the blonde. Her eyes danced over Mackayla's face for a moment, drinking in her appearance, and she moaned softly as she leaned in to claim her lips in a slow, sweet kiss, hoping the emotion she poured into the caress conveyed the words she was sure Mackayla was not ready to hear yet.

She settled herself against Mackayla's side and purred softly at the feeling of the blonde's fingers run through her hair.

"Mackayla," she whispered, her voice soft and positively awed as she let her right hand begin spiraling slowly around Mackayla's breasts, tracing an invisible infinity sign upon her chest.

The soft touch felt absolutely heavenly, and Mac sighed, her left arm falling up beside her head, giving herself over to Charlotte's touch. She groaned as the brunette's hand covered her left breast, squeezing gently as a deft thumb dragged back and forth over her nipple before moving onward, stroking up and down her stomach. The feather-light caress was so achingly tender that it made her heart skip a beat, and she whimpered beseechingly into Charlotte's kiss as her body strained toward her, needing more.

Charlie's breath caught in her throat as she felt Mackayla's leg fall open in pleading anticipation. She hummed against the blonde's lips as she ran her hand down her inner thigh as far as she could reach before she began working higher, drawing random, spiraling patterns on sensitive skin, causing goosebumps to erupt in the wake of her touch. The feeling of sticky hot arousal coating her fingertips drew a soft moan from her lips, and she tore her mouth away from Mackayla's so she could look into the blonde's eyes.

"Charlotte," Mac purred, her chest arching toward the ceiling as her hips began to rock with the fingers stroking lightly through her. She was already so close, and each gentle brush of Charlotte's fingers pushed her that much closer to the edge. Charlotte's forehead landed against hers, the brunette's hot breath falling lightly over her lips, and she groaned as she closed her eyes to focus on riding the wave building inside her.

An easy smile tweaked Charlie's lips as she gazed adoringly down at Mackayla. Everything about the moment, from the way Mackayla's eyes were scrunched tight as she focused on her building orgasm to the soft whimpers that fell from her parted lips, was perfect, and Charlie's heart swelled with affection as she eased two fingers into Mackayla.

"Oh fuck," Mac groaned, her hips rocking hard against Charlotte's hand in an attempt to take the brunette deeper. She shuddered as the heel of Charlotte's hand brushed against her clit and grunted, "God, yes."

"Beautiful," Charlie breathed. She sighed and curled her fingers, pulling them back over hidden ridges that made Mackayla twitch and cry out. Strong muscles tried to hold her in place as she pumped her fingers in and out, each thrust taking more effort than the last until she felt the telltale flutter that announced the blonde's impending orgasm.

Mac moaned, her body curling around the hand between her legs as her orgasm tore through her in violent spasms. She instinctively reached for Charlotte as her body shook and trembled, needing an anchor as she rode out her release. Lost in the haze of her pleasure, she was only vaguely aware of the soft kisses being pressed to her lips, her cheeks, and her chin as she gasped and shuddered with the force of her climax. When the last spasm eventually eased, leaving her feeling boneless and weak, she smiled up at Charlotte, whose hand was still draped loosely over her. "Oh my god."

"You can say that again," Charlie chuckled, licking her lips as she leaned in and kissed Mackayla tenderly. "Wow."

Chapter 28

Mac awoke before dawn the next morning, feeling exhausted and simultaneously rejuvenated, and sighed as she glanced at the alarm clock on the bedside table. She had texted Spencer the night before to let him know where she was so that he wouldn't worry, but she was still left without any clean clothes and a class that started in less than two hours.

"Stay," Charlie murmured, pulling the arm around her waist tighter. She closed her eyes and snuggled closer to Mackayla, relishing the feeling of the blonde's body pressed against her back. Last night had been wonderful and raw and powerful, and she wasn't ready to let it end. For all of their touching, they hadn't actually talked about what it was they were doing, and she was afraid that if she let Mackayla walk out her door, she might never see her walk back through it.

The sleepiness in Charlotte's voice made Mac smile, and she pressed a soft, lingering kiss to the brunette's shoulder. "I need to go home, Charlotte. I have class in a couple hours and no clean clothes."

"Skip it," Charlie argued, licking her lips as she rolled onto her back, careful to not dislodge Mackayla's arm that was holding her close. She bit her lip and reached up to run a gentle hand over her jaw, her fingertips gliding lightly over the blonde's skin. "Stay with me."

Mac sighed. It really was a tempting thought. "I–"

Charlie silenced her with a kiss. "Stay with me," she murmured, kissing her again.

The taste of Charlotte's lips was unfairly convincing, and Mac groaned as she rolled on top of her. She smiled at the way Charlotte's body relaxed beneath her, the brunette's left leg falling open wider as she straddled her right. "Aren't you tired?" she teased, smiling as she rolled her hips forward.

"I am," Charlie confessed, whimpering softly as Mac thrust again. "But I don't want to lose you."

The vulnerability in Charlotte's words made Mac's heart break, and she sighed as she saw, for the first time, how much this whole thing between them was affecting her. Charlotte had been so brazenly confident that it had honestly never occurred to her that it had been, at least partially, an act. "I'm not going anywhere," Mac whispered, smoothing a hand over Charlotte's brow. She sighed and brushed a gentle kiss across Charlotte's lips. "I'm done fighting how I feel about you."

Charlie's heart swooped into her throat and she couldn't help asking, "Really?"

"Really," Mac murmured. "I'm..." She sighed and leaned her forehead against Charlotte's. "I can't say that I'm not a little bit scared about this, but..." Her voice trailed off again, and she licked her lips as she searched for the words she needed to explain what she was thinking and feeling. "This thing between us is too strong to fight. So I'm done trying. I'm just going to trust that this will work. That we can work. Because living without you was hell, Charlotte Bennett." She smiled and kissed her tenderly. "And fighting how I feel for you was even worse."

"We're really going to do this?"

"We are," Mac whispered, pressing the softest promise of a kiss to Charlotte's lips. She knew that she should leave so that she could get to her eight a.m. class, but she couldn't find the willpower to do it. Not with Charlotte so soft and warm beneath her. Not when enchanting green eyes so full of fragile hope and boundless love were staring at her like she was everything the brunette wanted in the world.

Charlie stared unblinkingly into Mackayla's eyes as first her left hand, and then her right, were lifted above her head and pinned to the mattress, long fingers threading between her own. The emotion swirling in Mackayla's darkening blue eyes made her heart skip a beat, and she whimpered when the blonde rocked purposefully against her. "Mackayla," she breathed, her hips lifting to meet Mackayla's next thrust.

Mac's eyes fluttered shut and she moaned, squeezing Charlotte's hands as she kissed her tenderly. Her lips molded around the brunette's, and she felt her nipples tighten when Charlotte began moving with her, thrust for thrust, their fingers playing lightly together as they pushed each other closer and closer to the edge. Their kisses grew deeper, tongues boldly stroking and exploring as they lost themselves in the moment, and Mac groaned when she was forced to pull away so she could draw more than a quick breath. "Shit," she muttered, nuzzling the brunette's cheek as she gasped for air.

"Tell me about it," Charlie chuckled, a low groan rumbling in her throat when Mackayla's thigh pressed harder against her.

Mac's grip on Charlotte's hands tightening as she ground herself against the brunette. "You are so beautiful, Charlotte."

"You think so?" Charlie asked, the corners of her lips lifting in a shy, pleased smile.

"Mmm, I do," Mac murmured, capturing Charlotte's lips in a slow, deep kiss.

If her hands were not pinned above her head, Charlie would have been tempted to pinch herself to see if she was dreaming because, even after a night spent making love, this moment was almost impossibly surreal. Tears stung at the backs of her eyes as the weight of what was happening descended upon her, and she turned her head to the side to draw a shuddering breath in an attempt to keep them at bay.

The knowledge that this was real and that Mackayla really was willing to give her a second chance, combined with the feeling of Mackayla's body atop her own and the firm thigh rubbing so perfectly against her was enough to send her flying into release. Charlie came undone with a muted scream, moaning Mackayla's name over and over again as her body trembled with the pleasurable waves of her orgasm.

It only took Mac another two thrusts to fall over the edge as well, and she buried her face in the crook of Charlotte's neck, murmuring the brunette's name as she came.

Charlie smiled as Mackayla pulled back to look at her, and her breath hitched in her throat at the unfettered love she saw shining down at her. Strong fingers squeezed her own, and she smiled as she squeezed back, hoping that her own eyes conveyed the depth of her feelings as well as Mackayla's did.

The air between them grew thick with quiet emotion, the silence heavy with the weight of words left unsaid. Before the silence could become awkward, or one of them slipped and said the three words it was still too early to say, the alarm clock on the bedside table went off, shattering the stillness that had surrounded them with a burst of static, and Charlie bit her lip as Mackayla let go of her hand to turn it off.

"Goddamn alarm clock," Charlie muttered.

Mac laughed and nodded. "Exactly." She sighed and pressed a lingering kiss to Charlotte's lips. "How about this, I'll skip my eight a.m. and we can maybe grab some breakfast before your nine?"

Charlie smiled. "I'd like that."

"Good."

"Would you want to shower here? I have some sweats that might fit you."

"That sounds perfect," Mac murmured, nuzzling Charlotte's cheek. "And then, could you drive me by my place so I can get dressed?"

"I think I can manage that," Charlie agreed.

"I'm sure you can," Mac winked at Charlotte as she climbed out of bed. The sight of Charlotte spread invitingly across the bed, hair tousled, lips swollen, eyes dark with desire, made her want nothing more than to ignore her responsibilities and climb back into bed, and she bit her lip as she forced herself to resist the urge. Her eyes trailed slowly over Charlotte's body, and she blushed when she noticed the handful of light purple marks that dotted the brunette's neck and shoulders. "I...uh, left some marks."

Charlie grinned, her eyes skimming over an array of lighter bruises to land on a particularly dark one on Mackayla's shoulder that she only vaguely remembered making. "Me too," she said, chuckling as she rolled out of bed. She sighed as she lifted herself onto her toes to wrap her arms around Mackayla's neck, holding the blonde close, not wanting the intimacy of their night together to end just yet.

Mac smiled and looped her arms around Charlotte's waist, pulling her in tight as she pressed a kiss to her forehead. "Come on, Bennett," she murmured after a moment. "Time to start the day."

"I guess you're right," Charlie agreed, though she didn't make any effort to move.

The feeling of Charlotte's body pressed up against her gave Mac a wonderful idea, and she chuckled as she slid her hands over the perfect globes of the brunette's ass to give the firm cheeks a playful squeeze. "We can save time and shower together," she suggested huskily.

"I don't know how much time we'll save," Charlie replied, smirking as she looked up at Mackayla. "But I like how you think."

Chapter 29

Charlie sighed and leaned back in her chair as she looked out her office window at the snow that was falling, turning Blake's campus into a winter wonderland. The semester had officially ended the day before, and she honestly did not know where the time had gone. She could remember every moment she spent with Mackayla, but it didn't feel like there had been enough of them to fill seven weeks of calendar space. Time was going too fast, speeding by in a blur, and she desperately wanted it to slow down.

But that was, as Adam continuously reminded her, outside her control.

Her phone rang and she reached behind herself to grab it off her desk. She checked the caller I.D. and shook her head when she saw who was calling. "Think of the Devil," she muttered as she lifted the phone to her ear. "Hey, Snow."

"Hey yourself. How are things going in the Great White North?"

"Getting whiter," Charlie shared, her gaze lingering on the flakes that were slowly but surely stacking up on the outside of her windowpane. "It's snowing again. How's New York?"

"Overrun with tourists doing the Manhattan during the holidays thing. I have to go out of my way to avoid Rockefeller Center now, and lord help anyone who dares go near Thirty-Fourth and Sixth. But, whatever. Christmas spirit and all that."

"And yet, you refuse to come up here with me," Charlie pointed out with a grin.

"Like having to sit and watch you and Mac be all kissy-face, lovey-dovey, ooey-gooey gross is any better than dealing with tourists," he retorted. *"How is the wife?"*

"My girlfriend is fine, thanks for asking." A light knock on her door made her turn around, and she smiled as her eyes landed on Mackayla. The blonde looked absolutely adorable in her snow boots, jeans, and blue cable knit sweater that Charlie could see peeking out of her unzipped parka. She licked her lips when her gaze landed on Mackayla's, and she smirked as she watched the blonde mimic the action. "She's right here, actually. You wanna say hi?"

"She's there? Are you guys in bed?"

"No, we're not in bed. I'm sitting in my office."

"Well, damn, too bad."

"You are such a pervert!" Charlie laughed. "My god, man. Go get laid so you can get your mind out of my goddamn bedroom."

"Adam?" Mac asked knowingly as she sat down in the chair opposite Charlotte's desk. She smiled at the way the brunette rolled her eyes and nodded, and held her hand out. "Lemme say hi."

"I'm giving Mackayla the phone. You better behave yourself," Charlie mock-threatened before she handed the phone over to the blonde.

"Hello, Mr. Snow," Mac drawled as she lifted the phone to her ear.

"Lynn Turner parentheses Mac Thomas," Adam retorted. *"How're you doing, sexy?"*

Mac arched a brow and grinned at Charlotte. "He called me sexy."

"You are," Charlie agreed, shrugging as she refused to rise to the bait. "Incredibly, breathtakingly so."

"You are such a sweet talker," Mac murmured.

Charlie grinned. "And you're at your sexiest when you whimper my name as I–"

"That's enough out of you, Charlie Bennett," Mac interrupted, a light blush creeping up her cheeks as she easily imagined where Charlotte was going with her little description.

Adam laughed. *"What did she say? I know it was something good because you called her Charlie, and you only do that when she's in trouble."*

"None of your business," Mac retorted.

"You're no fun."

"I'm a lot of fun, just ask Charlotte." Mac smirked at the brunette, who was nodding in agreement.

"I would love to ask her. Put her on the phone."

"She's smart enough to not tell you anything, but feel free to go ahead and ask. I need to go input my grades and send them over to the registrar," she said, more for Charlotte's benefit that his.

He sighed dramatically. *"Fine. Whatever. I was tired of talking to you anyways, Lynn Turner parenthesis Mac Thomas."*

"Love you too, Mr. Snow," Mac retorted, blowing him a kiss through the phone before she handed it back to the brunette.

"You are incorrigible," Charlie laughed as she lifted her phone to her ear.

"Yeah, well, I try," he quipped. *"So, now that school is done for the semester, you have any big plans?"*

"Just the faculty holiday party tonight and then hanging out with Mackayla as much as possible over the break."

"Is she staying in Hampton for the holidays?" he asked, knowing that the blonde had gone back to California with Spencer for Thanksgiving, while Charlie had spent the holiday with her family in Boston.

"Yeah. We're going to do Christmas Eve here, and then drive down to my parents' for Christmas Day."

"You're finally bringing the girl home for Christmas."

Charlie grinned and nodded. "I am. And hopefully for many more to come."

"I'm happy for you, Charlie-girl," he murmured, his tone warm and full of gentle affection. *"Is anything else happening?"*

"Nope. Just getting ready for the holidays."

"Same here. Shit, I just remembered I need to run up to a meeting now, so I gotta go. Call you next week?"

"Sounds good. Later, buddy." Charlie sighed as she disconnected the call and looked through her open door and across the hall to Mackayla's office. The blonde was sitting at her desk, her laptop open in front of her and a stack of papers to her right, transferring the grades she had marked on the stories onto her computer. Her eyes traced the lines of Mackayla's face, gliding over her cheekbones and jaw, and she smiled as she watched her run a hand through her hair and shake her head at a paper as she flipped it over to reveal the one beneath it.

Blue eyes flashed up to look at her and she grinned and blew Mackayla a kiss. The small smile she got in response before the blonde returned the gesture made her heart leap, and she laughed as she opened up her laptop to go finish inputting her own grades before it was time to get ready for the holiday party.

Chapter 30

"You look...wow," Charlie murmured, licking her lips as she opened her front door. Mackayla was wearing what looked like the same tuxedo pants she had worn at the Mish-Mash, and beneath her open pea coat, Charlie could see that she had paired the trousers with a fitted cranberry red button down that was unbuttoned conservatively at her neck.

Mac eyed Charlotte's outfit for the evening with an appreciative smile as she stepped through the door to drop a soft kiss to her lips. The brunette was wearing a pair of killer black heels, a knee-length black pencil skirt, and an emerald green sleeveless blouse that made her eyes stand out even more than they usually did. "You too. Absolutely stunning. These are for you, by the way," she added, pulling a small bouquet of irises out from behind her back. Her heart leapt at the shy, pleased smile that lit Charlotte's face as she handed them over, and she made a mental note to do it more often.

"Thank you," Charlie whispered, biting her lip as she spun the bouquet in her hands. Irises had always been her favorite, and she felt her throat grow inexplicably tight at the thought that Mackayla had remembered such a trivial detail about her. "Really, they're gorgeous," she murmured as she leaned in to capture Mackayla's lips in a sweet, tender kiss.

Mac hummed softly and grabbed onto Charlotte's hips, holding her tight as their kisses grew deeper and more indulgent, tongues flicking and stroking against each other lazily as neither sought to pull away. The real world and all its responsibilities waited for them outside the front door, but for now, this was all either of them really wanted for the night, and they were both unwilling to let the moment end just yet.

"Hi," Charlie whispered between kisses, smiling when Mackayla's hands slid down to grab her ass. She held the flowers away from them so that they wouldn't be crushed, and reached up to run the fingers of her free hand over Mackayla's jaw. Her breath caught in her throat as she watched Mackayla's mouth fall slightly open as she ran the pad of her middle finger over the blonde's plump lower lip, and her nipples tightened at the way Mackayla's tongue poked out to lick it. "Fuck," she breathed.

Charlotte's breathy exhalation made Mac's stomach clench, and she groaned softly as she rested her forehead against the brunette's. Aas much as she would love to continue this, to leave the flowers in Charlotte's hand wherever they fell and take her to bed, she knew that they needed to at least put in an appearance at the party that evening. "Do you have a vase to put those in?"

"I'm sure there's something in the kitchen," Charlie said, pressing another quick kiss to Mackayla's lips. "We need to go, don't we?"

Mac sighed and nodded. "Yeah." A car horn punctuated her point, and she smiled. "Spence and his date are waiting for us, anyways."

"Bummer," Charlie muttered playfully. "If they weren't out there, I'd say we could just blow the whole thing off and stay in tonight."

"You're mean," Mac grumbled. She smiled and kissed Charlotte one last time before she forced herself to let go of her.

Charlie laughed. "You can't tell me you weren't thinking the same thing."

"Oh, I was," Mac assured her with a sly grin. "But it doesn't make you any less mean for saying it."

"What if I make it up to you later?" Charlie retorted, winking over her shoulder at Mackayla as she started toward the kitchen to look for a vase. All of her glassware was in storage in New York, and she really hoped there was something tucked away in one of the cupboards that she could use.

"Then all will be forgiven," Mac assured her.

"Good. Because I definitely plan on making it up to you later." Charlie sighed and forced herself to think of something besides Mackayla in her bed, because if she didn't, they would never leave the house. "So, tell me about Spencer's date. Is she an actual girlfriend, or just a flavor of the week?"

Mac shrugged and opened the cupboard above the refrigerator. A glass vase that looked to be a leftover from a flower delivery was sitting on the bottom shelf, and she grinned as she pulled it down. It wasn't fancy, but it would work. "I found one," she said, holding it out to Charlotte. "They've gone out a handful of times in the last month, which is really big for him. Huge, actually. And, to listen to him talk about her, I'd say it's pretty serious, but he's not quite ready to admit that yet. You know how he is, Mr. Player Extraordinaire and all that crap."

"I see." Charlie nodded thoughtfully as she filled the vase with water. Once full, she set it on the counter and carefully removed the flowers she had been given from their cellophane wrap. "These really are gorgeous, Mackayla," she murmured, smiling shyly up at the blonde as she fingered a delicate violet petal.

Mac smiled and stepped in behind Charlotte, who was still facing the sink. She wrapped her arms around the brunette's waist, holding her close as she pressed a soft, lingering kiss to the sensitive hollow beneath her ear. "I'm glad you like them," she whispered, kissing her again for emphasis. Outside, Spencer laid on the horn again and they both laughed. "Somebody is getting antsy," Mac muttered.

"Couldn't they just make out in my driveway for a while and leave us alone?" Charlie asked, only half-joking, and sighed when she felt Mackayla's arms briefly tighten around her waist before the blonde released her.

"You are more than welcome to ask him that yourself," Mac told her with a grin. She tilted her head toward the front door and added, "Let's go, beautiful."

"Ugh, fine," Charlie grumbled playfully. She carried the flowers she had just carefully arranged out to the living room so she could put them onto the coffee table where she would be able to admire them more often, and brushed her hands off on her hips as she turned to the foyer where Mackayla was waiting for her.

"Milady," Mac drawled, holding Charlotte's coat out for her.

Charlie smiled. It was still a new experience to have Mackayla act the gentleman for her. When they were in college, the blonde hadn't been comfortable enough with herself to assume such a role, and while she did not mind filling that part in their relationship, it was nice to be treated like a lady every once in a while. "First flowers, and now this," she murmured teasingly as she slipped her arms into her coat. "You spoil me."

Mac smoothed her hands over Charlotte's shoulders and leaned in to brush a light kiss across her cheek. "You deserve to be spoiled, Charlotte Bennett," she murmured, her voice low and smooth as silk. She bit her lip at the way Charlotte trembled ever so slightly at her words, and sighed as she rested her forehead against the brunette's temple. "You deserve the world."

A gentle smile lifted Charlie's lips as she leaned back into Mackayla. She closed her eyes and allowed herself to simply enjoy the closeness of the moment for a few heartbeats before she turned to kiss the blonde softly. "All I need is you," she whispered. Spencer honked again and she laughed. "And, maybe to get him out of my driveway," she added.

Mac nodded and reached for the door. "Shall we go?"

"We shall," Charlie agreed, biting her lip to keep from kissing Mackayla again as she walked past the blonde onto the porch. She locked up quickly after they were both outside, and smiled when Mackayla's hand slipped easily into hers as they walked down the path to the driveway. It was a simple gesture, just a small touch that told anyone who dared to look that they were more than friends, but to Charlotte, it felt like Mackayla was, in fact, giving her the world.

Chapter 31

The Blake University holiday party was held in the elegant red brick colonial mansion that served as the administrative building for the university. It was an open-house type affair, with each of the mansion's three floors dotted with open bars and tables that were loaded with a myriad of delicious looking *hors d'oeuvres*. Christmas music played softly in the background to set the mood as faculty and staff mingled, celebrating the end of yet another successful semester. It was a festive affair, laid-back despite the more formal dress of those attending the event, and Mac smiled against the rim of her wine glass as she watched yet another department chair and his wife approach Jack O'Connor and Charlotte. The Journalism Department Chair had swooped in and stolen Charlotte from her side not two minutes after they arrived, and thirty minutes later, he was still busy introducing the brunette to as many people as he could.

Charlie shot Mac an exasperated look over Jack's shoulder, and the blonde laughed as she smiled and waved at her.

"She is so done," Mac muttered under her breath.

"Yeah, well, you could always go save her," Spencer said, smiling as he handed Sara, his date, another glass of Chardonnay.

"I was going to, soon," Mac assured him. "Jack is just excited to show her off. You guys don't usually get guest lecturers with her credentials, and he deserves to brag a little."

"Yes, but this is the first time you've ever brought a date to this thing, and she's been hijacked," Spencer pointed out with a laugh.

"Yeah, well, thems the breaks," Mac drawled, rolling her eyes. She caught Charlotte shooting her yet another annoyed look, and she sighed. "Okay, fine. I'm going to go rescue her."

"You do that. I saw Jake and the Griffins go upstairs, so Sara and I will go try and find them so you two can spend some time alone," he cooed, waggling his brows suggestively. He laughed as Mac smacked his shoulder and grinned. "You hit like a girl. Look, if we don't see you for a bit, shoot me a text when you're ready to go and we'll figure something out."

"Will do. You guys have fun," Mac said, smiling at Spencer and Sara as she downed what wine was left in her glass and set it onto the tray of a passing busboy. "Wish me luck," she muttered as she started across the room to where Charlotte was shaking yet another hand.

Mac sidestepped her way through the crowd and managed to avoid all but one attempt at a conversation with a jovial, "Yeah! Happy Holidays to you too!" When she finally managed to get close to the corner of the room where Charlotte was standing, she was almost as relieved as the brunette seemed to be when she spotted her.

"Mackayla," Charlie murmured, interrupting the Physics Chair who was asking her about what she thought of the Patriots' chances in the postseason. "Hi."

Mac placed a discreet yet slightly possessive hand at the small of the brunette's back as she sidled up next to her, and smiled apologetically at the group. "Hello. I'm sorry to interrupt, but there is somebody I want to introduce Charlotte to and they'll be leaving soon, so I'm afraid I need to steal her away from you."

"Of course, of course," Jack murmured, smiling at Mac and Charlie. "I'm sorry to have kept her so long."

"It wasn't a problem at all," Charlie assured him. "It was lovely to meet you, Bob–" she shook the Physics Chair's hand, "– and thank you for introducing me around a bit, Jack," she said, smiling as she shook O'Connor's hand as well. "Happy Holidays."

"Happy Holidays," the men echoed, smiling.

Mac repeated the sentiment, and smiled as she and Charlotte turned away from them, the tips of her fingers playing lightly across the smooth fabric of the brunette's shirt. "You looked like you were enjoying yourself," she teased.

"Oh my god, that sucked," Charlie muttered, shaking her head. "I felt like a trophy being shown off. If I had to listen to him prattle on about my stupid National Magazine Award one more time, I was going to scream. Like it really matters that I have an Ellie sitting on my bookshelf at home."

"Yeah, well," Mac chuckled, "he's the chair of one of the smallest departments on campus, and landing you was something of a coup for him."

"Lucky us," Charlie murmured, smiling up at the blonde. She sighed and added, "So, who would you like to introduce me to?"

"Me, myself, and I," Mac replied with a smirk as she reached down and took Charlotte's hand into her own. "I was tired of sharing."

A familiar thrill shot through Charlie at the feeling of Mackayla's fingers lacing with her own, warm and pleasant, and she instinctively looked around the room to see if anyone was watching them. While she was glad that Mackayla seemed determined to not hide their relationship while they were in public, she had spent too many years in the cutthroat world of major media to be comfortable at a work function flaunting her sexuality. People at the magazine knew she was gay, and she had even brought dates to events, but idle touching like this was something that she just did not allow to happen. The men she worked with didn't go around holding hands and kissing their wives or girlfriends, and she had adhered to the same standard. It was part of the reason she had been welcomed into the boys club so easily. She hadn't tried to change the establishment; she had simply blended into it.

"Are you okay?" Mac asked, frowning at the way Charlotte had basically frozen beside her.

Though she knew that holding hands with Mackayla was okay and that there would most likely be no reaction to the sight of them together, Charlie still pulled her hand away from the blonde as she nodded. "Yeah. Of course." It was a lie and they both knew it, and she sighed at the thoughtful, wounded look Mackayla gave her. "I'm just…"

"Not ready to come out?" Mac supplied, offering Charlotte a wry smile.

Charlie groaned. She knew that the question had been meant to be playful, but it smacked of the bad history between them and she hated that the blonde was, in a way, right. "It's not that," she murmured looking around them for somewhere they could disappear to and talk. She spotted the women's restroom across the hall and tipped her head at it. While not ideal, it would at least afford them a small measure of privacy. "Come with me, please?"

"Okay." Mac nodded and shoved her hands into her pockets as she followed Charlotte across the large two-story entryway, around the towering Christmas tree that anchored the space, white lights twinkling merrily and ornaments shining brightly, and into the women's restroom. She watched as Charlotte ducked down to check for feet in the stalls, and she crossed her arms over her chest when the brunette stood back up to look at her.

The blonde's defensive posture made Charlie's stomach twist unpleasantly. The night had started out so well, and now she had managed to fuck it up. She ran her hands through her hair and groaned as she tried to find a way to explain herself. "I'm sorry," she apologized, knowing that it was at least a good start to what she was trying to say. "I'm just not used to being out, out at work functions. It was pure instinct for me to pull away from you, and I'm sorry."

"Why?" Mac asked softly, her arms dropping to her sides. "Why did you hide it when I thought you were out?"

The softening of Mackayla's posture made the knot of worry that had twisted itself in Charlie's gut loosen, and she licked her lips as she dared take a small step toward the blonde so that they were within arms' reach of each other. "I didn't hide, *per se*, I just didn't flaunt the fact that I'm gay either. I brought dates to events and stuff, and people knew that those women were with me, but I didn't rub anyone's faces in it. It was more…decorous, I guess you could say, to keep a careful distance and not make waves. I mean, it wasn't like any of the men I worked with were holding hands with their wives or girlfriends or anything, so my behavior wasn't at all beyond the bounds of normal. And when you took my hand just now, I loved it." She offered Mackayla a small smile to try and convey exactly how much she had enjoyed the light touch. "But my instinct was to pull away, and I did it before I could even really think about what I was doing. I can't tell you exactly how sorry I am that I did it and that it hurt you, but–"

"I get it," Mac interrupted. "I get it. And I guess I should apologize for not asking you if you would be comfortable with it first. I just assumed that since you never had a problem with me taking your hand when we were out in public or with friends, that you would be okay with it here."

Charlie shook her head. "I want to be," she murmured, reaching out and taking Mackayla's hand into her own. She looked down at the way their fingers fit together so perfectly and sighed. "You may have to be patient with me for a while as I unlearn a lot of the behaviors I picked up in New York. I don't want to hide the fact that we're together, it was just…"

"Instinct," Mac offered.

Charlie sighed and nodded, grabbing onto the word like it was a life raft. "Yeah."

"I get it." Mac smiled and used her hold on Charlotte's hand to pull the brunette into a light embrace. "It's fine, Charlotte. We're fine," she added softly as she slipped her hand out of Charlotte's so that she could wrap her arms around her.

"Thank god," Charlie whispered, closing her eyes as she tucked her head under Mackayla's chin, trying to get as close to the blonde as she possibly could. It was an almost bizarre switch in positions for them, Mackayla being more confident about their relationship than she was, and while she was annoyed at her own behavior, she couldn't help but be thankful that Mackayla had understood.

The door to the restroom pushing open and a surprised apology broke them apart, and Charlotte held Mackayla's eye as she again reached for her hand. "Should we go back to the party?"

Mac nodded. "Sure."

"Hey! There you are!" Spencer's jovial voice greeted them as the exited the bathroom.

Mac looked up at him and rolled her eyes at the smug, leering look he was giving them. "Don't even," she warned him.

"What?" he retorted, grinning. "Did you get a little *L Word* bathroom action happening in there? Because, damn."

"No," Charlie chuckled, shaking her head. "But thanks for the idea. Maybe next time."

"I don't think so," Mac muttered, giving Charlotte's hand a light squeeze. She was heartened by the fact that the brunette returned the gesture, and she found herself feeling grateful for her roommate's appearance. She could tell that Charlotte was still a little on edge, either because they were still holding hands or because she felt bad about what had just happened, and Mac knew that, for now, laughter would be the best medicine. Later, when they were alone, she could reassure Charlotte that she understood with soft touches and gentle kisses, but, for now, Spencer's goofy quips and sly grins were exactly what they needed.

"Too bad," Spencer laughed. "So, anyways, I was coming to find you because there are actual tables up on the third floor this year. You wanna come up?"

Mac nodded. "Sounds good to me. I was wondering what happened to that date of yours."

"Yeah, she's up at the table with everybody. Jake and Liam invented a drinking game where you have to do a shot for every hideous holiday sweater you see, and Sara and Heather are cheering them on."

"I didn't think the bar stocked hard liquor like that," Charlie said, frowning.

"They may have brought the tequila in with them. Allegedly," Spencer told her. "Or it fell off the back of a truck or something. You know..."

Charlie grinned and nodded. "Gotcha." They started up the stairs and she gave Mackayla's hand another light squeeze. It still felt weird to be so demonstrative in a professional setting, but the pleased smile that tweaked Mackayla's lips at the gesture was more than enough reward for her mild discomfort. "So, shots, huh?"

Spencer nodded. "Yeah. You want in?"

"I think I'll sit this one out," Charlie said, shaking her head.

"Feel free to go for it if you want," Mac told Spencer, grinning as she slapped him on the back. "I can drive us home."

Spencer nodded slowly. "You're sure?"

"Not a problem at all," Mac assured him. "I can either take Sara home first, or drop you two at our house, depending on what she wants, and then I'll take Charlotte home."

"And then you'll bring my car home sometime tomorrow," Spencer added knowingly.

"You'll be too wasted to need it tonight," Mac pointed out with a grin.

"All right then," Spencer said, clapping his hands decidedly. "Let's do it!"

Chapter 32

"Okay, I have to admit, this holiday party was way better than any holiday party I've been to before," Charlie said as she watched Spencer walk Sara up to her front door. He was unapologetically drunk and swaying from side to side a little as he walked, but the smile on Sara's face told her that the redhead found his antics amusing. Spencer, Liam, and Jake had ended up roping another two tables into their drinking game, which had expanded to include any kind of fashion faux pas. From pants that were too tight, to hideous ties, to dresses that would have been better left to somebody else to wear, nobody who walked in front of their table was safe from their drunken scrutiny. While it was not the most politically correct way to spend the evening, it had been thoroughly enjoyable.

Mac smiled and reached across the center console to lace her fingers with Charlotte's. "I'm glad you had fun," she murmured, giving the brunette's hand a gentle squeeze.

"Did you?" Charlie asked softly. She looked away from Spencer, who had managed to climb the three steps to Sara's front porch without falling down, and turned towards Mackayla. The blonde's features were highlighted in shades of gray, and Charlie's breath caught in her throat at the gentle affection she could see shining in her eyes.

Mac leaned over to brush a gentle kiss across Charlotte's lips. "I did," she assured her, kissing her again for emphasis.

The sound of drunken laughter and Sara's high-pitched, "Oh my god!" shattered the silence around them, and they both looked up to find Spencer sitting on his ass at the foot of Sara's porch steps. He had obviously fallen down them after kissing the redhead goodnight.

"Oh, shit," Charlie laughed, shaking her head as she watched Spencer try and get to his feet. He managed the task with a little help from Sara, who looked simultaneously concerned and amused, and when he started limping bravely back down the path, Charlie shared a quick look with Mackayla before they both hopped out of the car and hurried to help.

"You fall down there, Walshy?" Mac teased as she wrapped an arm around his waist to help steady him.

Spencer grinned and shook his head. "Nope. All good, dude."

"You have snow on your ass, dude," Mac pointed out with a laugh. "Seriously, how bad is it?"

"I think he'll be okay," Sara said, laughing in spite of the fact that her date was now hobbling to the car. "He just missed that first step and..." Her voice trailed off and she shrugged. "Boom."

"Yeah, well, if kissing you didn't make my knees go weak and my stomach do this crazy flippy-floppy thing, maybe I might have been able to see that first step better," Spencer retorted, too drunk to be anything but honest.

Charlie bit her lip to try and contain her grin when she noticed the way Sara was smiling in response to Spencer's confession. "I'll go wait in the car," she murmured, quickly disentangling herself from the situation.

"I can walk," Spencer grumbled, shaking off Mac's arm.

"Then I'll go wait in the car with Charlotte," Mac said, shooting Sara a look to make sure the redhead would be okay. She smiled at the way Sara was focused only on Spencer, and shook her head as she turned and hurried back to the car. A light snow had begun to fall, and it was much warmer inside the heated car than it was outside.

Charlie smiled as Mackayla jumped into the car and slammed the door closed after herself. "Your kisses make my knees weak and my stomach do a crazy flippy-floppy thing, too," she shared, chuckling as she leaned across the center console to kiss the blonde softly.

Mac laughed and reached up to cradle Charlotte's face in her palms as she deepened their kiss. A low hum rumbled in her throat as Charlotte's tongue stroked slowly around her own, making her stomach flutter pleasantly and her nipples grow hard, and she smiled when the need for a proper breath eventually forced them apart. "Me too," she whispered. She sighed as she leaned her forehead against Charlotte's. The words "I love you" were right on the tip of her tongue, aching to be said, but she didn't want to say them for the first time sitting in a car in her best friend's girlfriend's driveway.

"Good," Charlie whispered, her heart swooping into her throat at the blonde's admission. Their feelings weren't something they ever really talked about and, determined to not push Mackayla any faster than she was ready to go, Charlie had purposefully held back the three words she had been wanting to give voice to ever since Mackayla had backed her up against the wall in her foyer and admitted to wanting her. "I would hate to be the only one feeling this way."

"You're not," Mac assured her softly. She sighed as the back door to the car opened, letting in a few flurries and the sound of Spencer saying goodnight, again, to Sara. She pressed one last quick kiss to Charlotte's lips before she pulled away and turned to look at her roommate. "How ya doin' there, buddy?"

"I'm drunk," Spencer replied, nodding to himself as Sara pushed the car door shut after him.

※ ※ ※

"Yeah, you are," Charlie chuckled.

Mac laughed and rolled down her window. She flashed Sara a knowing smile and said, "I'm sure he'll call you tomorrow. I'll wait until you're inside before I leave."

Sara bit her lip and nodded. "Thank you. It was nice to meet you, Charlie," she said, leaning to her left to catch Charlie's eye.

"You too," Charlie replied, giving the redhead a small wave. She reached out and took Mackayla's hand into her own as Sara hustled back up the path to her house, and she sighed when Sara disappeared inside. It was late, she was tired, and she wished for nothing more than to crawl into bed with Mackayla and go to sleep.

A comfortable silence filled the car as Mac headed toward her house to drop Spencer off, and she gave Charlotte's hand a quick squeeze as she pulled into her driveway. "I'll be right back."

Charlie smiled at her and nodded. "Take your time." She then turned to Spencer and added, "Be good, Mr. Walsh."

"I'm always good," Spencer retorted, throwing his car door open with entirely too much force so that it bounced back at him. "Damn door," he muttered as he somehow managed to get his hands up in time to keep it from hitting him in the face.

"Easy there, buddy," Mac said, jumping out of the car, ready to catch him should he fall again. He thankfully made it out of the car without falling down, and she shook her head at him as she followed him up the walkway to their front door. "You wanna go upstairs, or just crash on the couch?" she asked after she opened the front door.

"Bed. My ass hurts."

"I bet it does." Mac chuckled and held him steady as he toed his shoes off onto the mat in the foyer. "You fell hard," she told him as she followed him up the stairs, just in case he missed another step like he had at Sara's house.

Spencer nodded and rubbed his tailbone. "I'm gonna have a bruise."

"Probably. Yeah."

"I bruised my ass."

"You did," Mac laughed, nodding as she steered him away from her room and toward his own. "Your room is this way, guy."

"I knew that," Spencer grumbled, frowning as he worked at his belt. He kicked his slacks off as he walked into his room, and flopped face-first onto his bed in his dress shirt and boxer briefs.

"I'll put a glass of water and some Tylenol on your nightstand for you before I go," Mac told him. He grunted out something that sounded like "Thanks", and she smiled as she hurried back downstairs to fetch a bottle of water. Once she was back upstairs, she grabbed the bottle of Tylenol they kept in the medicine cabinet of the hall bath, and set them both onto his bedside table. "You need anything else?"

He shook his head. "That's good. Thanks."

"My pleasure," she assured him, smiling as she leaned down to press a sisterly kiss to his forehead. "Call my cell if you need me."

"Okay."

"Okay," Mac repeated. She was almost out his door when he called her name. She turned around to find him in a relaxed plank position, looking at her with the most adorably confused expression on his face. "What do you need, Spence?"

"Does your stomach flip-flop when you kiss Charlie?"

Mac smiled and nodded. "Yeah."

"It means that I might love Sara, huh?"

"That's what it means for me, yeah."

He sighed and nodded as he dropped back onto the bed. "Yeah. That's what I thought. Have you told Charlie that you love her?"

"Not in so many words," Mac said, shaking her head.

"You should," he told her, yawning as he pulled his blanket up over his legs. "She's totally in love with you."

"I know," Mac murmured. She ran a hand through her hair as she watched him fall quickly asleep. She couldn't keep from grinning as she made her way downstairs and locked up after herself, and she was still smiling as she made her way through the snow to the driveway.

"You look happy," Charlie greeted Mackayla when she got back into the car.

"Spencer is in love," Mac shared.

"Not with you, I hope," Charlie quipped. "I would hate to have to go in there and beat his drunk ass for trying to take you away from me."

Mac laughed and shook her head. "Not with me."

"Well, good. Sara seems like a nice girl."

"She does," Mac said as she pulled out of their driveway and turned toward Charlotte's house. The falling snowflakes illuminated by the car's halogen headlights seemed to race toward the windshield, and Mac was glad that they would soon be off the roads in case the storm got worse. She sighed with relief as she pulled into Charlotte's driveway, the sight of the colored lights the brunette had strung along her roofline welcoming them home with a festive glow, and smiled at her as she pulled the keys from the ignition. "I still can't believe you got up on that roof to hang Christmas lights."

Charlie shrugged and opened her car door. "The hooks were already there. It took me ten minutes to do," she said as she climbed out of the car. She met Mackayla at the end of the walkway to her front porch and smiled as she slipped her hand into the crook of the blonde's arm. "I've never had a house I could decorate like this before. It was fun."

"Well, it looks great," Mac said. She looked up at the lights as she covered Charlotte's hand on her arm with her own. A soft smile tweaked her lips as she stopped in the middle of the path and turned to face the brunette, and she swallowed thickly as she lifted her right hand to tenderly cradle Charlotte's jaw. Her eyes danced over Charlotte's face before dropping to focus on her mouth, and she sighed as she leaned in and captured her lips in a slow, sweet kiss. The chill of the night air and the cold bite of the falling snow disappeared as she felt Charlotte's arms snake around her neck and pull her in closer. The moment was perfect, and her heart skipped a beat as she realized that here, now, was the time to say the three words she had been holding back from the moment she had admitted that this was what she wanted.

Charlie hummed softly when their kiss broke, and she smiled up at Mackayla as she opened her eyes. "Hi."

"Hi," Mac murmured. She licked her lips and, heart racing, added softly, "I love you."

Charlie beamed and leaned in to brush a feather-soft kiss across the blonde's lips. "I love you too." Her heart felt like it was going to burst with happiness when she pulled back to look at Mackayla. She had hoped that the affection she had seen shining in Mackayla's eyes was love, but to have that hope confirmed was the best Christmas present she had ever received, and she was determined to find a way to keep it. She would do whatever it took to be able to stay in New Hampshire with Mackayla. She laughed and crushed her mouth against Mackayla's, impervious to the snow and the cold as she kissed the blonde. "I love you too," she repeated, her tone soft and awestruck.

Mac smiled and brushed a quick kiss across Charlotte's lips. "Let's go inside, sweetie."

An expectant shiver rolled down Charlie's spine, and she nodded. "Okay."

Chapter 33

"I love you." Now that the words had been said, there was no holding them back, and Charlie murmured them repeatedly like a prayer as she slowly kissed her way down the regal column of Mackayla's throat.

Mac whimpered as Charlotte's teeth scraped lightly over her collarbone, and rolled her hips up into the brunette as a nimble tongue flickered across the hollow at the base of her throat. The feeling of Charlotte's breath landing in hot waves against her skin made Mac squirm, and a low groan rumbled in the back of her throat as a firm hand swept up over her side to palm her left breast, squeezing and rolling it in time with each gentle press of Charlotte's lips. Every touch radiated love, filling her with a feeling of contentment and warmth, and she was helpless but to submit to it.

"Charlotte," Mac moaned as the brunette's lips ghosted across the plane of her chest, the tip of Charlotte's tongue tracing a fine line down her sternum. The cool air of the room made goosebumps erupt in the wake of the sensual touch, and she arched up into it as Charlotte began kissing a meandering path around her right breast.

Determined to worship every inch of Mackayla's glorious body, Charlie took her time kissing her way around the blonde's breasts. It would have been easy to rush and bring her to climax, but that wasn't what Charlie wanted. She wanted to touch. To taste. To commit to memory every sound that fell from Mackayla's lips as she made love to her. To truly savor the taste of the blonde's skin against her tongue. She had been content to go along at Mackayla's pace, to let her take the lead in every facet of their burgeoning relationship, but no longer. Now that she was free to say exactly how she felt, she was filled with an almost primal need to lay claim to her prize with reverent touches, lingering kisses, and quiet words of affection. "I love you," she breathed as she brushed the lightest kiss across a straining nipple.

A low moan rumbled in the back of Mac's throat at the feeling of Charlotte's tongue sweeping boldly around her nipple, and she tangled her right hand in the brunette's hair, holding Charlotte close as her mouth enveloped her. Gentle sucks accompanied by teasing, perfect flicks of the brunette's tongue sent sparks of desire coursing through her body, and Mac let loose a shuddering breath when Charlotte switched her attentions to her other breast.

Even if Charlotte hadn't been repeating "I love you" over and over again, Mac would have felt those words in each brush of the brunette's lips against her skin. They were plain in every lick, every kiss, every gentle teasing suck that stoked the slowing building fire of need inside her hotter and hotter. They had made love many times in the weeks since she had appeared on the brunette's porch, but none of those other encounters had been quite this tender. Charlotte's touch was unapologetically reverent, like the brunette had been waiting to truly make love to her like this, and Mac felt herself respond more to that adoration than she did to the soft kisses being rained upon her skin. Her heart swelled with every press of lips against her, until it felt like it was about to burst from her chest.

Though Charlie could have gladly stayed where she was and lovingly attended to Mackayla's breasts for hours, she acquiesced to the light press of the hand against the top of her head that wordlessly asked for more and began kissing her way slowly down Mackayla's stomach. Her lips dragged lightly over the defined ridge of Mackayla's abdominals as she made her way down the blonde's body, and she whimpered at the scent of Mackayla's arousal as she peppered a string of light kisses down the line where her leg and torso hinged. "So beautiful," she murmured as she settled herself between open, welcoming thighs. Shell pink lips glistening with desire called her forward, and she licked her lips quickly as she leaned in to press that first intimate kiss to Mackayla's half-hooded clit.

The feeling of Mackayla's hips lifting off the bed, searching for more contact than that brief kiss made Charlie smile, and she sighed as she began painting the lightest kitten licks across her clit, coaxing the sensitive nub from its hiding place. "Stunning," she breathed as she felt it swell against her tongue, and she lifted her eyes to look up the long, lean length of Mackayla's torso to watch the blonde's face as she surrounded the bud with her lips and began sucking lightly against it. The sight of Mackayla's mouth falling open in a silent scream sent a jolt of arousal crashing wetly between her own thighs, and she let her eyes flutter shut as she lost herself in the taste, the feeling, the scent of Mackayla's body.

She loved looking into Mackayla's eyes as she brought her to orgasm, but more than anything else in the world, she loved this. The breathy cries that would escape Mackayla when she flicked her tongue over her just so. The rich, rumbling moans that would reverberate in the back of the blonde's throat when she pushed as deep inside her as she could. She loved the feeling of strong fingers fisting her hair, pulling her in closer even as Mackayla's hips rocked away from her because the sensation was just too much.

"Oh my god," Mac groaned, her back arching wantonly off the mattress as Charlotte's tongue began sliding slowly around her clit, teasing the bud with light then firm touches that left her guessing, always wondering what would come next. The heat that had begun to build low in her hips while Charlotte had played at her breasts was now spreading through her body, down her legs and up into her chest. Her pulse pounded violently in her ears as she was worked higher and higher, only to be brought back down again with gentled kisses and light breaths blown across her, holding her at that point of absolute arousal before Charlotte sent her soaring again. Release hit her hard and completely by surprise when an unexpectedly firm swipe of Charlotte's tongue over her clit, which was followed by the ghost of an "I love you" that she could feel in her very soul, sent her flying over the precipice of ecstasy.

Charlotte bit her lip as a smaller sympathetic orgasm rolled through her at the sight of Mackayla coming undone, and she swallowed thickly as she climbed back up her body to press a deep, lingering kiss to her lips. Strong arms wrapped around Charlie's waist, holding her close as she kissed Mackayla back to reality, and she smiled when dark blue eyes fluttered open to look at her. "Mmm, hi," she murmured.

Mac smiled and reached up to run a gentle hand over the curve of Charlotte's jaw. "Hi. That was…wow."

"I love you," Charlie whispered, brushing another soft kiss across Mackayla's lips.

"Love you too," Mac breathed, her face scrunching up as she tried to fight back a yawn. It had been a long day, and now that her body was so completely sated and relaxed, she was having a hard time keeping her eyes open.

Charlie smiled at the sight of Mackayla fighting off sleep and kissed her again tenderly. "Just go to sleep, my love."

"Nnn, you," Mac mumbled, shaking her head.

"Later, Mackayla," Charlie assured her. "We have all the time in the world."

Mac bit her lip to keep from yawning again and stared imploringly up at Charlotte. There were times when it felt like Charlotte's words were true. That they did, in fact, have all the time in the world. And then there were times like this, when her heart was racing a little too fast, reminding her of the fact that seconds were ticking away into weeks without her even noticing. "Do we?"

"Absolutely," Charlie murmured softly, her gaze steady and her tone unflinchingly confident. She sighed and lifted herself up to press a reassuring kiss to the blonde's brow. "Sleep, sweetie," she murmured against the smooth skin as she felt Mackayla yawn. To further entice Mackayla to give in to her exhaustion, Charlie slid back down her body and laid her head on the plane of the blonde's chest. She could hear Mackayla's heartbeat slowing as she reached down and pulled the comforter up to ward off the chill that had begun to seep into her skin now that the heat of their lovemaking had subsided, and she hummed softly as she felt Mackayla's hold on her waist loosen by a fraction, telling her that the blonde had fallen asleep.

Chapter 34

It was well after ten o'clock the following morning when Mac managed to force her eyes open. She smiled as she saw Charlotte lying on her stomach beside her, toned arms tucked up under the pillow and the blankets bunched just below her shoulders to ward off the winter chill that had settled in the house overnight despite the best efforts of the heater that was quietly humming in the background. Rays of bright winter sunlight shone around the edges of the heavy curtains covering the windows, burning golden streaks across the foot of the bed. Mac bit her lip as she carefully stretched, easing the sleep from her limbs, and she sighed softly as she relaxed and rolled onto her side to really look at Charlotte.

Hair tousled from sleep, sculpted shoulders peeking out from the wrinkled sheets, and toned arms folded beneath her pillow, Charlotte was an absolute vision, and Mac felt her heart skip a beat as she looked at her. She was continuously amazed by how much her life had changed in the last few months, and every single one of those changes centered on the determined, brilliant, beautiful woman beside her. She had been content before Charlotte arrived in Hampton. She had her friends, a job she loved, and the writing career she had always dreamt of that was just taking off. But she did not have this intimacy. This feeling of being completely adored. Cherished. She didn't have the security that came from having someone who loved her and craved nothing more than her love in return.

Being happy, truly happy, was still something Mac was getting used to feeling, and what made it so hard to accept was the fact that she was also painfully vulnerable because of it. She knew that everything she had found with Charlotte was, at this point, temporary. When June rolled around, decisions would have to be made. Big decisions. Life-altering, gigantic decisions. And she was terrified of what those decisions might bring. Charlotte spoke of forever the night before, and she dearly hoped that the brunette was right, but a small part of herself was just waiting for the axe to fall. For the curtain to close on their relationship and for Charlotte to walk away again, leaving her to find some way to survive the fallout. She was positively certain that she wouldn't be able to, and the thought of that absolutely terrified her.

Charlotte hummed softly in her sleep, drawing Mac's attention from the downward spiral of her thoughts, and Mac swallowed thickly as she forced herself to stop thinking of the *what ifs* that haunted her. It wasn't easy, but she tried to force herself to focus on the present. Because here, now, Charlotte was in bed beside her, and she could still feel the ghost of the brunette's lips and her whispered declarations of love on her skin.

She sighed and leaned in to press a gentle kiss to the swell of Charlotte's shoulder and, like the night that she had been unable to outrun her thoughts and had ended up on Charlotte's front porch, her world stopped spinning wildly out of control the moment she touched the brunette.

Eyes closed, she pressed kiss after kiss to Charlotte's shoulders and upper back, each one a silent prayer that asked for this happiness to not be taken from her. The thought of a future without Charlotte by her side was frightening, but feeling the warmth of the brunette's skin against her own calmed those riotous emotions. Here, she was happy. Charlotte was her anchor, keeping her grounded in the moment so that she didn't get lost in her own head.

The quiet purr that rumbled in Charlotte's throat as the brunette came awake made Mac smile, and she pressed a lingering kiss to the nape of her neck. "Good morning."

"Mmm, good morning to you," Charlie murmured, licking her lips as she rolled onto her back. She hummed softly under her breath as she felt Mackayla's hand slide across her stomach, strong fingers wrapping possessively around her hip, and she smiled as the blonde's lips descended lightly upon her own.

It was the perfect way to wake up on a cold winter's morning, wrapped in the arms of a beautiful woman and trading languid kisses that simmered with the promise of something more. Charlie groaned softly as Mackayla's tongue flicked imploringly across her lips, and she wasted no time opening her mouth so that their tongues could stroke slowly together. She reached up and cradled Mackayla's jaw in her palm as their kisses deepened, needing to feel as connected to the blonde as possible as her body began to pulse with need.

Mac smiled against Charlotte's lips as she released her hold on the brunette's hip and began drawing light, barely there, swooping, swirling lines over her torso. Her smile grew wider as Charlotte squirmed away from her touch when her fingers danced over a particularly ticklish spot, and she moaned softly as she felt Charlotte relax again as she moved on, the brunette's legs shifting ever so slightly beneath the blankets as she unconsciously opened herself for more.

Every gentle circuit of Mackayla's fingers over her skin sent tiny sparks of desire shooting through Charlie's body, and she moaned as the blonde's wandering touch began slowly spiraling around her right breast. Around and around, lightly touching, nails barely scratching. Higher and higher, each circuit a little smaller, a little tighter, until a single fingertip trailed around a dark areola.

The light touch was maddeningly erotic, and Charlie whimpered when Mackayla's thumb finally began stroking heavily back and forth across her nipple.

"So beautiful," Mac purred, smiling as she palmed the breast she had been playing with and gave it a gentle squeeze.

Charlie groaned as she arched her chest into the blonde's hand. "Mackayla."

The need evident in Charlotte's voice sent a wave of desire crashing wetly between Mac's legs, and she squeezed the brunette's breast again. "I love you," she breathed. She had felt a thrill run through her every time Charlotte had whispered those words the night before, and she wanted to make sure that the brunette knew that she was loved as well. "I love you," she repeated, giving Charlotte's breast one last squeeze before she moved on, slowly stroking her hand up and down Charlotte's abs.

"Love you," Charlie murmured, moaning softly as Mackayla's hand slipped lower to skate back and forth across her upper thigh. She rolled her left leg out wider, wordlessly offering all that she was, and her breath hitched in her throat as Mackayla's hand covered her. The hold was firm. Possessive. And just the thought of Mackayla claiming her like that sent a delicious tremor of anticipation rolling down her spine. "So much," she whimpered when Mackayla's hold tightened, the blonde's knuckle pressing perfectly against her clit.

Mac hummed softly and rocked her hand against Charlotte's center, her middle finger slipping deeper into the hot, slick desire that waited for her. Pride that she was the reason Charlotte was so aroused rocketed through her, and she bit her lip as she curled her finger to lightly tease the brunette's opening with just the barest amount of pressure. The idea to tease Charlotte like the brunette had done to her the night before was tempting, but the sight of Charlotte fisting the pillow beneath her head as her hips rocked up hard, searching for more, was too enticing to resist.

The hand between her legs shifted, and Charlie moaned as Mackayla pushed two fingers inside her. Long, steady thrusts made her writhe, and she opened herself further, trying to take Mackayla as deep as she could, wanting to feel as connected to her as it was possible to be.

Mac purposefully kept the heel of her hand away from Charlotte's clit on every thrust, wanting to see her come, but not wanting it to be too soon, and she hummed as she dropped her lips to Charlotte's throat. She smiled as she felt the rough rumble of Charlotte's "Oh god," against her lips, and sucked lightly over the sensitive spot beneath the hinge of Charlotte's jaw that never failed to make her squirm. "I love you," she whispered against the pinked flesh, punctuating the quiet promise with a teasing flick of her tongue. "Mine," she added softly, both wanting to lay claim to Charlotte and knowing how much the brunette loved being claimed.

Charlie's eyes rolled back in her head as her entire body reacted to Mackayla's words, and she nodded. "Yours, Mackayla. All yours."

"All mine," Mac repeated softly, her voice tinged with absolute wonder, like she still couldn't believe that Charlotte was truly hers. She licked her lips and swooped higher to claim Charlotte's mouth in a deep, probing kiss as she increased the force of her thrusts so that the heel of her hand slapped against the brunette's clit.

Charlie groaned as Mackayla's tongue plunged hotly inside her mouth, stroking heavily against her own. The hand between her legs pumped faster, harder, and she fisted the pillow beneath her head as she met each thrust eagerly. "Jesus," she gasped as Mackayla's hand landed forcefully against her, sending bolts of pleasure coursing through her body. "Mackayla."

"Charlotte," Mac murmured, nuzzling the brunette's cheek. "My Charlotte." She smiled as she felt the strong muscles around her fingers flutter. "My Charlotte," she repeated, brushing her lips over the brunette's ear. She was answered with a deep, keening moan, and the walls around her fingers clamped down hard, holding her in place as Charlotte came. Once the initial wave of Charlotte's orgasm passed, she stroked her through the length of her release, whispering quiet 'I love you's against the shell of her ear. When Charlotte eventually stopped trembling, Mac brushed an adoring kiss across her cheek as she slowly pulled out of her.

"Oh my god," Charlie whispered, smiling as Mackayla brushed a soft kiss across her lips. "Baby."

Mac smiled. "I love you."

"Mmm, love you too," Charlie murmured. She sighed contentedly as Mackayla kissed her again, slow and sweet and languid, like the blonde had when she had first woken up. It was the kind of kiss that made her want to never get out of bed, because everything about the moment was too perfect to give up. Her stomach, however, had other plans, and made itself known with a loud growl.

"I think somebody's hungry," Mac teased.

"Not me," Charlie muttered, lifting her head to claim Mackayla's lips in another kiss. Her stomach protested her argument with another loud growl, and she sighed as Mackayla laughed.

"Can I make you breakfast in bed?"

"Will we eat it naked?" Charlie countered.

Mac grinned. "Of course. Although, at some point today I will have to get dressed and take Spencer back his car," she added reasonably.

Charlie pouted playfully and shook her head. "If he wants it, he can drive your car over and trade."

"You just want to keep me naked and in your bed," Mac chuckled, dropping a quick kiss to the point of Charlotte's nose.

Charlie arched a brow challengingly and grinned. "Can you blame me?"

Mac smiled. "Not at all, beautiful. Having you in bed with me is perhaps my second favorite thing in the world."

"Only second?"

Mac nodded. "Yup."

"So what's your first favorite thing?"

Mac smiled sheepishly, knowing that her answer was ridiculously cheesy and sappy and over-the-top romantic, and shrugged. "Just having you here with me, Charlotte. Clothes off or on, in bed or out doing stuff, I just like having you here with me and knowing that you're mine."

"All yours," Charlie confirmed as she rolled into Mackayla and forced her onto her back. She smiled down into the blue eyes she so loved to drown in and dragged the pad of her index finger down over Mackayla's lips. "Forever yours," she promised.

Mac pressed a kiss to the finger against her lips and smiled, willing herself to believe that the forever Charlotte promised was actually attainable.

Chapter 35

Mac eyed Charlotte's parents' home with no small amount of trepidation, and sighed. She knew why she had agreed to spend Christmas with Charlotte and her family–it was something she could do for Charlotte now that she hadn't been able to do for the brunette when they were younger–and, when she had agreed to join Charlotte for the holiday, the idea hadn't bothered her at all. Spencer was back in California for the week with his family, so it made sense for her to go home with Charlotte. But now that she was here, standing on a wide red brick walkway in front of the Bennett home in Lexington, Massachusetts, staring up at the impressive two story French colonial that was bedecked with white Christmas lights and festive holiday wreaths, she was having second thoughts.

The night before, Christmas Eve, had been picture-perfect. Just she and Charlotte, exchanging heartfelt, inexpensive gifts and making love in front of the fire. Christmas Day, however, judging by the cars crammed into the long, sweeping driveway that fronted the Bennett home, was going to be something much different.

Finding Mackayla's nervousness about meeting her family utterly adorable, Charlie smiled and lifted herself up onto her tiptoes to press a reassuring kiss to the corner of the blonde's lips. "Don't worry, sweetheart. They are going to love you."

"Is it obvious?" Mac asked, looking down at Charlotte, who was beaming back at her. Her heart, which had been racing wildly out of control, slowed as she stared into the brunette's bright green eyes, and she sighed. "I'm sorry."

Charlie gave the lapels of Mackayla's coat an affectionate tug and shook her head. "You have nothing to be sorry about. I, however, would like to apologize in advance for anything my family says or does."

"Not exactly reassuring," Mac pointed out, chuckling nervously as she smoothed her hands over her jeans. The Bennetts did a much more casual Christmas than her family used to. "How bad will it be?"

"Eh," Charlie hedged, shrugging. She grinned at the way Mackayla's face went just a shade whiter and shook her head. "It shouldn't be too bad. Just try and ignore ninety percent of the things that my grandfather says, and you should be good."

"Charlie Bennett, you better not be making out on my front porch!" Charlie's dad hollered as he opened the front door in a pair of faded 501s and a red and black Wesleyan Dad sweatshirt. "I don't have the Super Soaker ready!"

Charlie looked up at her father and grinned. "You haven't turned the Super Soaker onto one of my dates since I was in high school and, let's be honest, Bobby was a dick. Making out isn't a bad idea, though," she added, winking conspiratorially at Mackayla. "Whattaya say?"

"Oh my god," Mac muttered.

"Get inside, you two, before you catch cold," Charlie's dad laughed, shaking his head as he beckoned the women inside.

The sight of Charlotte being enveloped in her dad's arms as she entered the house made Mac's heart ache just a little for what she had lost, but the brunette's delighted laughter made up for it. Charlotte was the spitting image of her father, from her rich chestnut-colored hair, though his was liberally flecked with gray, to her lean build and bright green eyes, and Mac smiled at the sight of them together. She was glad that Charlotte still had this connection—even if she no longer had it herself.

Charlie's father gave the brunette one last squeeze and smiled as he turned to Mac. "Hello, Mackayla."

"Mr. Bennett," Mac murmured politely, her posture straightening by a fraction.

"Jim, please," he said, smiling warmly as he reached out and pulled Mac into a light embrace. "I'm glad you could make it. I would like to apologize now for anything my wife does or says today."

Mac laughed in spite of her nervousness as she pulled away from him. "Thank you, sir," she murmured, biting her lip.

"Is Charlie here?" a new voice rang out, and by the way both Charlotte and her father rolled their eyes, Mac figured it belonged to the brunette's mother.

'I'm sorry,' Jim mouthed to Mac as his wife swooped into the foyer like a mini-tornado. Charlotte got her looks from her father, but the brunette quite clearly got her petite stature from her mother.

"Mackayla!" Charlie's mom enthused, smiling warmly as she strode past her daughter without a glance to pull Mac into a fierce embrace. "Welcome!"

Mac swallowed thickly and looked at Charlotte, who was just biting her lip and smiling at her. "Um, hello, Mrs. Bennett."

"Nancy," Charlie's mother corrected, giving Mackayla an affectionate pat on the back before she let go of the adorably nervous blonde. "It's so nice to meet you."

"You too," Mac murmured.

"Hello, mom," Charlie drawled.

"Yeah, hi," Nancy said, laughing at the exasperated look her daughter gave her. She sighed softly as she pulled her youngest into a tight hug and whispered, "I'm glad you got her to come with you."

"Me too," Charlie replied softly.

"Right, well," Nancy said as she released her daughter and turned to address both her and Mackayla, "your brothers and their families are in the family room playing video games, and snack-type food is in the kitchen if you're hungry. Everyone else should be here shortly, and then we can get started."

"What are they playing?" Charlie asked, eyes sparking with a competitive look Mackayla easily recognized.

"Mario Kart," Jim answered, shaking his head. "And don't play Will. He's good."

"He's six," Charlie retorted, laughing as she made her way over to Mackayla and looped an affectionate arm around the blonde's waist. She smiled at the way Mackayla leaned into her and gave her a gentle squeeze as she teased her father, "You can't beat a six-year-old?"

"Yeah, well, he has the whole flinging turtle shell thing down. Kid is vicious," Jim quipped, shaking his head.

Mac laughed and draped her arm over Charlotte's shoulders. She was still nervous, but the gregarious nature of Charlotte's parents was slowly dispelling those nerves.

"You two are so cute," Nancy cooed, clapping her hands excitingly.

"She is," Charlie agreed, smiling up at Mackayla. "Absolutely beautiful," she whispered, her smile widening at the light blush that tinted Mackayla's cheeks.

"Don't make me get the Super Soaker out, you two," Jim chuckled, waving a hand at his daughter and her girlfriend as he turned back toward the family room.

Charlie gave Mackayla's waist a gentle tug to spur the blonde into motion before she dropped her arm and started down the hall after her father. "You okay?" she asked softly.

"I'm fine," Mac assured her, reaching for Charlotte's hand. She wasn't quite ready for any displays of affection that were more dramatic than a simple hand hold, but, much like Charlotte at the Blake holiday party, she was determined to make an effort to do something that was just a little outside her comfort zone. "So, who's Bobby?"

Jim chuckled quietly and Charlie rolled her eyes. "An utterly failed experiment at being straight," she said, shaking her head. "He was the ultimate straight-girl prize: captain of the football team, student body president, the whole nine yards."

"Tell her the best part," Jim prodded, grinning.

Mac cringed and arched a questioning brow at Charlotte. "Do I want to know?"

"We, ah–" Charlie glared at her father, "–broke up when he caught me making out with the head cheerleader during one of his games."

"Oh." Mac nodded, pieces of this story coming back to her. "I remember you telling me something about that when we were in school."

"He started crying," Jim chortled, shaking his head. "And then went out and threw three interceptions to lose the game. I never did like that kid."

"Hence, the Super Soaker," Charlie added dryly.

"Exactly, baby girl," Jim laughed, winking at Charlie as they walked into the family room.

Mac looked around the room, her stomach fluttering nervously. All three of Charlotte's older brothers and their families were spread out amongst the floor and couches. Six adults, seven kids. The women were sitting on the sofa chatting, two of them had a baby cradled to her chest, and two of Charlotte's brothers and two of the kids had little steering wheels in their hands and were yelling at each other and the television as they played Mario Kart.

It was chaos personified, and Mac took a deep breath as she let the scene sink in.

"Aunt Charlie!"

Mac tried to see which of the children had yelled, but the announcement of their arrival had all the kids running toward them, yelling for their aunt. She bit her lip as she watched Charlotte greet the group *en masse* before singling out each kid for a hug, and she smiled at the sight of the brunette picking one of the little boys up in a tight hug and spinning him around as he squealed excitedly.

"Sis!" Charlotte's older brothers yelled, and then the brunette was screaming as they playfully descended upon her like their children had moments before, only now she was the one being squeezed and lifted into the air and spun around. All four of the Bennett children were nearly identical in their coloring, the only real difference between them all was that the boys were all about a foot taller than their sister.

"Oh my god, you jerks!" Charlie gasped, laughing as they finally put her down.

Mac laughed and shook her head.

"And you must be Mackayla," the eldest older brother drawled, grinning at the blonde.

"Behave, Ryan," Charlie mock-threatened as she moved back to Mackayla's side.

Mac nodded and held out her hand. "I am, but you can call me Mac."

The guys grinned and nodded, and shook her hand in turn as they introduced themselves and pointed out their wives and children. It was a lot to keep track of and Mac only managed to remember Charlotte's brothers' names–Ryan, Scott, and Zach– because of all the stories she'd been told about the antics the siblings had gotten up to when they were kids. Thankfully, there seemed to be no real pressure to do more than just smile and wave, and she felt herself breathing easier as she sat down on the end of one of the couches and Charlotte took the seat beside her. Her nerves eased as Charlotte leaned into her and she let out a quiet breath as she felt the brunette's hand settle upon her thigh.

"I'm sorry about them," Charlie murmured, biting her lip as she leaned her head onto Mackayla's shoulder.

"Why?" Mac smiled at the way Charlotte's hand had begun to stroke slowly up and down her leg and dared to press a quick kiss to the brunette's forehead.

"I know we can be a little overwhelming when we're all together."

Mac shrugged because, yeah, it was a little overwhelming– but mostly because she had never attended another family's holiday celebrations as "the girlfriend" and she was terrified of being deemed not worthy of Charlotte's love. "Not really. It's nice. You're lucky to have this."

"I know." Charlie nodded.

"Charlie, Mac, you're up," Scott announced with a grin as he and Zach held Wii steering wheels out for them. "Let's see what you got."

Charlie groaned and looked up at Mackayla. "You wanna play?"

Mac smiled and nodded. "Why not?"

Chapter 36

"And, last but not least, we have one for Mac," Jim announced, pulling a brightly wrapped package out from behind the tree.

Mac bit her lip as she took the box from Charlotte's father. Half the box was wrapped in the same metallic Santa-themed paper as the rest of the presents that had been handed out so far, while the other half was wrapped in a balloon print that was clearly a birthday print. While she knew that Charlotte was working on some top-secret plans for her birthday the following week, she was surprised that the brunette's parents had been told of the upcoming date. "I wasn't…"

"We know," Nancy assured her with a small smile. She waved a hand excitedly at the box and said, "You're the first girl Charlotte has brought home for the holidays–we had get you something. Now, go on. Open it."

"Yeah, Mac!" Charlie's brothers echoed laughingly. "Open it!"

Charlie could tell that her brothers were biting back innuendo-filled comments because of the kids who were huddled in the center of the room playing with their new toys, and she placed a discreet hand at the small of Mackayla's back. "You may want to get on that, Thomas, before my brothers let loose with the French Maid outfit and lingerie jokes," she murmured against the blonde's ear. "Even with the kids around, they can only hold back for so long."

"Oh god," Mac muttered, glancing nervously at Charlotte.

The urge to lean in and kiss Mackayla was nearly overwhelming, she was just so goddamn cute when she was flustered like this, and Charlie chuckled as she shook her head. "You're fine."

"Says you," Mac whispered, taking a deep breath as she worked her finger under a seam of the wrapping paper and began to tear it open.

"Why is her present wrapped different?" Hannah, Scott's eldest, asked.

"Because her birthday is next week," Charlie explained with a smile.

All of the kids perked up at the word 'birthday' and turned with excited smiles to Mac. "How old are you going to be?" they parroted.

Mac looked up from unwrapping her present and smiled. "Thirty."

"That's old," Hannah said, sounding simultaneously impressed and horrified.

"It is," Charlie agreed, laughing as she playfully tickled her fingers up Mackayla's back.

"You'll be there soon enough," Mac retorted as she set the last of the wrapping paper from her present aside. The lid of the plain white box gave no hint of what might be inside, and she took a deep breath as she opened the lid. She exhaled quietly as she saw gift cards from iTunes and Amazon sitting on top of a black North Face hoodie, and looked up to smile at Charlotte's parents. "This is awesome. Thank you."

"Our pleasure," Jim assured her with a pleased grin. He cleared his throat softly and looked at his wife. "Dinner?"

Mac frowned at looked at her watch. It was only two thirty in the afternoon.

"Everything's ready," Nancy answered.

"We do what my mother likes to call a lun-din," Charlie explained as everyone started getting to their feet. "Kinda like brunch, but for lunch-dinner, instead. This way everyone will be able to get home before it gets too late."

"I see," Mac murmured. She groaned softly as she pushed herself up off the floor and did some quick stretches to work out the kinks that had formed while watching everybody open presents. Charlotte's parents had gone out of their way to spoil their kids and grandkids, and the unwrapping process had taken a while.

Before Charlie could respond, her eldest brother swooped in and looped a playful arm around Mackayla's neck. "Sis, I'm just gonna steal your girl for a bit," he said. "Cool?"

"I don't think so," Charlie retorted, reaching for Mackayla's hand.

"Possessive little thing, isn't she?" Ryan teased, winking at Mac.

"Just a bit," Charlie allowed with a grin. "But, really, can you blame me for not wanting to let you guys at her without some interference?"

"You make us out to be monsters," Scott chimed in as he and Zach joined the group. "We were just going to give her the big brother talk, geez. She's the first girl you've ever brought home. We've been waiting for this moment for *years*!"

Mac smiled and gracefully slipped out from under Ryan's arm. "Ah, so that's what this is," she drawled, nodding as Charlotte leaned into her. She sighed and looked down at the petite brunette cradled against her side, and licked her lips as she looked up at Charlotte's brothers. "I know exactly how lucky I am to have her, and I promise I will treat her right."

"Works for me," Ryan said, clapping his hands as if to seal the deal.

"Don't fuck this one up," Zach told Charlie, pointing a playfully stern finger at her. "She's hot, smart, and kicks ass at Mario Kart."

"The ultimate trifecta," Charlie muttered, rolling her eyes.

Scott laughed and nodded. "Exactly. Or we could go with: way outside your league and amazing with the kids," he said, referring to the way Mackayla had sat on the floor all morning with one or another of the younger kids on her lap, "playing" video games with them so they didn't crash into the walls in perpetuity or start running the course backwards.

Mac bit her lip as she felt a light blush begin to creep up her neck. "I don't think—"

But she was interrupted by Nancy who had walked up on the group when Scott was talking about kids. "Do you want children, Mackayla?" she asked, smiling. "Because there is a very well respected sperm bank in Boston that—"

"Mom!" Charlie groaned. "No!"

"What? I've sent you countless links to their webpage, Charlie," Nancy said, waving her youngest off. "I want more grandbabies. They're the reward I get for not killing you four when you were teenagers."

Mac laughed and squeezed Charlotte's hand gently, assuring her without words that everything was fine. "I would like to have kids someday, yes."

"Excellent," Nancy chirped, beaming. She turned to Charlie and added in a hushed whisper that all of them could hear perfectly, "I like her. Don't mess this one up."

Charlie rolled her eyes and nodded. "Yes, ma'am."

"Good," Nancy drawled, winking at Mackayla. "Now, go eat. Boys, you need to supervise your children in the kitchen because if mashed potatoes end up on the ceiling *again* this year, *you* will be the ones cleaning it off."

"Yes, ma'am," Ryan, Scott, and Zach grumbled as they, as one, turned and headed for the kitchen.

"You two get to sit at the adult table," Nancy told Charlie and Mac.

Mac nodded. "Okay."

"Can't we go sit with the kids too?" Charlie asked. She usually hung out in the kitchen with her brothers because it was a lot more fun than sitting at the dining room table with her grandparents, aunts, and uncles.

"Nope," Nancy said, shaking her head.

"Damn," Charlie grumbled. She looked up at Mackayla and smiled. "You hungry?"

"Famished."

"Excellent. Grab your plates, and food is in the kitchen," Nancy said, patting Mac's arm affectionately.

The sound of a plate shattering in the kitchen had them all turning to look in that general direction, and Mac bit the inside of her cheek to keep from laughing as a chorus of "Not me!"s echoed from the room.

Nancy sighed and shook her head. "I didn't know he moved back in," she muttered, looking side-eyed at Charlie for a minute before she went to inspect the damage.

Mac looked at Charlotte as they made their way to the dining room for their plates and asked, "What was your mom talking about?"

"My mom used to joke that we had a ghost named Not Me who lived here because every time something happened and she asked us who did it, we all said 'not me'," Charlie explained as she picked up a plate and handed it to Mackayla.

"Ah," Mac murmured, nodding as she followed the brunette into the kitchen.

Once their plates were filled, they made their way back to the dining room, and Charlie bit her lip to hold back a groan as she saw that the only chairs left were across from her grandparents. She loved them dearly, of course, but she had been hoping to keep her grandfather away from Mackayla this time around. To let the blonde get her sea legs under her, so to speak, with the family before she was subjected to the unpredictable whims of her grandfather.

"Charlotte!" he boomed as she set her plate down across from him.

Charlie smiled and nodded. "Hey, grandpa."

"Are you still in New Hampshire?" he asked as Charlie and Mac took their seats across from him.

"Yep," Charlie said, glancing at Mackayla who was smoothing her napkin over her lap.

"You too?" he asked Mac.

Mac nodded. "I am. I teach at the university where Charlotte is guest lecturing this year," she answered politely.

"What do you teach?" Charlie's grandmother asked.

"Creative writing," Mac said as she split a roll in two and began to butter it.

"Do you also write, or do you just teach it?" Charlie's grandfather asked.

"I write as well, yes," Mac answered, glancing over at Charlotte. The brunette was eyeing her grandfather with a speculative eye as she stabbed at her salad.

"What do you write?"

Mac bit her lip and considered the different ways she could answer his question before finally deciding on, "Procedural crime fiction."

"Are there any lesbians in it?" he asked, leaning forward interestedly.

"Robert!" Charlie's grandmother admonished, slapping his arm.

Mac laughed in spite of the situation and nodded. "Yes, sir."

"I bet that would be a good book. I haven't read any books with lesbians in them, but I like watching the videos on the internet."

"OH MY GOD!" Charlie laughed, staring at her grandfather. "Grandpa!"

"Robert!" Charlie's grandmother scolded, shaking her head and looking like a flabbergasted parent whose toddler just said something outrageous. "My god, I can't take you anywhere anymore!"

He just laughed, shoulders bouncing with his own amusement, obviously pleased with the reaction he got from everyone. "What?"

Charlie's grandmother shook her head and smiled apologetically at Mac. "I'm sorry about him, he thinks he's funny," she muttered, rolling her eyes.

"It's fine," Mac assured her.

"See, she said it's fine," he chortled, reaching for his wine.

"It's not and you know it," Charlie's grandmother snapped.

"I'm just kidding around," he grumbled.

"Oh god, dad, what did you do now?" Nancy asked as she sat down at the head of the table beside her father.

"Why does everyone always think I'm the one who did something?" he retorted, grinning wickedly as he shoved a forkful of mashed potatoes into his mouth.

"Because you always are," Nancy pointed out rolling her eyes.

"Pot, meet kettle," Charlie muttered, earning herself a glare from her mother and a smile from her grandmother. She looked at Mackayla and grinned. "Aren't you glad you agreed to come home with me for this?"

Mac laughed and nodded. "Strangely enough, I am."

"I like this one," Charlie's grandfather said, grinning as he pointed his fork at Mac. "You should hang onto her."

"I intend to, grandpa," Charlie assured him.

"So does that mean you're leaving *Sports Illustrated*?" Nancy asked, shooting her daughter a quizzical look.

Charlie sighed and glanced at Mackayla who was biting her lip nervously and looking at her with an expression that was cautiously hopeful. She hated that she didn't have a plan in place, but, thankfully, she still had time. "I have to figure out what I'm going to do," she said, her stomach twisting a little at the way Mackayla's eyes dropped.

"You're supposed to be named Senior Editor soon, right?" Charlie's grandfather asked, oblivious to the tension that had sprung up across the table from him between his granddaughter and her girlfriend.

"That's the rumor, yeah," Charlie answered him, nodding. She reached out to place a gentle hand on Mackayla's thigh, and gave it what she hoped the blonde would feel was a reassuring squeeze. "But, surprisingly enough, I actually love living in Hampton and Mackayla can't leave there, so I gotta see what I can do. I still have a semester to figure it all out, so I have time. We have time," she amended, looking at Mackayla who was chewing her lip and pushing some food around her plate as either a distraction or an attempt to not appear so invested in the conversation that was taking place.

Robert nodded, seemingly content with Charlie's answer, and turned his attention to his daughter. "So, what's this I hear from your mother about you deciding you're going to try and become a yoga instructor now?"

Relieved that the attention was off of them, Charlie put her fork down and leaned over so that her lips brushed lightly against Mackayla's ear. "Are you okay?"

Mac swallowed thickly and nodded, forcing a smile as she turned to meet Charlotte's warm, questioning gaze. She would be lying if she said that she didn't wish that the brunette's answer to her grandfather's question had been more concrete, a solid 'Yes, I am leaving the magazine'–but she was comforted by the fact that Charlotte sounded like she wanted to find a way to make things work. "Of course."

It wasn't hard for Charlie to read the lingering unease in Mackayla's eyes and she sighed as she gave the blonde's leg another squeeze. "I will find a way to make us work, sweetie," she whispered, staring imploringly at Mackayla. "I promise."

"I believe you," Mac murmured, trying and failing to sound convincing.

"When are you gals driving back?" Charlie's grandfather asked, shattering the bubble that had formed around the two women.

Charlie cleared her throat softly and looked at her grandfather. "After dinner. It's a two and a half hour drive and I don't want to be on the roads too late."

Chapter 37

Charlie eyed Mackayla thoughtfully as she toed off her shoes onto the mat in the blonde's foyer, glad to be home despite the somewhat awkward tension that had made their drive back from her parents' house. She suspected that Mackayla's introspective mood was a result of her conversation with her family about leaving *Sports Illustrated*, she just wished there was an easy way to assuage the blonde's fears about their situation. This state of limbo they were in was not ideal, she knew, but the kind of life-altering decisions and changes that would have to be made to make things permanent took time to implement.

The quiet sigh that escaped Mackayla as she hung her coat on one of the hooks mounted to the frame of a long, horizontal mirror did not escape Charlie's attention, and she bit her lip thoughtfully as she considered her options. She had reassured her multiple times at dinner and then on the drive home that she would find a way to make sure they survived whatever fallout awaited them at the end of the school year, but the murmured *uh-huhs* and *I'm fines* that she got in response made her afraid that she was dangerously close to losing Mackayla back to the walls the blonde had for so long kept erected around her heart like a fortress.

That was something she could not let happen and, knowing Mackayla as she did, Charlie knew that the best way to try and reassure the blonde with actions, rather than words. She stepped closer to Mackayla, noting that her blue eyes were tinted with shades of gray and just a little bit haunted, and hummed softly as she reached up to run the pad of her right index finger across the soft swell of Mackayla's lower lip. The feeling of Mackayla's breath cascading around her finger made Charlie's stomach clench with anticipation, and a low hum rumbled in the back of her throat as she lifted herself up to claim Mackayla's lips with her own.

A small noise of surprise escaped Mac at the feeling of Charlotte's lips against her own, but she wasted no time meeting the light caress, her hands surging forward to wrap around Charlotte's hips and drawing the brunette against her. She had expected Charlotte to confront her once they were home, demanding to know why she was so standoffish when it was perfectly understandable for the brunette to not have all the answers right now, but this almost desperate seduction was something she had not expected.

And her reaction to it was both powerful and immediate.

She groaned as Charlotte steered her backwards, and a soft whimper escaped her as her back hit the front door. The feeling of Charlotte's body pressed against her own sent expectant shivers tumbling slowly down her spine and she gasped as the brunette's hands covered her breasts, squeezing tentatively at first and then more firmly as their kisses grew deeper and more demanding.

Charlie moaned softly at the feeling of Mackayla's nipples pressing into her palms, and shifted her grip so that she could run the pads of her thumbs over them. "I want you," she husked against Mackayla's lips.

Mac nodded and tightened her hold on Charlotte's hips. "Okay."

Charlie smiled and gave Mackayla's nipples a light pinch. "Good."

More often than not, when they were together like this, they made love. Slow and sweet, with gentle kisses raining reverently down on soft skin as fingers stroked, teased, touched, and thrust with a quiet passion that brought them to slowly the edge of ecstasy before lovingly nudging them over.

This, however, was not one of those times, and Mac groaned as she felt Charlotte's hands slide down her stomach to fumble with the button of her jeans. "Jesus. Bed?"

Charlie shook her head. "Need you now," she murmured throatily, flicking her tongue over Mackayla's parted lips as she popped the button on the blonde's jeans.

"Oh god," Mac whimpered, and then she found herself unable to say another word when Charlotte's mouth claimed her own with an unrelenting passion that left her struggling to stay upright as every muscle in her body fluttered weakly in the face of the brunette's onslaught. She helped Charlotte as best she could as the brunette's hands flew over her body, tugging, pulling, removing clothing and tossing it carelessly aside, and she barely noticed the coolness of the door against her back as she leaned against it. She wanted to ask Charlotte what had brought this on as her jeans were tugged down over her hips, but the sight of the brunette kneeling before her, normally bright green eyes dark with desire as they stared at the apex of her thighs, made her forgot how to breathe, let alone speak.

The scent of Mackayla's arousal was as hypnotic as it was intoxicating, and Charlie groaned as she hastily finished pulling the blonde's jeans off and added them to the messy pile of clothes on the floor around her. "Beautiful," she hummed, using her hands to spread Mackayla's legs before her.

Soft curls glistening with desire beckoned her forward, and she licked her lips instinctively as she leaned into taste, a low moan tearing itself from her throat as Mackayla's arousal coated her tongue. She ran her hands up the backs of Mackayla's thighs and she tilted her head back as she tried to take as much of the blonde into her mouth as she could. Mackayla's hips bucked against her mouth and she groaned as she slid her right hand down to the back of the blonde's knee and lifted it up over her shoulder. With Mackayla now more open in front of her, she surged forward, pushing herself closer as she thrust her tongue into tight velvet walls.

"Fuck!" Mac grunted, reaching down and tangling her hands in Charlotte's hair for balance as the brunette began to alternate fucking her with her tongue and lapping almost roughly against her. Broad, heavy licks swept over her clit, causing her hips to buck and her hands in the brunette's hair to tighten as her body tried to decide if it wanted to get closer to Charlotte's mouth or further away.

Closer was the inevitable answer every time, her hips desperately rolling forward to rock against the brunette's face before canting backwards when it became too much, only to repeat the movement again and again and again until she finally came undone with a scream, Charlotte's name echoing around foyer as her body shook and trembled with her release. She sighed contentedly as the mouth against her gentled, a soft tongue brushing lightly over her as she rode out her climax, and she groaned when she felt Charlotte finally pull away.

Charlie smiled up at Mackayla's dazed face as she pushed herself up off her knees. She let her fingertips draw light trails up the front of the gasping blonde's thighs as she stood to her full height, and she grinned as she lifted herself up onto her toes to capture Mackayla's lips in a slow, deep kiss.

A low groan rumbled in Mac's throat at the taste of herself on Charlotte's tongue, and she finally relaxed her hold on the brunette's hair to loop her arms around the smaller woman's shoulders as their tongues stroked lazily together. "Fuck, Charlotte," she breathed when the kiss finally broke, her skin erupting in goosebumps as her body began to cool after reaching its peak.

"Maybe later," Charlie murmured, smiling and lifting her left hand to trace the perimeter of Mackayla's right breast. Dark eyes held hazel captive as she spiraled her fingers around the mound, the circuits growing tighter and tighter until she was stroking the circumference of an engorged rosy nipple. She hummed approvingly at the way Mackayla's eyes fluttered at the soft touch, and couldn't resist giving the nub a gentle pinch. "Hi."

"Oh god," Mac moaned, her hips bucking into Charlotte as electricity shot through her, ending in a fresh wave of arousal crashing between her legs.

Charlie grinned and slid her right hand between the blonde's legs to let her fingers play in the wetness that was pooled there. She ran her fingers back and forth through soft, swollen lips, coating her fingertips with the blonde's desire as she let her slowly get used to the idea of more. Because she definitely wanted more. She wanted to look into the beautiful blue eyes she loved so much as she once again brought Mackayla to the edge of ecstasy and sent her flying. "I'm not done with you yet, gorgeous."

"Shit," Mac muttered, licking her lips as her body began to rock slowly with Charlotte's fingers that continued to stroke slowly through her. A low moan tore itself from her throat as she felt the brunette's fingers dip down to press lightly against her, pushing into her with shallow thrusts. She was still breathing heavily from her last orgasm, struggling to fully recover, but she couldn't contain the, "God, please, Charlotte," that fell from her lips as she tried to thrust herself down onto the brunette's fingers.

Unable to resist giving Mackayla what she so obviously wanted, Charlie groaned and sheathed two fingers inside her. Velvety heat surrounded her and she muttered a raspy, "I love you," as she reached up with her free hand to pull Mackayla's head down to her level so she could claim the blonde's lips in a scorching kiss. "You are so goddamn sexy," Charlie murmured when she pulled away. She smiled as she began pumping her fingers slowly in and out, loving the way Mackayla tightened around her, trying to pull her deeper and hold her there.

Mac's head fell back against the wall with a heavy thud, and she laced her hands together behind Charlotte's neck as her hips rolled to meet each of the brunette's thrusts, which were steadily increasing in force and tempo. "Charlotte," she whimpered, her eyes rolling back in her head as the brunette's fingers curled inside her.

It was an undeniable power trip to have Mackayla like this: stark naked, her beautiful body pinked with arousal, and gasping for air; and Charlie purred softly as she flicked her tongue across Mackayla's parted lips. "What do you need, baby?"

"You." The word was more of a groan than anything else, but Mackayla didn't care. She just needed Charlotte.

"I'm yours," Charlie whispered, thrusting harder for emphasis. "Forever yours, sweetie. I promise." She felt herself clench at the low, needy moan that rumbled in Mackayla's throat in response to her words, and used her chin to turn Mackayla's head to the side so she could brush her lips over the delicate shell of the blonde's ear. "All yours," she breathed.

"Fuck, Charlotte," Mackayla grunted, her eyes rolling back in her head as Charlotte's words washed over her like a caress, making her nipples grow even harder as a fresh wave of arousal spilled from her to coat the brunette's hand.

Charlie braced her left hand on the wall beside Mackayla's head and began thrusting even harder, ignoring the way the muscles in her forearm were burning with the effort she was expending as she fought to bring the blonde to climax. "You are absolutely stunning like this," she murmured, letting her eyes sweep over Mackayla's body.

Mac groaned and bucked hard against Charlotte's hand.

"Gorgeous," Charlie breathed.

A small ripple tore through Mac's body and she whimpered. "Please."

"Jesus," Charlotte breathed, her body tightening sympathetically as she fucked the blonde as hard and as fast as she could.

"Oh god, Charlotte!"

"That's it, sweetie," Charlie encouraged, curling her fingers so that she massaged hidden ridges with every thrust. Her voice trailed off as Mackayla screamed and began spasming around her fingers. She stalled her hand as the first wave rocked through the blonde, causing a smaller, yet no less staggering, orgasm to rip through her, flooding her panties as she let out a soft cry of release.

She stroked Mackayla through the length of her orgasm, drawing it out as long as possible. When the final spasm left Mackayla breathless and weak, Charlie smiled as she pulled out and pressed herself up against the blonde, pinning her to the door until she found the strength to stand on her own.

"My god, Charlotte," Mac husked, once she finally managed to catch her breath.

Charlie chuckled and nodded. "You liked?"

"Mmm, loved," Mac assured her, tangling her hands in the brunette's hair and pulling her in for a kiss. "But you have way too many clothes on."

Charlie grinned cockily. "Do you really have the energy to do anything about that now?"

Never one to back down from so blatant a challenge, Mac smirked and reached down to undo the zipper on Charlotte's jeans. She slowly pushed them to the floor, leaving the brunette's long, toned legs on display, and wasted no time yanking her shirt off as well. Charlotte's bra was next to go, and Mac's tongue swept impulsively over her lips as her eyes zeroed in on perfect mocha-colored nipples that were already peaked, pebbled, and waiting for her. She reached up to cradle Charlotte's breasts in her hands, weighing them, swiping her thumbs back and forth over the swollen tips. She moaned softly as she bent down to take one into her mouth, sucking on the nub as she reached down to shove the brunette's panties to the floor.

She stroked her hands up and down Charlotte's thighs as she licked, nipped, and sucked on her breast, and she sighed as she let her right hand slip between her legs to play in the warmth and the wetness that had collected there.

Charlie groaned and her hips bucked against the blonde's hand. "Mackayla, baby, please."

Mac smiled and lifted her head to capture Charlotte's lips in a slow kiss, looping her arms around the brunette's waist and picked her up. Charlotte's legs wrapped around her waist as she carried her on shaky legs over to the small pallet of blankets that were still piled in front of the hearth from the night before. She giggled at the quiet grunt that fell from Charlotte's lips when she all but dropped them both onto the blankets, and she swallowed any protest Charlotte might have made by reclaiming her lips in a deep, probing kiss. She slid her right hand back between the brunette's legs, and she smiled as her fingers stroked through the slick warmth she found there.

"Mine," she murmured as she ran her fingers through the length of the brunette, loving, as she always did, the feeling of soft swollen lips gliding around her fingertips.

A sympathetic orgasm wasn't nearly enough to leave Charlie feeling sated. Proud, yes. A little relieved, most certainly. But not sated, and she groaned as she rolled her hips up into Mackayla's hand. "Please."

"What do you want?'"

Already too far gone to the blinding need that was buzzing through her body, Charlie didn't hesitate. "Fuck me."

Mac moaned softly and stared hard into Charlotte's eyes as she deftly thrust into her with two fingers. "Good?"

"So good," Charlie grunted, leaning back to try and take Mackayla even deeper.

"Yes, you are," Mac agreed, smiling as she used her hips to drive her next thrust even further into the brunette. She could tell by how tight Charlotte already was that she was close, and she bit her lip as she began thrusting harder and faster, eager to make her come as quickly as possible.

The sight of Mackayla kneeling between her legs, breasts swaying with every thrust, the taut muscles in her forearm flexing powerfully between her legs, fathomless blue eyes dark with lust as the blonde fucked her, fingers curling, rubbing, stroking, making stars flash behind her eyes as she raced flat-out toward orgasm had Charlie moaning loudly and chanting almost indecipherably as she blindly sought the explosive climax that was just beyond her reach. And then Mackayla's hand landed between her legs just that little bit harder, slamming roughly against her, and she screamed as her entire body seized, curling in on itself as orgasm swept through her.

"There you go, baby," Mac murmured encouragingly, gentling her thrusts as she eased Charlotte through her climax. She hummed softly as she leaned in to kiss her, mouths open, tongues stroking sloppily together while the brunette shook and trembled with release.

"Oh my god," Charlie moaned, smiling up into twinkling blue eyes as her orgasm finally began to ease. "Wow."

"Yes, you were," Mac whispered, kissing Charlotte softly. "I love you."

"Mmm, love you," Charlie purred, reaching up and pulling Mackayla down to her level again so she could kiss her.

Their kisses gentled after a time and Mac grunted softly as she tugged a blanket free from the pile to cover themselves with. "Not that I am at all complaining," she said, nodding for emphasis, "but may I ask what brought all that on?"

Charlie shrugged and reached up to run her fingers through Mackayla's hair as the blonde settled against her side. "I just wanted you. Today was crazy and I am so glad that you went with me and I just…I dunno. I just wanted you."

"You have me," Mac murmured, smoothing a hand over Charlotte's jaw. She just prayed that their time together lasted beyond June. "You have me."

Chapter 38

By the time Mackayla's birthday rolled around the following week, Charlie was ready. It had taken more private cooking lessons than she cared to admit to perfect the dish that she had found online that she was sure Mackayla would love, but Henry was a patient teacher, and she had eventually managed to prepare the meal properly for the first time the day before. To be safe, though, she had spent a few hours earlier that afternoon in the kitchen at Shenanigans while Mackayla was at the gym, trying the recipe one last time just to make sure that she truly did have it down pat. And she did. The portobello lasagna was bubbling happily away in the oven when the doorbell rang.

Charlie's footsteps automatically matched the beat of the Melody Gardot song that was playing from her laptop, which she had set discreetly on one of the shelves beside the fireplace, and she hummed along with the melody as she padded through the living room to the foyer. She peeked through the window beside the front door, and a slow, pleased smile tweaked her lips at the sight of Mackayla standing on her porch looking simultaneously nervous and curious and excited. The blonde had abided her request and dressed up for the night in a pair of black slacks and a pale blue oxford left open at the neck, and Charlie felt her stomach flutter when she noticed the way Mackayla had purposefully mussed her hair. She always found Mackayla beautiful, but the sexy, bedhead style the blonde was sporting now made her think of long, lazy mornings making love, and her fingers itched to run through those messy strands as she kissed Mackayla senseless.

"Hi," Mac murmured when Charlotte opened the door, smiling as her gaze swept over Charlotte's body. The brunette was stunning as usual, barefoot, and wearing the dress she had worn to the Mish-Mash. She licked her lips as her eyes traced the swath of skin between the Charlotte's breasts that the dress left on alluring display, and she hummed softly at the feeling of Charlotte's arms sliding around her neck.

"Hi." Charlie's eyes danced over Mackayla's face, noting the way the blonde's eyes had darkened by a fraction at the sight of her in her dress, and she smiled as she pulled her down into a slow, sweet kiss. "Happy birthday."

Mac bit her lip and smiled. "Thank you." She ran her hands lightly over Charlotte's sides and added, "So, are you my present?"

"If you're lucky," Charlie laughed, tapping Mackayla on the nose with her finger. "Dinner is almost ready. Would you like a glass of wine?"

"That sounds great." Mac glanced apprehensively toward the kitchen as she pulled her boots off and set them on the mat beside the front door. "You cooked?"

Charlie rolled her eyes at the uneasy edge to Mackayla's voice, but she couldn't blame her for being skeptical. She had managed to burn Rice a Roni the last time she cooked for her. Though, to be fair, that had more to do with Mackayla kissing her neck than her lack of culinary prowess. "I did," she said, glancing back toward the kitchen.

"Wow," Mac said, trying to sound impressed, but only managing to come across as mildly terrified.

"It'll be amazing, I promise," Charlie said, shaking her head as she reached for Mackayla's hand. "Come on."

Mac allowed herself to be pulled toward the kitchen, and her eyebrows rose in surprise when she saw that Charlotte had gone all-out in setting the dining room table. A large bouquet of red roses sat in a fancy crystal vase in the center of the table, and there were dozens of cream-colored candles of various heights and thicknesses set around the vase, all lit and adding a warm glow to the room. "Wow, Charlotte," she breathed, this time sounding exactly as impressed as she had tried and failed to sound earlier.

Pleased that Mackayla seemed genuinely awed by the arrangement, Charlie smiled and gave the blonde's hand a gentle squeeze. "The flowers are for you, but since I made you drive over here, I figured it was better to use them to set the table than hand them to you at the door where we would then have to put them in a vase and everything."

"They're gorgeous," Mac assured her, her heart feeling impossibly full at the effort Charlotte had gone through to make the night special. "Thank you," she added softly, leaning down to brush an appreciative kiss across Charlotte's lips.

Charlie ran a gentle hand over Mackayla's jaw and sighed as they broke apart. "You're welcome." Her stomach fluttered as Mackayla nuzzled her cheek, the blonde's hands sliding easily around her waist and pulling her in close, and she purred when Mackayla's lips once again landed atop her own. The kiss was gloriously unhurried, lips idly clasping together, tongues circling languidly, and Charlie swore softly when the kitchen timer started to beep and broke them apart.

"That's probably important, huh?" Mac murmured, unable to resist kissing Charlotte one last time before she let the brunette go.

"Only if you would like dinner to be edible," Charlie said, flashing an apologetic smile as she started for the kitchen.

"Edible is always a good thing," Mac quipped as she followed Charlotte into the kitchen where the timer was still beeping relentlessly. She leaned against the sink and watched

Charlotte bend over to pull a glass dish out of the oven, enjoying both the way the brunette's dress hugged her ass to perfection and the smell of whatever it was she had made. "May I ask what we're having, or is it a surprise?"

"Spinach salad and portobello lasagna," Charlie said, setting the glass baking tray onto the stovetop and closing the oven door. Her stomach growled quietly as the rich scent of tomatoes, cheese, and mushrooms filled the kitchen. "Wine, of course," she added, grinning at Mackayla as she lifted an already open bottle and poured the blonde a glass, "and you have to wait for dessert."

"And you made all of it?"

Charlie handed Mackayla the glass of wine she had just poured and said, "Everything except the wine."

Mac glanced at the label on the bottle on the counter and arched a brow in surprise. The wine was one of her favorites, from a small vineyard in Central California that Spencer had introduced her to, and something Charlotte had not served before. "You've been talking to Walsh."

"Just a little, amongst other people," Charlie admitted with a wink. "So, I was thinking we could just make our plates here and carry everything into the dining room. Is that okay?"

"Perfect," Mac murmured, nodding as she picked up Charlotte's already filled glass of wine. "I'll put these down and be right back."

"Just take those out and have a seat," Charlie countered, dropping a quick kiss to the blonde's lips before she shooed her out of the kitchen. "I have this."

"But–" Mac began to protest, but she was cut off by another sweet kiss that made her heart flutter.

"Go sit that scrumptious ass of yours down at the dining room table, birthday girl," Charlie commanded with a forceful, yet playful nod of her head. "Or you don't get dessert," she added, smirking suggestively.

Mac feigned a dramatic sigh and rolled her eyes. "So demanding."

"You love it," Charlie retorted, winking sassily at the blonde before she turned to pull two plates–the only settings with the exception of their wine glasses not already out on the dining room table–from the cupboard above the dishwasher.

Unable to resist the sight of Charlotte standing on her tiptoes, calves beautifully defined, firm cheeks of her ass straining against the fabric of her dress, Mac walked over and draped herself over the smaller woman's back, carefully holding their wine glasses away from them so she didn't spill. "I love you," she murmured, dipping her head down to brush her lips over the side of Charlotte's neck, using the tip of her tongue to tease the sensitive hollow beneath Charlotte's ear that never failed to drive the brunette wild, and hummed softly as she felt Charlotte's hips roll back into her. "But okay," she added softly, nipping lightly at her throat before she pulled away so abruptly that Charlotte actually swayed slightly on her feet despite the fact that she was still leaning against the counter.

"You're mean," Charlotte grumbled, rolling her eyes as she shot a playful glare over her shoulder at the blonde.

Mac grinned. "You love me."

"I do," Charlie laughed, grabbing a dishtowel off the counter and swinging it playfully at Mackayla. "So very, very much. But you need to stop distracting me."

"As you wish," Mac replied, stealing the trademark line from Charlotte's favorite movie and offering the brunette a gallant bow before she spun on her heel and all but sauntered out of the kitchen. She chuckled softly at the "So goddamn sexy" she heard Charlotte mutter behind her back, and sighed as she set the glasses she was carrying down onto the dining room table.

Her eyes slid slowly over the table, committing each and every element to memory. Her most recent birthdays had been spent with Spencer and their friends, drinking and hanging out. And, while fun, those celebrations paled in comparison to the night Charlotte had already created for her. She had been in the brunette's house for barely more than ten minutes, and she already knew that this would be the birthday she would remember for the rest of her life. Charlotte's dress, the roses, the candles, the wine, all of it was almost too perfect to believe, and she just barely resisted the urge to pinch herself to make sure she wasn't dreaming.

"Everything okay?" Charlie asked softly, biting her lip nervously as she entered the dining room to find Mackayla frozen beside the table, a wholly inscrutable expression on her face.

"Everything is perfect." Mac nodded as she turned to watch Charlotte set their plates onto the table. The lasagna smelled delicious and she smiled as she quickly moved to pull Charlotte's chair at the head of the table out for her.

"You're the birthday girl, I'm supposed to be doting on you," Charlie argued weakly, a pleased smile tweaking her lips as she smoothed her dress over the backs of her legs and sat down.

Mac bit her lip and quickly took her seat beside Charlotte, her heart beating erratically as she reached for her hand. "You are," she murmured, stroking her thumb over the back of the brunette's knuckles. "I can't remember the last time my birthday garnered this much attention."

"Every year from now on," Charlie promised softly.

Mac smiled, willing to let the promise go without challenge for now, to share Charlotte's unwavering belief that they will find a way to make things work without worrying about the details of how, exactly, they were going to manage the task. She gave Charlotte's hand one last squeeze before letting it go, and she drew a deep breath as she picked up her silverware. "So, um, is this a new recipe?"

"It is," Charlie said, folding her hands on her lap as she watched Mackayla take a tentative bite of lasagna. "So…?"

"Delicious," Mac murmured, nodding, her taste buds in portobello, ricotta, and tomato heaven. "Seriously, Charlotte," she added, smiling at the way the brunette puffed up at the compliment.

"I'm glad you like it." Charlie beamed and picked up her own silverware.

It didn't take either of them long to clean their plates, and Mac sighed happily as she leaned back in her chair to sip at her wine as the food settled. "That was seriously amazing," she repeated, for what seemed like the thousandth time, but she just could not get over the fact that Charlotte had cooked actual food and that it had been so good. "I'm beginning to think your whole 'I can't cook' thing is just a ploy to get out of cooking."

"Hardly," Charlie scoffed, rolling her eyes as she pushed her plate toward the center of the table. "That dinner was the result of two weeks of Henry's exceedingly patient tutelage and more failed attempts than I care to admit."

Though she had wondered how, exactly, Charlotte had managed to create such an incredible dish, Mac was genuinely surprised that the brunette had sought help to learn how to make it. If anything, knowing that Charlotte had gone to Henry to learn how to cook this dinner for her made it even more special because of the thought and effort the brunette had put into the whole thing. "You're incredible."

"Yeah right," Charlie muttered, the earnestness in Mackayla's tone making her blush. She shook her head and leaned down to retrieve the small package she had hidden under the table before the blonde had arrived. She immediately noticed Mackayla's eyes on her when she straightened back up, and she cleared her throat softly as she ran a hand through her hair.

Second Chances

"Anyways, happy birthday, sweetheart," she said, licking her lips nervously as she handed the present to Mackayla.

"You didn't have to get me anything," Mac murmured as she obediently took the box from Charlotte, pushing up from her seat to press a quick kiss to the brunette's lips. "Thank you." The candlelight reflected dully off the silver paper, and she bit her lip as she slipped her finger beneath the tightly folded seam on the side of the box.

"I hope you like it." Charlie reached for her wine glass to cover up her nerves. They had agreed to keep their exchange at Christmas casual, but she had made no such promise for Mackayla's birthday and had gone a little overboard in her shopping.

Mac carefully finished removing the wrapping paper from the present and set it onto the table as she looked at the sky blue box in her hands with a speculative eye. The words *Invicta Subaqua* were emblazoned in silver across the lid along with a stylized dragon. She did not recognize the name, and she shot Charlotte a curious look as she carefully opened the box. And then her breath caught in her throat when she saw the absolutely gorgeous watch that lay inside, nestled amidst camel-colored suede. It was large, obviously a man's watch, stainless steel with what looked like a copper accent around the face. The face of the watch itself was impossibly ornate, the different mechanical workings set above the flat face and cast in hues of copper, blue, and gold so that each element stood out against each other and the silver background of the face itself. It looked expensive, exceedingly so, and Mac bit her lip as she looked up at Charlotte. "It's too much."

"It's not," Charlie assured her gently, smiling with relief that Mackayla seemed to like the gift despite her protestations. "Adam knows a guy in the jewelry district back in New York, and I got the watch at cost. It's not a Timex or anything, but I didn't pay anything close to market price, so don't worry about that. And it's engraved, so I can't return it anyways."

"It's engraved?" Mac asked, looking back down at the watch.

Charlie nodded. "On the back of the face."

Intrigued, Mac pulled the watch from its nest, idly noting the *Skeleton COSC* that was stamped across the inner lid. She opened the clasp and slid the watch off its bolster, and her breath hitched when her eyes landed on the engraving Charlotte had hinted at. Two hearts, joined together at the point to create a stylized infinity symbol, her initials etched into the center of one while Charlotte's anchored the other. She looked up at the brunette and swallowed thickly, her eyes stinging with tears she refused to let fall. She had a feeling that even 'at cost' the watch in her hands was anything but cheap, but the engraving made it priceless.

Her heart swelled with affection as she leaned forward, searching for a kiss, and she sighed happily when Charlotte met her halfway. "Come here," she murmured, the breathy request falling in gentle waves against Charlotte's lips in between languid kisses, and reached out beseechingly to tug the brunette closer.

The desperate edge to Mackayla's plea had Charlie moving immediately, sliding out of her own chair, and allowing the blonde to guide her onto her lap. She hummed softly as she cradled Mackayla's face in her hands and reclaimed the blonde's lips in another deep, lingering kiss, and couldn't help but smile when she heard the watch land on the table with a quiet clatter half a heartbeat before Mackayla's arms wrapped tightly around her waist, holding her close. "So, do you like it?" she murmured.

"I love it," Mac assured her softly. She sighed and ran her right hand up Charlotte's back to tangle her fingers in the silky strands of the brunette's hair, using that hold to pull her back down into another kiss. "Let me show you how much?"

Charlie smiled, both pleased and aroused by Mackayla's response. "Dessert?"

"Dessert can wait," Mac muttered, shaking her head. She trailed the fingers of her left hand up Charlotte's stomach to lightly rake her nails up and down the narrow swath of skin that the brunette's dress left exposed. She felt Charlotte shiver with anticipation, and she smiled as she curled her fingers beneath the fabric to tease the soft swell of Charlotte's breast. "I want you."

"It's your birthday," Charlie husked, moaning softly as the backs of Mackayla's fingers dragged over her nipple.

Mac's lips quirked in a pleased, wolfish grin. "Happy birthday to me," she murmured, continuing to lazily run her fingers over Charlotte's rapidly hardening nipple as she pulled the brunette down into a deep, searing kiss.

Chapter 39

Charlie looked out the window of her office as she lifted her phone to her ear and sighed as she listened to the call ring through. The old adage that time waits for no man was painfully true, and she was left wondering how her calendar was telling her that it was already the middle of February. She could remember every minute she had spent with Mackayla over winter break. The trips they had taken to a local ski hill where the blonde had teased her relentlessly about being "old" because she preferred skis to a snowboard. The nights they spent wrapped around each other on the couch or in bed, kissing, touching, or just sitting together in silence, simply enjoying the other's company. She remembered fondly the days they had spent together doing the mundane, everyday type things like cleaning and laundry and grocery shopping that just needed to be done. She could remember it all, and yet she could swear that somebody was playing a cruel joke on her because there was no way two months had passed since the end of the fall semester.

And yet, they had. The simple fact that they had was undeniable, evidenced by the throng of students out her window that were hurrying to their next class, heads bowed down against the cold northern wind that was whipping across campus.

Her call was answered just before it was undoubtedly kicked to voicemail, and though she was determined that this was the only course of action available to her, the knowledge that she was actually going to make her move from New York to New Hampshire permanent had her stomach twisting with nerves.

"Snow Realty."

"Anna Snow, please," Charlie murmured.

"May I ask who's calling, please?"

"Charlie Bennett," Charlie answered, biting her lip as the receptionist put her on hold. She found it oddly fitting that Sara Bareilles's song *Brave* was the dead air filler as she waited for Adam's sister to pick up.

"Charlie Bennett. How are you doing? Is my brother behaving himself? How's New Hampshire?"

Charlie smiled, easily picturing the curly-haired brunette's sweet smile. Anna was the opposite of her twin brother in almost every sense imaginable, but she had the same big, open, caring heart that he did and that was just one of the reasons Charlie loved her. "I'm well. Last I heard, Adam was behaving himself. And New Hampshire is great. That's actually why I'm calling you." She took a deep breath. "I want to sell my condo."

Anna whistled, and Charlie could just imagine the thoughtful look that the brunette was undoubtedly now wearing. *"Okay. We can use the pictures I took when we listed the property for rent, so that will make things easier. And, thankfully, the lease on your condo is a month-to-month, so we'll just have to notify your tenant that it'll be going up on the market and that will basically be their thirty day notice that you'll be terminating the lease, though there's a good chance they might be willing to stay until we close on the sale. And I'll have to get them to sign off for showings and stuff, but they seemed pretty cool when we signed the rental docs so I don't see that being too much trouble. If they don't sign, I will have to wait to list until they have vacated the property to begin showing it, though. Are you okay with that?"*

"I kind of have to be," Charlie muttered, running a nervous hand through her hair.

"Do you know what you would like to get for it?"

"I honestly don't know what places like mine are selling for," Charlie said, biting her lip as she heard Anna's keyboard clatter to life over the phone.

"Okay. I'll pull some comps and we can go from there. How quickly do you want to sell?"

"The quicker the better," Charlie said, running a hand through her hair. "I need to be out of my place here by the second week of June, so I would like to have things finalized before then."

"Okay. Let me do my thing, talk to some of the other agents in my office who have people looking in SoHo, and I'll see what we can do. I'll have my assistant track down your tenants and notify them that you will be putting the condo on the market, and to try and get them to sign off on allowing me to show the property provided I give them 24 hours notice. I'll call you later today with what I think will be a good list price and, once you give me the okay, I'll email you the listing docs for you to sign and email back to me. And then we'll get rolling on this. Sound good?"

"Sounds completely overwhelming, but yeah," Charlie muttered.

Anna laughed. *"Yeah. I know. But, judging by what Adam was telling me over Christmas–this is a good thing, right?"*

"It is," Charlie agreed, nodding as she spun around in her chair to look at Mackayla's closed office door. The blonde was teaching at the moment, no doubt surrounded by fawning graduate students who simply adored her, and that alone was enough reason for her to know that she was doing the right thing. She could write sports articles anywhere. Mackayla *belonged* at Blake. "You would love her, Anna."

"I'm sure I would," Anna replied warmly. *"Adam adores her, you know."*

A soft, wholly pleased smile tweaked Charlie's lips and she nodded. "Yeah, I know."

"So, have you given notice at SI?"

"That's next on my to-do list," Charlie groaned. "I'm thinking I'll be able to drive down Friday morning after my nine o'clock class and pop into the office that afternoon. They've been good to me and I don't want to do something like that over the phone. It just doesn't seem right."

"No point burning bridges you don't have to burn," Anna agreed.

Charlie nodded. "Yeah, especially because I'm thinking I'm going to try and freelance. It wouldn't be smart to totally alienate myself from one of the biggest magazines I could sell articles to."

"Exactly. Have you told my brother about this?"

"Not yet. I mean, we talked some more about it all over New Years when he was up visiting, but I haven't told him that I'm actually going to do it. He was supposed to be dropping hints for me at the magazine that something like this could be happening, though."

"Softening the beach. I like it," Anna drawled. "Okeydokey, cutie. I need to get going if I'm going to sell your condo so you can live happily ever after in the middle of nowhere. So, I will call you later."

"Sounds good, Anna. Thanks," Charlie murmured, smiling as she disconnected the call. There were still so many details that needed to be worked out before she could really call Hampton home, but it was a relief to just know that she had taken that first step.

She pursed her lips thoughtfully as she leaned back in her chair, her gaze focused on Mackayla's office door. Despite Mackayla's continued assurances that she was fine, Charlie knew that the blonde was growing increasingly nervous about the tenuous nature of her residency in New Hampshire. It was in the little comments that would crop up in conversation, and the almost wounded look that would flash in Mackayla's eyes whenever she mentioned New York or anything to do with the magazine.

The blonde had taken to running again, wearing out the treadmills at the gym when the weather was bad, or taking to the streets on the still rare days that temperatures got above twenty. And, while Charlie was sure that this was something that would help ease Mackayla's fears and cut down on her stress, she knew that the kind of limbo that she was now stuck in–condo going up for sale but not sold, no real plans for where she was going to live in Hampton after her lease ran out–could also increase Mackayla's stress levels tenfold.

She already laid in bed alone most nights from about two until four, listening to Mackayla aimlessly pace through her house, a beautiful ghostly specter gliding from room to room, lower lip caught between her teeth, dull blue eyes shining with the promise of tears. It was not hard to imagine what would happen if Mackayla became even more worried about their future, she would be going to bed alone every night as the blonde slowly but surely pulled away from her in order to try and protect her own heart. And that was something she would not let happen.

A knock on her door drew Charlie from her thoughts, and she smiled as she spied Mackayla, cheeks pinked from the cold northern wind, leaning lightly against the doorframe. "Hey, beautiful. How was your class?"

Mac smiled and nodded. "It went well. They're all really getting into their projects and it's cool to see them so excited. What has you looking so thoughtful this early on a Tuesday morning?"

"Just…stuff," Charlie answered, deciding in that instant to handle things on her own. Her heart clenched at the way Mackayla's smile dimmed by a fraction at her evasive answer, and added quickly, "What would you say to taking a trip down to Manhattan with me this weekend? We can leave after our morning classes and be there before five. Stay in a fancy hotel and just get lost in the city? Eat some amazing food? Maybe catch a show or something?"

"That sounds fun," Mac murmured, brow furrowing with confusion. "Did something happen that you need to go back?"

"Not at all," Charlie lied. "I just want to take my beautiful girlfriend to the city for the weekend and spoil her rotten. Is that okay?"

Though Mackayla wanted to press and ask Charlotte why, exactly, the brunette was so determined to go to New York, she was simultaneously terrified of what the answer might be, so she did not push. A romantic weekend away sounded lovely, even if she was certain that there was an underlying reason to the impromptu trip. "Okay then," she said, trying her best to sound pleasantly surprised. "You'll have to let me know what I should pack."

Chapter 40

Mac swallowed thickly as she stood beside Charlotte and looked up at the gleaming glass and steel building that housed the New York Offices of *Sports Illustrated*. Ever since Charlotte had invited her on this impromptu trip, there had been a strange distance that had erupted between them. At first, she had thought that she was simply imagining it, that the tension she felt was simply a manifestation of her persistent insecurities about their relationship, but then Charlotte had started leaving the room to take certain phone calls, and she had caught the brunette staring wistfully at her profile on the *Sports Illustrated* webpage on more than one occasion. Clearly, something had changed. Something big. But she hadn't a clue as to what that change was.

All she knew was that it terrified her.

The drive down to the city had been quiet, and the feeling of Charlotte's hand on her thigh had done little to dispel the apprehension that was twisting her stomach in knots. Whenever she had managed to work up the courage to ask Charlotte if everything was okay, the brunette's smile was always too bright and her answer too forced to be believable.

A horn honking jolted her out of her thoughts, and she bit her lip as the traffic on the street behind her surged in waves, engines revving and rumbling, while strangers flowed around her like she was a boulder in a stream, interrupting the unending flow of humanity that refused to be stemmed. She had been to New York before, of course, but she was surprised by how much the crush of people and traffic bothered her when it never had before.

She looked down at Charlotte when the brunette squeezed her hand gently, and tried to force herself to smile. The unshakable feeling of unease that had haunted her for the last few days grew tenfold at the nervous excitement she could see dancing in Charlotte's eyes, and she knew that whatever it was that Charlotte needed to do inside those gleaming glass doors was the entire reason they had driven to New York. Their "romantic getaway weekend" was simply an excuse to cover up whatever ulterior motives had called Charlotte south.

"You ready to go in?" Charlie's brow furrowed as she took in Mackayla's anxious expression. She knew that she had been wrapped up in her own head for most of the last few days, but for the life of her, she could not think of a single thing she had done to set the blonde one edge. She had been so careful to act the same as she always had, so that she wouldn't alarm Mackayla in any way, and it pained her to see that she had so obviously failed. She cleared her throat softly and added, "Or, would you rather wander around the city while I pop inside? Or go back to the hotel? I'm sorry if I made you feel like you had to come with me to the office–I just figured that since I was in the city that I could pop in and say hello to some friends."

Mac's heart *kathumped* heavily in her chest, and she glanced around at the strangers that continued to stream past them. The opportunity to avoid whatever was about to happen was too good to pass up, and she latched onto it like it was a life raft. "Would you mind if I just went back to the hotel?"

"Not at all," Charlie murmured. She reached up and ran a gentle hand over Mackayla's jaw, her eyes filling with concern as she felt the blonde tense beneath her hand. "Are you okay? Did I do something wrong?"

"You didn't do anything wrong. I'm just a little tired from the drive," Mac lied, swallowing thickly as she saw a look of pure disbelief flash in Charlotte's eyes. And, in reality, Charlotte hadn't done anything wrong. Charlotte was allowed to hold private conversations, just like she was allowed to think about the life she had left behind to come to New Hampshire, or simply get lost in her own head for a while. Nothing the brunette had done was wrong. It was just that those otherwise innocent behaviors combined with her own insecurities to create a perfect storm inside doubt and suspicion inside her mind.

She cleared her throat uncomfortably and added, "Go see your friends. I'm sure Adam is dying to see you, and I'll just be waiting for you at the hotel whenever you're finished."

Charlie knew that she should go with Mackayla, but she also knew that Billy would be leaving in less than an hour to head upstate to go visit his grandchildren for the weekend, and she needed to talk to him before he left. She did not want to have to make this trip again, but if Mackayla needed her to leave, she would. She would leave and then either come back in a few weeks or simply tender her resignation over the phone. She cared more for Mackayla's happiness than any bridges she might burn by not telling Billy in person that she wasn't going to be returning to the magazine. "You're sure?"

"Totally sure," Mac said, forcing a weak smile as she leaned in to drop a quick kiss to Charlotte's frowning lips. "I'll see you soon."

"See you soon," Charlie murmured. Her stomach twisted uncomfortably as she watched Mackayla disappear into the crowd, and she knew that, whatever it was that was bothering the blonde, she was going to have to fix it–and soon.

The lobby was nearly empty as Charlie strode across the marbled expanse to the bank of elevators on the far wall. A soft sigh escaped her as she followed two men she did not recognize into the car when it arrived, and she pushed herself back against the far wall, her eyes focused on the tiny strip of numbers above the door. Her mind spun with possible reasons for Mackayla's odd behavior, and yet she did not have a clue as to what had set the blonde off.

She had thought that everything was going well. Her apartment was already listed and Anna had called her that morning to tell her that there were already a handful of showings scheduled for that weekend. The only thing left for her to take care of was to give her notice at the magazine, and she would be free. Free to move to New Hampshire permanently. Free to find a new job that would allow her to stay with Mackayla.

Stepping out onto the thirty-seventh floor was a surreal experience, and Charlie drew a deep breath as she stepped out onto the bustling floor that had been her kingdom. Her life. She had given everything she had to the magazine, done everything she could to see both it and her career thrive, and yet this was the first time she had ever wandered through the maze of desks and cubicles, printer stations and water coolers with her heart intact.

"CHARLIE BENNETT!" a familiar voice boomed from across the floor.

Charlie grinned as she spotted Adam standing in the doorway of her old office waving at her. She knew that he had taken over the space along with her duties, and she laughed as she started toward him. "Do I know you?"

Adam just shrugged and smiled as he watched Charlie make her way across the floor, stopping to say hello to familiar faces on her way. When she finally reached his office, he held his arms out and said, "Hey, Bitch."

"Whore," Charlie retorted, smiling as he pulled her into a quick embrace.

"Where's your woman?" he asked, frowning. Charlie had called him the day before to ask if he would show Mackayla around the building a little while she spoke to Billy, so the fact that the blonde wasn't with her was definitely noteworthy.

Charlie shrugged, sighing as she ran a hand through her hair. "She, uh...wanted to go back to the hotel and rest up a bit."

Adam frowned. "Is everything okay?"

"I thought it was," Charlie said, shaking her head. "I almost went back with her, but I really want to talk to Billy and get this all over with, and..."

Adam nodded understandingly. "All right. So, as much as I would love to spend time with you, you need to go see Billy right now. And then you need to get that sweet little ass of yours back to your hotel and fix whatever it is that is wrong."

"I know," Charlie sighed. "I just don't know what I did to piss her off."

"Just watch out for flying footwear," Adam warned sagely as he pushed her toward the stairs. They were always faster than the elevator anyways, and this way Charlie wouldn't have to make her way back through the maze of desks and cubicles that were full of people who looked eager to catch up with her. "Go talk to Billy, and then get back to your girl. Call me later."

"I will," Charlie murmured, giving him one last quick hug before she hurried toward the stairs. "Thanks."

Chapter 41

Charlie knocked lightly on Billy Davis's door to get his attention and smiled when he looked up from whatever report it was that he was reading, his kind brown eyes lighting up at the sight of her. "Hey, Billy."

He laughed and waved her inside. "Charlie Bennett. I wasn't expecting to see you darkening my doorway until June. How's it going, kiddo?"

"It's going great," Charlie said, her pulse pounding in her ears as she sat down in one of the visitor's chair opposite the Senior Editor's desk. Out the windows, she could just make out the top of Radio City Music Hall's iconic neon signage, and she sighed as she folded her hands on her lap to hide the fact that they were shaking. Between her worry about Mackayla and her nerves about what she was about to do, she was an absolute mess. "That's actually why I'm here."

Billy leaned back in his chair, his expression curious as he waited for her to continue.

Charlie cleared her throat and gave Billy a small, apologetic smile. "I'm not going to come back when the school year's over. I'm going to stay in New Hampshire."

He nodded thoughtfully and steepled his fingers in front of his mouth, his gaze unblinking as he studied her. "You're sure?"

"I am. I…you see, I met a girl," Charlie said.

"I see," he drawled, a knowing smile lifting his lips. "In New Hampshire?"

Charlie nodded. "Yeah. She's a professor at Blake, and I can't ask her to give that up, and I don't want to lose her again, so I need to be there. In Hampton."

"You do realize that you were going to be named Senior Editor when I retire next year, right? I just want to make sure you know what you're giving up."

"I know," Charlie assured him. "But, I want her more than I want to be Senior Editor. She's the one, Billy. I actually dated her in college, but the situation wasn't ideal then and we just didn't make it." She sighed, a soft smile tweaking her lips as she remembered how she had met Mackayla for the second time. "I actually crashed into her my first day in New Hampshire. I had no idea she was up there and I literally sideswiped her car with the little U-Haul trailer I was towing."

"You did not," Billy laughed.

"I did," Charlie said, running a hand through her hair and smiling sheepishly at the memory.

"Way to make a second first impression," Billy chuckled.

"I know, right?" Charlie replied wryly.

His smile softened and he nodded. "What are you going to do up there? Keep teaching?"

"I wouldn't necessarily be opposed to teaching, I actually like it a lot, but I haven't spoken to the university about it." Charlie shrugged. "I was actually hoping to maybe do some freelance for you guys, kind of like what I did with that national team article in October."

"I think we can manage that easily enough," Billy agreed. He sat up straighter in his chair, his demeanor becoming more serious as the conversation switched back to business. "Would you want to just take a step back to just being a Senior Staff Writer without any of the editor responsibilities? You don't necessarily have to be here to do that. You may have to do a little traveling from time to time, but you would get more articles, which would make your income a little more stable..."

Charlie smiled. "You don't want me selling stuff to ESPN."

"Damn right I don't," Billy retorted, grinning. "What do you say?"

"I think that sounds great," Charlie said, nodding. "Thank you."

"I'm sorry to see you go, Charlie, but I'm happy for you," Billy said, his tone warm and fatherly as he pushed himself to his feet. "You were a damn fine Assistant Editor, and you would have been amazing in this job, but I can respect the fact that you're going to do what's right for you. Treat this girl of yours properly, all right?"

"Yes, sir," Charlie murmured. "Thanks for everything, Billy. Really. It was an honor to learn from you."

"I'm gonna miss you, kiddo." Billy shoved his hands into his pockets and sighed. "Give Janet a call when you're ready to start writing for us again, and we'll set you up."

"I will," Charlie said, swallowing thickly as she took that first step back toward the door. "Thanks again, Billy."

He smiled and waved at her to go. "I'll be talking to you soon, I'm sure."

Charlie nodded and spun on her heel, her footsteps light as she made her way back down the hall to the elevators. Her pulse, which had been racing throughout her entire conversation with Billy, finally began to slow as she stepped into the elevator and, as the doors slid shut, blocking the executive's floor from her view, she couldn't keep from grinning.

She had done it. There was nothing left to anchor her to New York. She was free.

Now she just had to figure out what was wrong with Mackayla, and fix it.

Chapter 42

Going back to the hotel alone was probably the stupidest idea Mac had ever had. Granted, this way she did not have to watch Charlotte with her old colleagues, but at the same time, she had nothing to distract her from the cacophony of thoughts echoing inside her skull that made her feel like she was slowly but surely going absolutely insane. At least at the office, she would have been surrounded by people, and she had no doubt that Adam would have done his damndest to both amuse her and embarrass Charlotte. Here, in their stunning room that overlooked Central Park, which undoubtedly cost more money than she cared to know about, there was no such reprieve from her thoughts.

She tried to busy herself with unpacking their bags and exploring the suite, but those two tasks combined took less than twenty minutes and then she was left once again looking for something to occupy her mind. Going for a run, no matter how much she wished she could, was not an option because she had not brought any of her workout things with her. She had anticipated a romantic weekend away, despite her concerns about the reason for the trip, and so the only cardio she had expected to do was in bed. With Charlotte. Where shoes and running tights and sports bras were entirely unnecessary.

"Damn it all to hell and back," she muttered, shaking her head. She wandered idly from the sitting room to the bedroom portion of the suite and dragged the armchair that was nestled in the corner of the room beside the armoire over to the windows that provided a breathtaking view of Central Park. She dropped heavily into the chair once it was where she wanted it, her body sagging against the back as she unsnapped the band on her watch and slid it off of her wrist.

The watch was warm in her hands and she sighed as she flipped it over to look at the design Charlotte had engraved into the back of the metal casing. She had taken great pride in wearing the watch, drawing strength from the knowledge that Charlotte's promise of forever was pressed against her skin, sliding across her wrist like a caress every time she moved her arm. She sighed as she ran the pad of her index finger over the stylized infinity symbol, around and around, again and again. Usually, the repeated action had a calming effect, but this time, it just set her even more on edge as memories of Charlotte's recent behavior flashed across her mind in time with each swoop and swirl of her finger over the engraving.

The sound of the door to the suite opening barely registered with her, and she jumped in her seat when she heard someone clear their throat softly behind her. Pulse racing, she scrambled to her feet, even though she intuitively knew that it would be Charlotte standing behind her, yet she still fisted the watch she had been toying with as she spun around. Whether the move was to protect the watch or to get ready to hurl it as a weapon, she did not know, and she swallowed thickly as she looked at Charlotte. The brunette's cheeks were pinked from the cold, her emerald eyes shining with a mixture of concern and excitement, and even as Mac anticipated having her heart broken, she found herself awed by the beauty of the woman before her.

It was impossible for Charlie to miss the defensive set to Mackayla's posture, and she licked her lips nervously as she took a careful step further into the room. "Hey. It's just me," she added quickly, holding her hands up to show that she was not a threat.

Mac nodded. "How'd it go?"

"It went better than I expected," Charlie answered truthfully. "It was nice to see everybody." Okay, that part was a lie, but had she actually stopped to visit with everyone she had intended to, it would have been nice. "Adam says hello."

"How's he doing?"

Charlie shook her head at the flat, toneless quality of Mackayla's voice. "What's wrong?" she asked instead of replying to the blonde's question."

Everything, Mac thought, wrapping her arms around herself even as she answered, "Nothing."

"Mackayla," Charlie sighed. Her heart clenched as she noticed that Mackayla was shaking ever so slightly, and she took a deep breath as she dared to take another step into the room. "What's wrong?"

"I don't know, Charlie," Mac snapped, all of the worry and fear and anger that had been building inside her since Tuesday morning exploding vehemently. Her fist clenched harder around the watch she was holding and she hugged herself tighter. "Why don't you tell me?"

"I don't know what's wrong!" Charlie threw her hands in the air. "I don't know what I did! I've been working my ass off for the last few days trying to get a bazillion things done so that I could surprise you with everything being wrapped up in a tidy little box, and I don't fucking know what I did wrong! Just tell me what I did so I can fix it! Please," she added, her voice cracking with emotion as she stared beseechingly at Mackayla.

Mac froze, biting her lip as Charlotte's panicked pleas cut through the anger that was coursing through her veins and made her actually stop and listen. "What do you mean?"

Charlie frowned. "What do I mean about what?"

"What bazillion things have you been trying to get done?"

Charlie swallowed thickly and ran a hand through her hair. "I put my condo here up for sale, and I just tried to quit my job at the magazine," she explained with a shrug. "I thought that was the easiest solution to the New York-New Hampshire problem."

The fury in Mac's eyes dimmed and she shook her head. "Why wouldn't you just tell me that?"

"I wanted it to be a surprise so that you wouldn't have to worry about any of it," Charlie murmured, her panicked pulse slowing to a more regular rhythm as Mackayla's expression softened. "I know you've been freaking out about it all, and I didn't want to add to your stress levels with the details of everything. Adam's sister is selling my condo, and I just got voluntarily demoted to Senior Staff Writer for the magazine so that I can work from New Hampshire."

"So you're not running away again?" Mac asked softly. She bit her lip nervously, her eyes filled with hopeful tears that were threatening to spill free as she searched Charlotte's face for the answer she so desperately needed to hear.

Charlie smiled and shook her head. "No, I'm not running away," she murmured, licking her lips as she quickly closed the distance between herself and Mackayla and pulled the blonde into her arms. "I'm not running away," she repeated softly, punctuating the reassuring words with a gentle kiss. "I'm running toward you, sweetheart."

A slow, shy smile tweaked Mac's lips as her heart soared up into her throat, relief sweeping through her in a tidal wave that made her actually sway on her feet. She licked her lips as she finally reached out for Charlotte, wrapping her arms around the petite brunette's waist and holding her close. She had been so convinced that she was going to lose Charlotte despite the brunette's promises, that she was suddenly feeling lightheaded with the knowledge that she had been wrong. She was not going to lose Charlotte.

Her mind jumped back to that fateful day in August when Charlotte had sideswiped her in downtown Hampton as she claimed Charlotte's lips in a slow, sweet kiss that was overflowing with love, and she could not help but think that this was meant to be. That they were destined to find each other again when they had both matured enough to make things between them work.

Call it fate. Call it destiny. Call it serendipity or kismet, she knew, as Charlotte's mouth opened beneath her own and the brunette's tongue flicked lightly across her lips, that she was exactly where she belonged.

Epilogue

Mac worked at the sink in the kitchen of the house she and Charlotte had closed escrow on three days before, humming along with the music from outside that filtered through the open windows. Six months had passed since that day in New York when Charlotte had told her that she was moving to New Hampshire permanently, and it was now exactly a year to the day that she had first run into the brunette again in downtown Hampton.

"Fuck you, Charlie Bennett!"

Mac looked up from the black bean burgers she was busy making at the sound of Adam's indignant cry, and laughed. He had been sunbathing on the deck when Charlotte had apparently decided to dump a bucket of water on him, and now he was chasing the brunette around their new backyard, flip-flop held threateningly over his shoulder as he took aim at her. "Dodge and weave, Charlotte!" she hollered through the window.

Charlie slowed down to flash Mackayla an arrogant smirk, and swore loudly when Adam's shoe hit her in the back of the head. "Shit! That really hurt, you ass!"

"And a bucket of ice water being dumped on me was pleasant?" he retorted.

Charlie laughed. "Yeah, probably not," she conceded.

"You're really sure you want to marry this one?" Adam hollered jokingly up at Mac, who was still watching them through the window. He had driven up two days ago in a U-Haul with all of Charlotte's things that had been in storage in New York, and had spent the last couple days helping move furniture and boxes.

A large, wholly indulgent smile lifted Mac's lips, and she nodded as her eyes dropped to Charlotte's left hand. Though the brunette was too far away for her to see the ring she put on that oh so important finger earlier that morning, just knowing it was there made her stomach flutter pleasantly. "Absolutely."

It had seemed only right that, after everything Charlotte had done for their relationship, she be the one to propose. And, once she decided that she was going to do it, she knew that she had to do it today. On the anniversary of the day Fate threw them together and gave them a second chance at happiness. It had been an understated proposal as they lay in bed earlier that morning, sharing lazy kisses and soft touches in their new bedroom, and yet, it was more romantic than any grand gesture she could have come up with simply because it was so honest and pure. There wasn't one thing about the moment that was manufactured, it was simply her, laying her heart open for Charlotte and asking the brunette to be her wife.

"Mac and Charlie sitting in a tree," Spencer chimed in from his lounge chair on deck where he was sunbathing beside Sara, "K-I-S-S-I-N-G."

"That doesn't sound like a bad idea at all," Charlie quipped, laughing as she ruffled Adam's hair before she jogged up the three short stairs to the deck.

Mac wiped her hands off on a dishtowel as she watched Charlotte saunter across the deck and into the kitchen, the brunette's eyes twinkling with affection, and licked her lips as strong, tanned arms wrapped around her neck. "Hey," she husked, grabbing hold of Charlotte's hips and pulling the petite brunette into her.

Charlie grinned. "Hey, yourself," she whispered, her eyes fluttering shut as she lifted herself onto her toes and claimed Mackayla's lips in a slow, sweet kiss. She laughed at Adam and Spencer's jeering catcalls, and groaned loudly when, in response to the boys' teasing, Mackayla pushed her back against the counter, pinning her there. Mackayla's mouth opened against hers and their kiss, which had been relatively chaste, grew heated in an instant, and then Charlie was aware of nothing but Mackayla. The press of Mackayla's body. The way the blonde's tongue stroked with a fervent passion around her own. The house could have been burning down around them, and she would not have noticed a thing.

So much had changed since she had sat at her kitchen table and decided to take a sabbatical from *SI* to move to New Hampshire and teach for a year, that it felt like it was a lifetime ago. In a way, it was. She was finally happy, truly happy, and it was all because of Mackayla. A low hum rumbled in the back of her throat when their kiss reached its inevitable end, and a soft smile tweaked her lips as she ran a gentle hand over the slope of Mackayla's jaw. "God, I love you."

"Love you, too," Mac murmured, sighing contentedly as she pressed a lingering kiss to Charlotte's forehead. Out the window, she could see the boys setting up the lawn dart game Spencer had found at a garage sale earlier in the summer, the one with the pointed metal tips on the darts that couldn't be found anywhere anymore because they were too dangerous. Everything about the moment was perfect. From the feeling of Charlotte in her arms, and knowing that the brunette really was hers forever, just like the engraving on her watch promised, to the sight of Adam and Spencer sword fighting with the lawn darts, she could not have imagined her life turning out any better than it had.

Adam yelled as Spencer's "sword" smacked across his knuckles, effectively shattering the moment, and Mac laughed as she dropped one last quick kiss to Charlotte's brow before she stepped back so that she was no longer pinning her to the counter. "The children are getting out of hand," she drawled, tipping her head at the backyard.

"Can't we just let them kill each other?" Charlie joked. She ran a lazy finger down the middle of Mackayla's chest, tugging on the fabric of the blonde's tank top, and smiled seductively. "We can just leave them to their own devices and christen the kitchen instead."

"While that sounds like a lot of fun," Mac murmured, eyes twinkling with amusement as she dipped her head down to kiss Charlotte softly, "we have company."

Charlie smirked. "Later?"

Mac nodded. "Absolutely."

Second Chances

Second Chances

Acknowledgements

Many, many thanks to Jade for the lovely cover art and the reassuring pats on the head when I needed them; to Rae D. Magdon for your editing prowess and for making such a valiant effort to curtail my love for super-long sentences (you mostly succeeded); and, lastly, to Wye for giving this thing its first legit test-run.

CPSIA information can be obtained at www.ICGtesting.com
Printed in the USA
LVOW11s0805050716

495092LV00001B/217/P